Cauda Equi-Not

Life's a Bitch, and her name is Cauda Equina

Bethany Taylor

FISHER KING PUBLISHING

CAUDA EQUI-NOT

Copyright © Bethany Taylor 2019

ISBN 978-1-910406-94-6

Published by
Fisher King Publishing
The Studio
Arthington Lane
Pool-in-Wharfedale
LS21 1JZ
UK

www.fisherkingpublishing.co.uk

Cover illustration by Bethany Taylor

This book is dedicated to every person who was with me through the real cauda equina journey and is still here to tell the tale now. I was a nightmare, I still am, you are amazing, thank you.

To the extraordinary NHS team at Harrogate Hospital and Leeds General Infirmary, who never once suggested that putting me down might be a better option.

I am indebted forever

Chapter One

I hate it up here. I swear to god it's haunted, and if it isn't yet, then one of these days Stabby Joe will come out of his secret, dingy, hidey place and kill me, so it will be soon enough.

Stabby Joe is the man we are all utterly convinced lives here, in the cinema and taunts us after hours, a legend really, but it becomes ever more convincing with each shift I work - especially in the screen upstairs. Up here, in "the box", it feels like a different planet; you can see below you, through the projector window, in to the screen itself. It's dark with no lights, no people, no noise, mostly just your own reflection on the glass, reminiscent of Vader's first moments in Empire Strikes Back - Christ on a bike, he's such a badass! The box is where we keep the projectors, where the history of cinema magic happens really, we have an old, original movie reel style one in the corner which fascinates us no matter how many times we've all played with it. And we really shouldn't play with it.

The whole space is dusty and unkempt, cardboard boxes strewn across the room filled mostly with tack left by previous management and the old projection staff, but there's some fun bits too. Old film reels, lovingly stacked then abandoned, and of course the current film set up: no more manual labour, it's all electrical and fancy - too many buttons to press (and forget to press, oops.) It's a job everyone loves to do though, when it's time to open and nobody fancies filling popcorn warmers or touching raw hot-dogs - BLEUGH, or when you don't want to be the first person to serve a scabby teenager who thinks they're entitled to watch a certificate 15 without an ID. Naturally, however, when it's closing and it's dark and there's only three of you in the building, it's got fewer perks! So has working with your best friends. As much as it has its benefits (of which there are hundreds), there is also a giant downfall when you're on the late shift and it mostly consists of them finding any way possible to scare the shit out of you. And I know that, right now, when I shut the lights off in this crap heap and lock the door, somebody is going to be lying in wait in the screen to scare the bejesus out of me.

In order to get out of projection you have to descend the stairs into the screen itself. Ahh yes, just as I suspected, the bastards have turned my safety lights off. The safety lights should be the only thing helping me to see because once you close down projection all the other lights go out with it. Right, be brave, as Sophie in the BFG would say. I like to imagine, stood at the top, I'm on the tallest peak of a mountain; I always fancied Kilimanjaro when I was in school I just still haven't gotten round to it yet. It's not like I've ever felt the need to rush considering it's the only thing on my bucket list anyway. Remembering suddenly I'm not on one of the greatest peaks in the history of the world I walk directly down the centre of the aisle, swiftly, quietly and try not to cry. Must be prepared for an ankle grab or a scream and don't lose your cool - not that I ever had any in the first place...

'You utter bastards!' I laugh, as I leave the screen, unscathed. Eli is creased in a ball against the wall, as I burst through the door, escaping what I thought was my impending doom. His long brown, pony tail is getting eaten by his tongue, as he struggles to contain his hysterical laughter - I hope he chokes on it!

'I bet you were shitting yourself,' he manages to breathe, pulling the hair from his face.

I shoot him a, 'ha-ha, very funny, all I can do now is mock your laugh' kind of face, like the meme of a little kid that circles the internet, and watch as Adam, the boss man, locks the management office across the foyer. I can see he wants to laugh, but he won't because he doesn't want to break his clear authority - I'm pretty sure he just doesn't like me, but everyone else begs to differ. Once Eli is off the floor, and now kindly apologising with the offerings of bringing me lunch tomorrow (lasagne please!) Adam leads us down the stairs to the staff exit and I do my best not to 'accidentally' trip them both up on the way.

'It was his idea, not mine.' Adam protests, 'you know I wouldn't try and scare you like that,' his arms are in the air as he goes to shut down the lights for the ground floor. Eli and I make our way out the door and wait for him to return and arm the alarm.

For September it's already cold and I'm wishing I'd brought a coat, but I will not look weak and chilly like a pathetic wimp, I will watch the goose bumps on my arms erupt into small Kilimanjaro's of their own and continue to save face by lying to Eli when he asks if I need to borrow his jacket. I watch him drape it over my shoulders anyway. He's a good egg really, not my type at all though, usually. A ponytail full of thick caramel hair hangs by his shoulders and his skin hints of a natural tan, it could just be filth in the wrong light and I'm sure if you couldn't smell his Paco Robane from half a mile away you'd probably think it's the latter. He's a bit on the short side, too, I mean, I'm only 5ft 2inches, but he's got to be like only 5ft 8 inches and everyone knows the importance of height, right? It's not just his looks, of course, that would be totally shallow of me, which I'm not, I swear! Overall he's really an alright guy, he's kind and sometimes pretty funny, we seem to have similar taste in films (not a hard task when I love most things), but that's about as good as it gets mostly. There's nothing breathtaking about him, there's nothing homelike about him either. He doesn't make me want to jump his bones or bear his children, not that I'm sure I even fancy either of those things, but still, it's just not like it is when I'm with Tom.

Tom and I met at my old work about a year ago now, he is tall, distractingly dark and handsome, great arms, and eyes like an Island in the Indian Ocean - clear blue with a sunshine ring round the pupils. Somehow though, he still had a thing about him that made him seem goofy, like he wasn't totally well kept together, or not as much as he looked. He was so professional and proper I had to break him, see what was under the quiet, important colleague, see if I was right and really he was just a lad. Of course, I'm not great at small talk and the first time I got a chance I insisted we go dancing. I love the old movies and the courting process that my grandparents always harp on about - meeting someone, asking them to go to a dance with you, falling in love and living relatively okay without harming each other for sixty years... perfect. I hardly knew a thing about this man and here I am, a little blonde, baby faced, just turned 21-year-old, asking him to go dancing with me. Well, a few weeks later we did our generations version of going dancing, and by that, I mean doing it in his car - classy. Since then we have continued to "dance", but a year later we have progressed - I'd like to think. We're not together, but we're not, not together, if you know what I mean - we go for dinner, to nice places and local places and we have picnics and sleepovers and we care about how each other's days has been and, although we no longer work together, I see him more now than I did before. We've met each other's friends and I've met his mum and sister, we go out for each other's work nights, having both changed jobs, everyone in both places thinks we're together with neither of us correcting them. He's my plus one even when I don't need one and even on those days I don't feel like I want one. I know when I put it like that it sounds as though we're together - but we're not. I don't even want a boyfriend.

'You know he doesn't hate you.' Eli states, matter of fact. We just waved Adam off in his taxi and he didn't wave back so naturally I insist he must despise me. 'He's got a bloody great big crush on you and you know it... Everyone does.'

'He CLEARLY doesn't!' I make a throwing up gesture with my mouth, holding my hand to my neck. 'I'm not crush worthy and he is very obviously only interested in work- don't be a dick!' Eli goes to protest, but I can't let him, 'trust me, he wouldn't waste his time.'

I always thought Adam was nice enough. Quiet, brooding. He didn't really understand the banter thing very well and that's basically the only language I speak, but he was easy enough to get on with most days. Not someone I'd ever think of that way and I'm sure I wasn't for him either. Regardless, it's not like I'm even interested in boys. I know when you're in your twenties they're supposed to be men, I just struggle to find anyone that's worthy of the title. Besides, there's far more important things in life, like what I'm going to have for my third round of dinner tonight.

As Eli's taxi pulls in, I hand him back his jacket and shut the car door behind him. I feel guilty for almost wishing he was made from boyfriend material once the cold breeze hit my shoulders, but I swiftly backtrack to dinner and get my phone out to text Tom.

'Long. Ass. Day. Going to Mick and Lily's for my gazillionth meal (is it technically breakfast now it's after 12?) - I hope you've eaten and work didn't suck too terribly, see you this week?'

You know those couples that everyone talks about and hashtags "relationship goals" all over? John and Chrissy Teigen, Amal and George Clooney, Rapunzel and Flynn Rider, okay, maybe that last one is just me, but still, you get the point. Mick and Lily are my real-life version and, to be frank, a hundred times better than the others. I have only known them as long as I've been working at the cinema, about eight months now, but they're two of my favourite people. Lily is the sweetest, badass; the total opposite of me in personality, she's quiet and polite and yet super protective and fierce, like one of the Queen's Corgi's I imagine. Mick is less subtle, in the best way. He will never let Lily, or anyone else he cares about, get walked over and he works so damn hard, he's so passionate it inspires you to be a better person just because his energy makes you feel like you can be. It's hard to explain to someone that's never seen them or witnessed them together, but you know the kind of love in "Up" where Carl, even in his old age, still finds a way to keep his promises to Ellie? It's that. They would do anything for anyone, they're so kind and generous and you can see in everything they make and do, that it is done with so much love. They were meant for each other and trust me, I don't usually say icky shit like that, but they bring out the mush in me! Love is for co-dependent sissy's who can't bear to be independent for a split second, these two are the only exception. Fight me on it, I dare you.

'Here', I type in WhatsApp to Lily, even though I'm technically still on the bridge. By the time I get to the other side and cross the main road, which is traffic-less in the early hours, it will have given her time to fight with Mick about who's turn it is to open the door, then get down the three flights of stairs and let me in which overall equals less time stood out in the cold for me - genius I know. Even if it did take them a few extra minutes to get to the door, it would give me time to gaze longingly into the restaurant window below them. Lost in a world of food, as per usual. I step off the bridge and down the curb metres from their front door, when I'm abruptly and rather painfully stopped in my tracks… 'Ow. Jesus, Mary and Joseph. Ow. Bollocks'.

Chapter Two

Okay, breathe... deeper... 5,6,7,8,9,10. You're okay. Maybe. My eyes are full to the brim with water. I'd say I'm crying, but I would have no clue why. I don't think I did anything, I didn't step funny, I didn't slide off the curb, I didn't skip like I usually would so why in the name of the god I don't believe in, does it feel like I'm the priest in the Omen that the church spire has just ripped through? I'm pretty sure I'm shaking, it's probably not helping, but I also don't think I have much control over it, I can't move. I mean, I cannot physically take a step without feeling, well, I'm just not exactly sure what I'm bloody feeling. PAIN! Grey's Anatomy watching side of brain take over please. Sharp and dull pain in lower right side from back to foot, it can take no pressure or weight from even arm movement without causing significant agony throughout. No physical trauma, no impact or accident has occurred - diagnosis - sciatic pain due to increasing old age, rest up, should be fine in the morning... if I ever get my fat ass out of the road and into a bed! Lucky for me there's no cars approaching, maybe I wouldn't mind at this point.

'Why are you standing in the road crazy lady?' Lily let out a giggle that makes me totally jealous that I sound like a donkey when I laugh, or an evil Santa! She's standing in the doorway when I finish my 'wish I could get hit by a car' thought.

'Buddy, I can't move!' A heavy breath escapes my nostrils as I speak, as if I'm laughing with her about how silly it feels to say that out loud.

'You what?' She's still smiling, but has started to walk

over, I suspect she thinks I'm having her on. I try and step towards her in a vain attempt to push through the pain, but it cripples me to laugh. I can no longer explain what's happening, just hysterically laugh and cry until I, with a super strong Lily as a second bannister, make it up the three flights of stairs into their living room, and collapse, literally, on the couch.

Poor Mick's face is a picture, eyes wide with one eyebrow practically hiding in his hairline like the plastic surgery patient in Just Go With It. The pair of them questioning what in the hell I've done, whilst suffering the 'second-hand giggles' from me. Second-hand giggles are great fun because it's like totally free enjoyment! Think about it, you have no idea what you're happy about, just because someone else is happy it makes you happy and is that not just the purest kind of happiness there is? Unfortunately, at this point I think it's become mostly pain, tears and shock with every minor movement. I couldn't bend my body to sit naturally on the sofa, so instead, I opted for a fish out of water approach, which, in my head, is just throwing yourself onto the space, flopping like a wet fish in someone's hand until you're "comfortable". This isn't comfortable. I find that if I lean completely on my left side and don't move my right arm, the left side goes dead, and I don't feel a thing - this is the best it's going to get it seems. After sufficiently creasing with laughter and answering their many questions, it's almost 1am and I'm exhausted, but I'm too scared… to move to go home so I'm just going to wait it out. It's just a pulled muscle anyway I imagine, not even sciatica. I'm sure it will be fine soon and I convince the guys that it's nothing serious and suggest we whack a film on. Surprise, surprise, the people that work in the cinema love watching films in their down time.

That's one of the main reasons I adore my job. It's not something I ever dreamed I would want to do, and it's certainly not something I planned. On a whim one day, after one of my many solo movie experiences - it's the best way, I promise! I had made a joke to someone behind the counter on my way out about how I'd love to work there just to watch the films for free, I was immediately handed an application and told to bring in my CV. So i applied, got the job, and continue to adore film and cinema, maybe even more so now since I don't have to pay to watch movies. It's so nice knowing you can watch whatever you want whenever you want and gives you even more of an excuse to go on your own, not that you should need one. I do everything on my own and it's liberating as fuck. I repeat, who needs a man?

By the time Wreck-it-Ralph is over, it's 3am and I should eally be "making my way down town, walking fast, faces pass and I'm homebound..." no, no Vanessa Carlton, I should be making my way home. Home. I have work in six hours and it takes thirty minutes to walk from the flat back to my house on the other side of town, based on this I'll only be getting about four hours sleep if I set off right this second! Urgh! My brain makes a vain attempt to kick my body into gear to stretch off the couch, but nothing reacts. My limbs are refusing to respond to any signals that aren't pain, even breathing too heavily at this point seems to be making a bold statement.

'I think I'm stuck...' I sigh, trying not to let my voice break. I give a half-arsed smile that could also be considered a grimace depending on the way you look at me.

'Do you think maybe we need to call an ambulance?' Lily asks, Mick agreeing with vigorous head nods as she says it, you can just tell they're having a telepathic conversation about what to do with me. I, too quickly, decline their suggestion of emergency services. For starters it's 3am and I'm exhausted, I refuse to be stuck in a crappy, hospital waiting area for the rest of the night just to be told I've pulled a muscle and they can do naff all. Also, I have work tomorrow (well, today) and I'm not going in on no sleep, not for a fifteen-hour shift. We swiftly conclude that, no, I really cannot move, but I'm in "luck". I'm currently perched on the pull-out sofa bed, so all they must do is rag it out from beneath me and let me land-hopefully safely. Fun. At the count of three with one on either side, they yank the mattress from under my fat bum. Between them they've got the strength of two Mr Incredibles, but it still astounds me they're able to take my weight, especially after all the dinners I've eaten. When they drop the base in place I kind of roll with it, landing on my side like a scared little hedgehog. I haven't shaved in a week, so I probably feel like one too, but thankfully I'm fully clothed and nobody need find that out. There's a brief pause in movement as I let out a wail, causing them to freeze and let me have a minute to ecover from the agony. "Agony! Beyond power of speech! When the one thing you want, is the only thing out of your reach!" Not really the time for singing, but even in my suffering, I can't help myself to belt out some 'Into The Woods', Mick joins in. Once I'm settled and they've got the duvet and arranged my cushions; one under my side to prop me up, one under my knees for support and a shit tonne by my head because I like to feel like the queen I am... they scold me on how when I wake up, if I'm in the same pain, I am under strict instruction NOT to go into work and I am to wake them and go to the hospital... blah blah blah. I feel like I'm being told off by my parents, but it's adorable and I love them - maybe more than my actual parents, they certainly give more of a rat's ass. I try and argue that although they are technically my supervisors when we're in work, we are in fact, not working right now and nor will they be in tomorrow, so if it comes to calling in sick I can't exactly say they've told me not to go. How unprofessional.

I think they've stopped listening to me though, Mick plonks a glass of juice and the TV remote next to my make-shift bed as Lily turns the light out. 'If you need anything, just shout, or call us, our phones will be next to the bed, okay? And we mean it, no work tomorrow.'

The lounge door closes behind them, followed by their own bedroom door being slotted into its frame. I love staying here, usually in a more fit state, but regardless, it's like a second home. There's character in every corner - spaces designated for different TV memorabilia and favourite superheroes and art. My favourite is the Disney DVD movie collection, endless possibilities of cinema magic. The lounge is the best room in the house, when you close the door it feels like a labyrinth, somehow it gets bigger even though there's only just enough space for the sofas and the TV! The other Brucey-bonus about the place is the location, right over the bridge from work and around the corner from the beloved McDonald's - even though the only thing any of us like there is the breakfast and we're never up early enough to get any. That's the problem when you're so used to going to bed after 3am.

Speaking of time, it's now getting on for four and I'm still wide awake... I just need to sleep, maybe that will take the pain away, the catch being, however, I can't sleep because of the chuffing agony I'm in. I scan the room for things to count under the light of the TV; maybe if I count the mountain of Tsum Tsum's in the corner it will send me into slumber-land? Or the DVD's? A-ha, DVD's are the answer, but I won't be counting them. I can see the box is still atop the Xbox from my last visit and for the first time I'm happy to see it. Tarzan 2. This bloody film has been the bane of my life for months, I made the mistake of saying I'd never seen it and so now I must watch it, but every time I do I am asleep before the first five minutes are over, the first five minutes. It's my Achilles heel in an all-nighter and just what I need to send me off tonight. I reach for the controller and press play. The infamous castle shows and I naturally turn towards the screen, forgetting myself for a moment. The pain sears through me and tears overwhelm by eyes. I really hate crying.

Chapter Three

Shit. One hundred times shit. What time is it? Ugh! The sun is beaming through the little window next to the TV, we must've forgotten to shut the blinds last night and now my eyes are paying the price. I feel as though I've been asleep for decades, I've never felt more alert in my life and yet I only went to sleep after 4am and I haven't heard my alarm go off. Or have I? Bollocks. I rummage next to me to find my phone, which, now I mention it, hasn't been on charge all night so who even knows if it's on.

I am honestly so stupid sometimes there are no words, I don't like to play the dumb blonde card, but this morning that's my plea. Thankfully, the Blackberry buttons can be felt under my neck, and yes, I have a Blackberry, I traded my 'shattered into smithereens' iPhone 5 for it last week. At the time I was feeling nostalgic, but now I'm just feeling annoyed that the buttons have given me a bad neck. When I see the time shining brighter than the bloody sun off my screen I jolt up so fast you could mistake me for Flash. One small issue with that is: OW OW OW BASTARD, JESUS, MARY AND JOSEPH, OW! I stifle my cries knowing Mick and Lily will still be sleeping and try not to move more than an inch whilst I gather myself. Apparently, I haven't slept off my "pulled muscle" and it's much worse this morning. Once again, my eyes are full to the brim with tears, my body is rejecting any motion or pressure on the entire right side, so it looks as though my arthritic left joints will be taking the brunt of it. It's bad enough having arthritis at twenty-two, but now an old lady back spasm, oh I'm so desirable it hurts. Suddenly my mind is playing images of Lily and Mick circling my head like a bad movie; 'under no circumstances are you to go to work tomorrow'. Now, as it happens, I'm still in my work uniform, badge and all, from last night's shift and... it's 8.25 – thirty-five minutes until today's shift starts.

With my best efforts and as little movement as I can manage, I put the sofa bed back together and spray some random 'So... something' spray that I found in the side pocket of my bag. I check my face briefly in the mirror in the hall-way as I make my way out the front door and to the top of the staircase, what a sight for sore eyes. My face is blotchy from crying, gross, emotional tears, my hair is still plaited from two days before and the grease is finally starting to show, what a picture. I smudge yesterday's eye-liner into today's smoky eye, because I'm a boss bitch, then I tie my hair in a messy bun that makes me look way more Ms Trunchable than it does chic, but at least I tried. Now if conquering all those insignificant morning tasks left me feeling like I was surely dying, I can't possibly imagine what attempting the three flights of stairs below me was going to feel like. As long as I don't tumble down them I'm sure it can't be that bad?

Wrong. Twenty-five whole minutes it took me to walk down three flights of stairs, out the door and over the bridge to the staff doors. That's a trip that, any other time, only takes five minutes at a push, in fact, I think the Google Maps time is only four minutes and we all know they're slow as a parked car. Now, stood at the entrance to work, waiting for Adam to come and let me in, I feel like I may collapse if it wouldn't cause me so much pain, but also, strangely accomplished. What a success, I only must make it through fifteen hours of work and the half an hour it takes to walk home, then I will be fine.

When the door finally opens, Adam doesn't give me more than a second glance before turning back inside. It's not until we're ascending the stairs up to the office that he realises I'm not behind him and I'm hobbling metres away. His eyes scan me up and down thoroughly, like a medical robot, before he asks if I've done my ankle in. To distract me as I tackle the stairs, I focus on telling him that I'm totally fine: I just think I've pulled a muscle and although I can't really move, I probably shouldn't be here. Of course I'm going to stay anyway because I'm a stubborn piece of shit and by the time we reach the office I'm getting a lecture about how you should look after your body. He still hasn't even motioned that I should go home though and unless he says it first I'm staying - even if I can't stand up straight.

Because of my crippled state, I have managed to avoid filling the popcorn warmers this morning and render myself useless for any site checking responsibilities, whoop! There's still no discussion about me going home, despite the fact the other manager that is in has done nothing but question how I'm going to cope all day. I know I'm supposed to be the adult here and say I'm unfit for work, but surely if they have identified it and not done anything about it, there's no reason I should have to be the one to send myself off sick. It will only come back to haunt me later. To start my shift, I must trek all the way back down the stairs to the front of the counter. I make it to the first till two minutes before Adam comes down to open the front doors and God do I wish I had a chair. Health and Safety doesn't allow it, apparently. The second the doors are unlocked there are flocks of elderly men and women queuing at my desk. You can smell them before you can see them, that parma violet mixed with old must smell, utterly delightful, really. It's days like today you are oddly grateful for the overbearing stench of popcorn that you can never wash out of your clothes, or your hair, at the very least, it's good for masking the smell of old people wee. It takes twenty minutes to get them all through the queue and into the screen before the next bunch of guests arrive for the 10:20 showing of BFG. Ah small children and their hyper stressed parents - someone bring back the biddies. By the time they've gone through, I'm dead on my feet. I mean, I was before I even got here, but now, an hour in and I'm flagging desperately.

'Why don't you go for a break, or at least for a sit down?' Eli shouts from the back, as he's putting the biscuits away. It's been so manic this morning we've not had much chance to catch up, but I've managed to briefly fill him in on the back situation between guests - it sort of helps my case that I look like shit and am having to lean on the wall for constant support.

'You really do look awful, why are you here? You're too proud.' Peter is also on with us today, a total gem of a boy, started the same time as me and so we're kind of buddies. 'I don't know why they haven't sent you home, do you want me to ask?' There's no way I would leave them if we're going to be rammed like this all day, that would be cruel, and I wouldn't be able to relax knowing my absence was causing them stress. I shoot down the idea that Peter fights my battle by reminding him he should know better than to think I wouldn't do it myself if I felt it necessary. Also, that

I am a mental head and would much rather spend the day winding the pair of them up with my fabulous singing of every song I remember the words to. I do reason with them though and accept their offer of giving me first lunch break. Usually, on a fifteen-hour working day, I like to take my first break as late as possible, so the rest of the day goes fast, but realistically today is going to be moving at snail's pace regardless, so first lunch it is.

Hand on the rail, right foot up, left foot up, pause for breath, and repeat. I seem to have mastered the art of walking upstairs without crying, if I keep stopping to breathe between steps. There's only thirty-eight up and thirty-eight down every time I need a break. My left leg has become stiff from being the main support so far, the muscles are shaking from holding this hefty body weight all day and the spasms are causing my spine to twinge in distress with every pulse. It's not even worth the effort of getting up the stairs by the time I get to the staff room. All the chairs are spongy and thin, I don't even know what colour they are from stains and dust over the many years they've been dumped here. The room itself is a shit hole, wallpaper pieces everywhere, rubbish that has "missed" the bin and to make it worse, it smells like someone was cooking fish in the microwave days ago; regardless of all the signage that passive aggressively says not to do dumb crap like that. Please. I did toy with the idea of going into the manager's office on my break, so I'm not sat on my own, but Eli has brought me that lasagne and I'll be damned if I must share it.

Get in ma belly, (in the voice of Fat Bastard - I think I

look like him now too after that!) It took me a while to finish because I opted for a laying down position over two chairs to rest my back as much as possible, but then didn't want to choke and die so I had to eat slowly, in little bites. I've got Eli's coat over me as a blanket and twenty minutes left of my break, better check and make sure my phone hasn't died.

'Woman, you better not be at work' A WhatsApp from Lily... whoops. My phone is on thirty percent and it's only ten past two so I decide to respond with a simple 'Maybe...' She's going to kill me when she gets hold of me, I know it. As I am writing my reply I get another message 'WHY DID YOU MAKE THE BED?!' Oh hell, now I'm really in bother, I was trying to be polite! Ah well, she can shout at me tomorrow, we're on shift together then. I spend the next fifteen minutes fiddling with my phone. There's not any apps or anything installed because I try to not be always using it and the more rubbish I download the more likely it is to be in my hand, it's good practice. It's not like anyone other than Lily messages me anyway, Tom does probably once a day or so and we will have a little chat about how our respective days have gone, but nothing elaborate. I notice that I haven't heard from my parents even though I stayed out last night, that's not exactly a shock, but it does always bother me. If I can have the decency to tell them I'm staying out surely then can give me a 'k'? I contemplate calling, but decide to sack it off, it's time to get back downstairs anyway and I can't be bothered with the fight.

Chapter Four

It's gone midnight by the time I get out, it's hard to believe I lasted my whole shift. Come the afternoon it had significantly quietened down, there's not that many people who frequent a cinema during school time on a Thursday. I'm honestly shocked I'm still standing, I have used multiple people as crutches all day; Eli's been holding me up with his shoulder and an arm, letting me squeeze his hand when it got painful, Peter let me lean against his back like a trust exercise for a bit just to even me out when my left side seized up too. Adam has stayed in the office most of the day, probably just watching us on the cameras. It's only just really occurred to me that when Eli is here he doesn't talk much, maybe it's not me he doesn't like after all.

Regardless, it seems I am crutch-less on my walk home. I had the chance of a taxi, staff taxi - paid and everything, but my pride got the better of me, as it usually does. No, no, don't worry about me, I've lasted all day, what's a thirty-minute walk home? Really, I'm fine. I had protested only ten minutes ago in the office to anyone who would listen. Now I'm wishing I'd just swallowed my damn dignity and taken the lift when it was offered. I suppose I could call my parents and beg for one of them to come and get me, but again, I can't see it being worth the fight. I sent Lily another message during a pause in my walk, 'Managed the full shift-check me out! On my way home now, see you in the morning! Oh, and thanks for letting me crash, literally! Ha-ha!' She doesn't reply immediately, but when she does it's another telling off and a warning not to go into work the next day if

I'm still suffering - pfft she thinks I'm going to listen?! I opt for texting my parents, too, just to say I've done my back in and I am on my way home, not to forget about me and to leave the porch light on, please! I sent it to both of them just in case one of them wants to please ignorant. I also text Tom whilst I'm at it, trying to keep it short, but sweet, totally casual and like I don't even care if he replies - because I absolutely don't care, he can do what he wants. We're not together.

'Hey mister, hope you've had a good day today? I'm working till close on Saturday if you are? Fancy a Sunday lie in?'

Up the driveway the porch light is off. I check my phone and notice the message has been opened and clearly ignored. Pushing the door shut as quietly as i can behind me, i slip off my popcorn filled shoes on to the rack. I see the light from the parents' bedroom die a sudden death. It was glowing through the gap in the bottom of the door onto the entry way laminate, but I imagine it was turned off so I would assume they were sleeping and didn't get my message... turn off your read receipts next time. I lock the door, both latches and with my key, then head up to my room. My bedroom is in the loft because we live in a converted bungalow, and although I never cared to have the upstairs to myself, I was never allowed the bedroom downstairs "in case someone breaks in", my dad would argue, as if they wanted to protect me. I know I'm upstairs because with me all the way up here, they can pretend I don't exist and like they never had their little accident baby. Parental neglect aside, I do have a relative amount of space if I wanted to do something with it, but I mostly just use it to make dens. There's an en suite bathroom so I don't have to worry about going up and down to disrupt them with my urge to urinate; I'm most glad for that tonight because these stairs are killing me in this state! All that's left is a little kitchenette and it's like a bedsit. If I had a fridge and an oven up here I'd never leave again. I did ask my dad once, for a fridge, but he said the cost of electric for me to have one would be too extortionate - much like that cruise around the Caribbean the pair of you went on when I was ten, no?

I can't remember the last time I was this grateful to see my bed, it's only a single, I keep meaning to buy a double, but worry if I ever move out it won't fit wherever I go. The quilt is a double, duck feather down and the sheets are woolly to accommodate my skin that is usually as cold as my heart! I have also got a bit of a soft toy problem, in which I have far too many and I feel guilty if I don't sleep with them all at once. There's Mr Bear, a 5ft cappuccino, cuddly dream boat, better than any man! Then, in no particular order, there's Mushu, Gaston, Pascal, Alien, Kanga, Pooh, Tigger, Flynn and Rapunzel, Gus Gus, The Cheshire Cat and a little pink giraffe, lovingly, named Gilbert - he was my only Beanie Baby and he's the longest standing member of the clan, the only none Disney member, too, but he's an honorary at this point. Tonight, however, I'm sorry to say to the lot of them that they'll be sleeping on their own in the den I was living in the other night. Apart from Mr Bear though, I think I can use him as back support. I lay him on his side and burrow backwards into him, keeping my left side into the bed and pulling a squishy arm around my neck, then dragging one of his legs between my knees as further spine support. I feel as comfortable as I can, I think, as I turn the TV on to the last DVD I was watching.

'Out the door, just in time, head down the 405, gotta meet the new boss by 8am', the Scrubs title sequence plays and I lip-sync along with it for a minute until it automatically starts the episodes on "Play all". I don't make it through the first episode before I'm asleep - I knew I should've set the timer.

I know I don't believe in the Lord our Saviour and all that, but do we think if I prayed hard enough to make up for the last twenty-two years of ignorance that he'd forgive me and make my back better ASAP? Didn't think so. No sign of improvement this morning and to make things even more annoying I can't seem to have my morning wee. I better not have a UTI as well, I haven't had sex for nearly two weeks, but with that now on the brain, I check my phone to see if Tom has replied.

'Won't be able to do a Sunday morning lie in, in work at 7, but if you don't mind an early start? I finish at finish tonight so I'll call you later. Have a good day'.

Bugger. Ah well, at least I can still see him and it gives me something to look forward to with another fifteen hour day ahead. I always forget his hours are as silly as mine, I suppose security work is more hard work than I give him credit for, even if he does spend most of his days eating snacks behind a camera. My skin is flushed from reading his name on my screen and suddenly I feel like a ridiculous person, a warm, happy person, so I decide not to reply right away as a punishment to myself for being such a loser.

lthough, it isn't his fault... *'looking forward to it!'* ... I shouldn't have put the exclamation mark, but it's sent now so sod it, that'll teach me. As I hobble down stairs, rucksack in hand - I daren't put it on my back, I'm starting to think that going in to work in this state isn't going to help. Already dressed in a clean uniform and a brand new face of makeup, being half way down the stairs at this point means that at I'm going whether I should be or not.

'Right, I'm going to work,' I tell my parents who are feeding each other croissants off the kitchen counter, 'I'm on until close so I'll be home late, please leave the light on for me if you can.'

I try not to sound too passive aggressive, letting a smile jump from my face to let them know I didn't mean anything by it.

'Well you know when you text that late we're asleep Pip, so we didn't actually get your message until this morning when it was too late.' The way she eyes my dad at the point she says "asleep" makes me cringe a little.

'Try to message us within good time next time.' Dad pipes in, I wonder if he'll ask about my back since they now claim to have read my message.

'Pee Pee, can you book us two seats for the new film adaptation of Girl on a Train, please when you get to work, premier seats remember. Thanks.'

No mention of my back, but a favour asked using the world's worst nickname. Of course. My full name is Philippa Ingrid Parker, but everyone I know just calls me Pip, I don't know if it's short for Philippa or just my initials, but either way it's better than Pee Pee.

They're not usually cinema go-ers, my parents, but

anything my mum has read, my dad will watch in film. When it's over, he will say how wonderful it was and she will compare it directly to the book and say it was shit. Following that, they then argue incessantly about why my dad should read more and how she's tired of explaining poor plots to him because they failed to follow the book and now the whole thing makes no sense. The one thing I do agree with my dad on, is how a book should never directly be compared to a film. It's a different form of media altogether so it can't possibly be the same. Either learn to respect it for what it is or stop going to watch them. I always say I never got anything from my parents, I must've been found in one of the bushes next to the driveway, but actually, I got his love of film and her stubborn nature - lucky me.

Naturally, the first stop on the way to work, even when I can hardly move, is the Co-op at the top of the hill. Meal deal for lunch? Yes, please! I opt for a triple cheese sandwich, a Cheesestring and a Tropicana multi-vitamin. Heaven only knows I'm not getting the nutrients I should from my excessive cheese intake. Do I look like I care mister cashier man? Purely rhetorical because I most certainly do not. I have to cram it all in to my tiny Kate Spade bag that mum bought me from her "girls trip" to Ibiza. It's fake, of course, she could only afford the real one for herself, but I like to use it for work instead of my real Michael Kors. I don't care too much if wannabe Kate smells like popcorn and sadness at the end of a day.

I cried all the way to work on the bus, I couldn't help it. With every bounce and pothole I felt like I was shattering into a million pieces like Mike TV on Willy Wonka, only this wasn't getting pixilated this was torture. Usually, when

I press the bell to get off, I stand and walk to the front before the bus stops so I can jump right off. Not today. I wait until the driver has stopped completely before standing, using the pole for leverage and saying 'I'm so sorry' to everyone for holding them up - still crying. As I go to step off the lowered step, my phone starts vibrating and playing 'Up the Junction' by Squeeze. Hurriedly stepping off the bus I scramble for my phone, which is underneath my sandwich in my bag. The cheese strings fly out and land in the road, but I can do nothing about it except cry harder. Oh shit, better wipe my eyes and pull myself together - it's Lily.

'Hey buddy, I'm nearly there now, I thought I started at 9.30 today or was it supposed to be nine? I'm so sorry I'm literally outside I just got off the bus I just have...' before I can finish telling her I only have to cross the road and I'm there, she cuts in.

'Buddy, you are not coming in today, go home.'

'But I'm here! I'm okay, I just have to get across the road!' My best efforts to argue are failing me and I can hear my own voice breaking as I try and convince her of my wellness.

'I can see you from the office window - that is you trying to pick up a Cheesestring from the floor with your foot isn't it?'

Of course it was me, I consider this some of my best multitasking to date; crying from debilitating pain, convincing my manager I'm able to work today, holding a phone in my only good hand and using my only good leg to successfully pick up a Cheesestring. I'm like a monkey!

'You're obviously not fit for work today, I've spoken to the other managers and you're not coming in, get yourself to the doctors and let me know what they say, okay?'

On a normal day I resent that my quack is based in the town centre, but I've noticed today is a different kind of day and right now I'm just pleased it's only a ten minute walk around the corner. Maybe twenty at this pace. Waving goodbye to Lily, who is still watching in the window for me to leave, I head straight across the bridge toward the surgery. BEEP, BEEP! I haven't even made it half way over before a car pulls up next to me.

'What in the hell has happened to you?! Get in!' It's my best friend Annie, we've known each other since we were two, but only got really, super close when we got to secondary school. She's the sister I didn't have - lucky for her! I take a minute with lots of grunting and heavy breathing to climb into the passenger seat, the cars behind started beeping and I could tell she's getting nervous for being in their way.

'Where are you going?' she asks as she pulls back into the traffic.

'Well, I'm supposed to be going to the quack,' I say, then briefly and rapidly explain what's happened as she drives multiple times around the roundabout. When I finish she pulls off in the opposite direction of the doctors.

'It's super busy down there, I've just been to pick up some files and it's heaving.' Annie works as a secretary to paediatric consultants at the hospital and there is nobody I think that is better suited for the job. 'I'm heading back to the hospital anyway so I think I'm better off dropping you at A&E?' She asks the question, but I know there is no response necessary, she's asking to be polite because she feels bad for commandeering the route without going back and forth for ten minutes first about who's going to make the decision.

Chapter Five

I told Annie there was no need to come and sit in A&E with me, that she should get back up to work and I'd text her the details. As much as I could tell she didn't want to leave me, she also didn't want to be late for work and with my blessing she felt a little better about abandoning me. I kid, of course, she has not abandoned me, even if that is what I shout to her as she scurries down the corridor.

As I turn into the accident and emergency department I am greeted with what seems to be a fairly busy waiting room for a Friday morning. There are a couple of screaming toddlers to my right in the children's waiting area, both with an army of adults, each, fussing over them, showing them all the different books and toys and pretending to understand how they're feeling even though they have no clue what is wrong with them. Christ on a pancake, it's infuriating enough when you have a cold and everyone tells you how they sympathise with how awful it is - like NO JANICE, you do not know how my body is responding to this cold, back off! I bet those poor little munchkins are only crying now because a rally of dumb adults are pretending to know what is going through their little brains, I'd be crying harder just to give them all a headache; it's certainly working on me and I've not done anything wrong, I don't think.

I join the queue with only one man in front of me and he seems visibly okay so fingers crossed he's just got a bit of concussion or something. Not that that's a good thing to have either I suppose. When it is finally my turn, I hesitate for a moment, worried that I may fall over or collapse in two if I try and move suddenly. I tell them my name and the reason for my visit; he had the audacity to ask if I'd gone over on my ankle before I'd had chance to answer his question and so I took great pleasure in explaining that is not the case at all. I acknowledge that it will be a wait time of two hours then gingerly turn to take a seat.

The worn, blue hospital chairs are lined down all the walls in the waiting area and then two rows run back-to-back down the centre creating a partition. There's only about enough room for people to squeeze sideways through to the other chairs so I knew that section was off limits for me, far too much hobbling around to get over there. Not only that, in the corner were two teenage girls, in school uniforms that I didn't recognise, talking loudly about their drug dealing boyfriends and getting weed later. Not to be a baby, but teenage girls are scary and drug dealers aren't my forte so I opted for the seats directly facing the children's bookshelf, facing away from the distorted television and the "cool" kids.

Next to me, an elderly gentleman with a big bald head and little round shoulders, started coughing, what sounds like, his guts up. Do you have to ask somebody if they're alright because they're your hospital waiting room neighbour? Will he even be able to answer me if he's coughing to death? Thankfully, before I can open my mouth and make a giant tit of myself, the little lady to the right, opposite us, stretches a hand out to his wobbling knee. I think the cough is going right through him. To make things a bit more awkward, I am completely uncomfortable in my current position, but I daren't shift my body on the left side any further in fear it seems I am trying to lean as far away from the man as possible. Slowly, I fidget around, making clearly overly dramatic groaning sounds and sighing with every flinch. I am trying to make it perfectly clear that I am only moving due to lack of comfort, only I think, now, I've made too much eye contact. I look away, hanging as far over the left arm of the chair as possible without causing further injury - grateful there's nobody else sitting in the chair that side of me, otherwise it might look like I was trying to do something a bit naughty. I think I'd really put my back out doing that!

'Excuse me, young lady?' The presumed daughter of the coughing man, reaches over and tries to make eye contact with me. 'Excuse me, are you alright?'

'Sorry, I didn't realise you were talking to me! Is everything okay?' I could feel my cheeks burn as I lied about not understanding it was me she wanted to communicate with. Of course, I knew, I was just hoping she'd not be persistent. And I'm a shoddy excuse of a liar.

'Yes, sorry to bother you. It just looks like you're having some trouble with your back?'

'Oh, right. Yes, kind of. I think I've just pulled a muscle, nothing dire.'

'Well, I've had troubles with my back before and I just think you could benefit from a cushion behind you for support. Here, let me.' The overly friendly, and frankly unqualified, back specialist stood up and takes my little bag from my hand. She leans in behind me and tries propping it against my back on the right side - the side I'm clearly trying to avoid putting pressure on!

'Lean back and try this, I know it's not exactly a soft pillow, but it should help a little?' Her eyes are focused intently on my movements as I slowly ease myself onto my leather bag, the sandwich box protruding through the front into me. I try so hard not to wince, but my eyes squeeze closed and my teeth bare together, sharply inhaling through the discomfort. I quickly force a smile and say thank you, it is actually more comfortable now and I appreciate the help. Unfortunately though, that's another lie. It hurts even more than I imagine having a pineapple rammed up your bum might and don't even get me going again on how much I cannot tolerate unrequested assistance and opinions. Thanks, but no thanks.

'Philippa Parker, please!' Wiry grey hair can be seen over the top of a clipboard; below a plump frame sporting a nurses uniform and some black Crocs. You know, not the big clunky ones, the slimmer version that aren't as immediately humiliating, but Crocs, nonetheless. As the clipboard lowers, I can only smile into the featureless abyss that is facing me, hoping she acknowledges this as, 'I'm coming just give me one-hundred years to stand up'.

'Do you need a wheelchair?' She is asking it as a question, but it demands itself an irritated statement of, 'you'd be saving us all some time if I could just push you in there.' I politely decline and side step as quickly as possible into the box room indicated by a bony hand. The triage nurse will see me now. We both take a seat either side of the desk and she begins to take down my details from the clipboard as I get as comfortable as I can. It's a tiny room, I'd quite like to see more than four people get inside without suffocating to death. Plastered across the little wall space, are posters of the human body and unrealistic pain charts - please don't try and convince me that just because someone is smiling it doesn't mean they're experiencing no pain, honestly who made this shit? I try my best to grin from ear to ear to prove a point, but even though I can't see my face I have a feeling it just looks like I'm smelling a sour fart and trying to be discreet about it. Before she looks up I let my face drop again.

I spent about five minutes going through my medical history and what had happened to make me come in to the hospital and the whole time I could've sworn she was just thinking about what she was going to have for tea - until I mentioned my morning wee failure. I don't really know what made me remember it to be honest, when she first asked if I'd had any problems with my bladder or bowel (Urgh, the word makes me sick - MOIST I can handle, but bowel - gross!) I'd said no, but then I was wittering on about my morning and it just slipped out. Of course, she scalded me for denying I had experienced any symptoms previously, but said she'd be right back because she had to go speak to a doctor. I've been in with the triage nurse a few times before this and the usual drill is to take some notes then kick us back to the waiting room to wait another two hours to be taken into a bay and seen by a doctor, I've never seen anyone else or myself experience the nurse running off for a quick chat before she lets you go. Four and a half times I watched the big hand on the very loud clock trickle around the hour, that's on top of the time I'd already waited before I had even started counting.

When she finally returned she had a wheelchair for me and a rather good looking care assistant to take me away in it - he could've been taking me anywhere and I'd have gone quite happily. I'm pulled into a bay straight away and three members of staff are rallied to help me onto the bed.

It's a standard white sheet, hospital bed with the sides up to stop me rolling out considering my most comfortable position is way over on my left, holding onto the cold metal for support. Thankfully, I'm not left long before a doctor arrives. She is easily the nicest person I've spoken to so far, chirpy, blonde, petite with surprisingly manly hands for such a tiny frame. Unfortunately an annoyingly prominent feature I wish I'd never noticed as she explains she needs to do some very invasive tests. I have only known her five minutes and she's already asking to put fingers in places I don't even let boyfriends go. As much I'm reluctant, I kind of have to let her do it, at least she's not a man, a really attractive man.

'Can I just borrow you a minute Si?' My doctor, that I have been okayed to call 'Shannon', is whispering through my curtain in to the corridor whilst I get as far over on my side as I can. My head is facing the floor, I don't really feel like looking anyone in the eye right now, so all I can see is a pair of trainers by my head as a firm hand rests on my shoulder. Shannon stands behind me and I can feel them together, pulling my work leggings down around my bum, pants and all. 'Now, I just need you to tell me when you can feel me touching you, okay?' I try and keep my head focused on the floor to not compromise when I can feel and when I can see. This 'Si' character appears to be wearing some fancy Nikes to work today, let's hope I'm not suddenly violently ill all over them!

'Can you feel this?'

'Feel what?' What a stupid thing to say, no would've sufficed.

'What about here? Do you know where my finger is?'

The more I think about it the more stressed I can feel

myself becoming, it hadn't occurred to me that I couldn't feel things, I don't suppose I'd been really thinking about it, but now it was making me nervous. My eyes filled a little causing a single tear to slide off my face and onto the nice white trainers under me. My hand began to tremor against the railing.

'Don't worry Philippa, or do you prefer Pip? I only have one more thing to check, in a moment I am going to be putting my finger inside your bottom and I will ask you to squeeze as hard as you can for me, you might find it uncomfortable so I'm going to use lots of cold jelly, you've been warned! Simon can hold your hand if you need to.'

'Pip is fine, thank you and...' I look up to face Simon, it's the super attractive care assistant that wheeled me in and now he's about to witness me losing any last hope of dignity- talk about being mortified! Oh well, I no longer care what anyone thinks, 'I don't need my hand holding, I'm a big girl - in every sense of the word quite obviously, I've got more rolls than Greggs, but I'll be fine thanks though.'

They both laugh and continue to try and make me feel better by talking about some people they treat who struggle to even stand up because of their rolls; I know it doesn't sound too professional, but it makes me laugh and I appreciate them trying.

When I've done what she asks, she cleans up the jelly mess and they get me re-dressed. As they're pulling my trousers back up Shannon lets me know that she's going to see if she can get me in for an MRI scan this afternoon so they can have a better look at what might be going on and that she'll be back to let me know what is said. She hands me my mobile from my bag then Simon leaves too, much to my approval. Great, no signal. Luckily they pulled the curtain back slightly when they left so I badger everyone who passes until I am given the phone from the ward. I use it to call Annie. When she answers I get to hear her work voice, smooth, soft and sickly sweet. She is due to finish work at 16.30, which is in the next couple of hours, so she says she'll come down and keep me company for a while until we know what's going on, then she'll take me home if that's where I'm headed. We both agree that it probably is where I'm destined, because there's usually very little they can do for a bad back, apart from a finger job apparently.

Chapter Six

Dur. Dur. Dur. Dur...Thank you Baby Cheesus for the gift of ear plugs in this time of need. MRI scanners are loud. 20th Century Fox at the start of a film, loud, only this isn't a tune you can sing along with. I don't even know why they asked what kind of music I wanted through the headphones they put on me because over the whirring of the gradient coil, I can't hear a thing. It took three people to get me from my bed to the 'MRI safe' bed and then on to the machine itself. They had to use a PAT slide because any attempt at movement at this point is just making me cry and cry again. Piercing my ice cold skin is a drip through which I'm receiving intravenous paracetamol to help target the pain quicker whilst we wait for the morphine to kick in. Oromorphe tastes like sick on a spoon so I hope it works quick enough that they don't have to give me any more.

I got taken from my bay just before four o'clock so I'm hoping by the time I'm done Annie will be waiting for me - preferably with my Cheesestring in hand, I'm suddenly starving. The machine stops grinding and the sudden silence is deafening. Through the headphones a voice sings that it's all done and they're coming through to get me out. As my football head emerges from the tunnel, there are seven members of staff waiting to PAT slide me back over onto the bed and to wheel me out. That's a lot more people than they used to get me in, I must've been an extra well behaved patient, I did refrain from pressing the panic button after all.

'It will be surgery.' I hear the technicians talking through the doors I'm parked by as I wait for a porter to come and take me back to A&E. They're talking about the guy in the machine who must have some rare problem because there's only one bloke in the room who knows what it's about and has ever seen it before. What it must be to see these curious things like that on a daily basis, to be watching what is happening in someone's body and not be able to do anything about it. After what feels like forever, two men stroll in to the unit to take me back to my bay. They don't seem to be in a hurry, but they do apologise for taking so long to get here, the morphine must be working because I'm able to respond with a quippy, 'An apology is all well and good, but we all know you're not really sorry unless you bring a girl flowers!' They laugh and I feel better for being funny, it's who I am and when I'm crying in pain, I do not feel like myself at all.

'They told me you had gone home, I thought you were going for an MRI, I thought it was your spine? I've had to leave because they said you're not here... let me know what's going on! Love you! XXX'

What in the hell? En route back to the A&E department, my phone buzzed with a message from Annie. Once I have been gently slipped back onto my bed in the bay and I'm comfortably waiting for the MRI results, I begin my harassment to borrow the ward phone again. But, before I get chance to get hold of it and call Annie, Shannon pops her head around my curtain. 'Hi Pip, I've just been looking at your MRI and we need to have a chat.' She pulls the curtain behind her and steps toward my bed.

I cannot hear a word she is saying. Her lips are moving, her hands are demonstrating, but I can only hear my own blood pumping in my ears, loudly. Surely not, they weren't talking about me, they were talking about him, HE had to have an operation, HE has the rare, horrible illness that no one has a clue about... not me.

'An ambulance is on its way for you and you'll be taken through to the Leeds General Infirmary where they'll do the operation. I'm so sorry I can't give you more information, but it's not something any one here has physically seen before today and I don't want to give you the wrong information when you'll be seeing the specialist who can tell you all about it.' She sounds so sorry for me and I can't fully understand why, my brain is still only trying to remember more of what the MRI techs said in case I missed something.

'So, I am going to Leeds now and they will send me a letter in the post to have an operation with them another time after I've seen the specialist today?'

'Pip, you're having an operation tonight, now, when you get to Leeds, they need to operate as soon as possible. This is serious and it's very important that you call someone to go with you. I'm sorry I can't give you any more information, I just don't want to wrongly inform you.'

I think my eyes are glazed over at this point, not with tears, just with thoughts. So many words rolling across my face like the Stars Wars opening sequence, only much faster and far less concise. What does any of this actually mean? I manage to ask for the phone to call someone to be with me, I don't usually require other people for this sort of thing, but since the doctor said I should, I feel I need to take her word for it. She is the professional after all and I have been unusually emotional today. My first dial is Lily.

She didn't let the phone ring more than twice before she answered, and it wasn't until I heard her voice that I had a complete meltdown. My voice broke and my face became Victoria Falls. I'm surprised she could understand a word I was saying, but that's true friendship for you, even through all the blubbing, she can understand me better than most. I tried to explain as best I could about what was going on and as I talked it out I lead myself, and her, to the conclusion that it was probably a slipped disk and I was going to be fine. I'd obviously never slipped a disk before now, but from what I understood it was fixable and not that bad in the long run. Pulling myself together and clocking the time at nearly 17:30, I had to get off the call and dial Annie, she'd be worried sick by now. I promised to keep Lily in the picture and she promised that her and Mick would be straight through if I needed them.

Annie's phone rang twice as long as Lily's, but she answered in just as much of a panic. Even though I wasn't calling from my phone she knew it was me, she recognised that I would be calling from a No Caller ID if I was still in the hospital - doesn't miss a trick that one. Again, I explained what had happened, only this time I was much calmer; I think talking myself down into it being a slipped disk had really helped, as well as talking it out with my biggest support systems. At this point, there's only Tom left to tell, if I even need to? We're not together and so it doesn't affect him if I'm in the hospital or not, why would he care and why should I feel like I can rely on him, anyway? Annie's voice is steady, she's clearly in panic mode. Anyone else would think she's totally unfazed, but much like when she sneezes, I'm the only one who can tell it wasn't a cough, and now, I'm the only one who can see straight through her logical responses and read the distress in her words.

'Have you called your parents? Do you not think they should be there? Will they come with you in the ambulance?' I don't even know why she asked that last question.

'Shit, you're right, I should probably call them, not that they will give a rats arse anyway!'

'Don't be like that, give them some credit, you're having an operation, I'm sure they'll care!' I let her think she's right before I cut the call off, again, promising to keep her in the loop. Mum and Dad are next on my list.

I'm genuinely shocked that dad even answers his phone, until I remember it's dialling in as an unknown caller and not my own phone number. He is far too nosy not to answer when someone he doesn't know calls, I'm the same.

'Hello, can I help you?' His favourite and only way that he ever answers his phone, even when he can read his caller ID and see it's me!

'Hi dad, it's Pip...' I don't get chance to continue with what I need to say before he's cutting in...

'Oh Pee Pee, why is your number not working on this stupid car phone? Honestly, I keep meaning to take this thing to get looked at,' he grumbles to himself, wittering on about how he's due an upgrade about now, surely. He isn't. 'Anyway, can you make this quick as we're on our way to the open evening at The Spa and I want to call them to let them know we're going to be a bit late, traffic is madness and this town just gets worse and worse.' I can hear mum talking over him whinging about how she was late out of work too and that she's in dire need of a relaxing massage because she's just SO stressed - cleaning is harder work than it sounds you know!

'Can you just listen to me a minute?!' I snap at them for

being so rude, I was the one that called them and if they wanted me to be quick then they should start listening to me in the first place. 'I'm at the hospital and I'm waiting for an ambulance to take me to Leeds so I can have an emergency operation on my back. I don't know what I've done or what the operation entails, but it sounds maybe like a slipped disk or something. They're on the way for me now and I'll be having the operation when I get there. The doctor said I should call somebody to be there with me so that's why I'm ringing.' Phew, and breathe! There's a short silence that I don't expect before my mum comes on over the speaker.

'Pip, we're almost at The Spa now, we're never going to be able to get all the way back to the hospital before your ambulance arrives, I'm sure...'

'I tell you what, don't worry about it, I can call Lily and Mick and they will come through, or Annie. I'm sure there's someone else who will do it, you enjoy your evening and I'll let you know what they say.' My voice is curt and cold, but I add an edge of 'no really it's fine' just to see if I can get some guilt out of them. I should've seen this coming really. Of course they'd rather have a night at the spa than sit in the hospital with me, their only child, who wouldn't? I know even if they don't come I won't be calling anyone else. I will manage on my own, no question, I do everything else solitary so what's so different about this, it's just an operation. I can't see it being a problem if I get a taxi home when they're done cutting me open, as long as I'm not driving myself. They might be keeping me over night anyway. Suddenly, dad pipes up.

'No, no, it's not that we don't want to.' His protest is weak. 'It's just that we've had this planned and we'll have to call them and lose the deposit, although, actually we are nearly there so maybe we're better off just going in and explaining; we might even get the money back if we say what's happened to you.'

'Good idea,' mum chirps.

'We won't be there for the ambulance, but we'll come to the hospital as soon as we can. Unless you can call us and say you're going in before we get there, then there's not really any point in us being there just to sit around. But if we don't hear from you we'll be there when we can. How's that?

'Fine, don't put yourselves out, I'll let you know what they say, but I have to go because I'm using the ward phone and the ambulance guys are here for me now.'

Mum mumbles something about, 'see, told you we wouldn't have made it in time.' I hang up before I say any more.

Chapter Seven

Stella was not a fantastic driver. She was clearly a skilled paramedic, very strong and witty, not fazed by much and had a response for everything. She had a "stellar" figure, too - get it?! Even in those unflattering forest green, uniforms you could tell she worked hard on her appearance, but her driving was poor. Ian, on the other, was a bit of a wet blanket in comparison. A short, red headed... boy, rather than a man, I'd say. His frame was safe for small children in that all of his edges were round and the only thing he had that made him stand out as a person was his dangerously spiky hair - think Gareth Gates era! No jokes, no charm, no personality at all really, just a bit of a stick up his bum about rules and regulations. 'Please don't rest your legs against the side like that, if we hit a bump and you knock yourself I don't want anyone to end up in trouble.' He would come out with little remarks like that the entire journey to the LGI, an hour's drive, even in an ambulance.

Upon arrival We were informed a bed would be ready for me on the spinal unit and so when we arrived we were sent straight upstairs. This is not a hospital I've ever been to, not that I frequent them, of course. It's not that the place was unsanitary, it just looks like it's not been washed, the paint is old and the railings are wobbly and the floors are permanently marked from dodgy bed wheels. It's well used, to put it nicely. Once out of the tiny staff only elevator, we trail down some ever expanding corridors until we reach the ward, I'm moving in to L27.

The woman on the phone said that a bed was ready for me

when they called to say I was here, however, pulling me into the expected bay, there wasn't a bed in sight, so what now? Do I sleep on the floor here? Out of nowhere, a little woman appeared, donning a light blue nurses tunic and, you guessed it, crocs. She was talking two-hundred miles per hour and I only managed to catch something about not expecting me yet, even though they'd had over an hours warning of my arrival. Once she'd put some sheets on a bed for me, white with a knitted blue blanket, she enlisted the ambulance crew to help PAT slide me across, it took 2 extra pillows under my legs to get me comfortable, but they did their best. I was left to my own devices for a short period of time whilst the crew went to hand over to the nurses station and get someone else to come and check my vitals. On their way out, Stella and Ian come back by my bed to say goodbye and wish me luck, just as I was wishing they didn't have to leave so soon, the little nurse came back with the blood pressure machine.

The bay I've been put in is quite big compared to the ones back at home, I'm in the bed closest to the door as you walk in so I can see down to the nurses station if I squint hard enough. Opposite me in bed number eight, a fragile frame of a woman, is slouched half way down the raised bed, her neck forward so I can only see the top of her matted grey head. If she was heavy enough to have chins she could use them as a cushion right now. From her surroundings she seems to have been here a while; there's lots of boxes of fruit scattered on her table at the foot of her bed, grapes, mostly. There's also a few vases of flowers on the tall cupboard next to her, I smelt the lilies before I could see them.

Behind the stained curtain to the right of me, there's a putrid smell of poo coming from what I gather is bed number six. I have zero view because, thankfully, the curtain is closed, I can just see the wheel of the commode from beneath the trim. This can only mean she must be sitting on it closer to my side of the bay than I'd like to think about. I imagine her as a younger, plump woman, in comparison to the woman in bed eight. Short, unkept hair, most likely dark, with a bum that just about fits on the bedpan. Her grunting only enhances my mental image of her nearing gorilla territory, so I turn my head away and focus, instead on the nurses station.

'I'll buzz you in.' I watch as the nurse at the desk presses a hand against the button on the wall to let someone in. It's after visiting hours, just gone eight thirty, so I can only think it is my two favourite people coming to finally see me.

The sound of her best, black heels echo down the corridor. 'Stewart and Ann Parker here for Philippa Parker, she was brought in via ambulance earlier on?' The nurse, who I will keep note of in my "people who cannot be trusted" pocket book from this point forward, walks my parents down to my bed, bringing my painkillers with her. I reluctantly take the morphine and let it stain my mouth with its ill taste, I hope I don't have to take too much more of this before they fix me up, it's vile! I then proceed to let the nurse explain to mum and dad who we're waiting for and that we will get more information as soon as possible. In the meantime, they will need to do some paper work to admit me and get me in a gown, just to speed up the process before they take me to theatre. She scurries off behind the curtain next to me to assist the lady who, by now, has finished on the toilet and insists she'll be back in a jiffy.

Mum is the first to sit down, she takes the large arm chair

next to the head of my bed and dad props himself on the end of my mattress by my feet, not too careful to miss my toes.

Again, I go through the story of how I got here, tired of explaining myself at this point and pretty exhausted in general, hospitals are no walk in the park and I'd been in one since 10am. Silly, to complain though. Mum has been at work for a full seven hours today and as she keeps saying, she could've used that massage at the spa because her back is just killing her from the bending down. Dad contributes to this lovely story by reassuring me they will have their deposit back in three to five working days and it's a good thing I am in the hospital otherwise they wouldn't have had a chance of getting a refund - you're so very welcome, glad I could finally be of some use to you both.

Although it certainly feels like a lifetime of making small talk, it's only over an hour before I finally get to meet the registrar they've all been talking about. Her name is Rachel and so far, she's my favourite person here. She doesn't look too much older than me, maybe seven years or so, she has boxy glasses on and dark brown hair tied back in a short, pony tail. Her height dominates her presence in the room, demanding attention, but she's only interested in speaking to me.

'Hi Pip, I hope it's okay I call you that? I'm so sorry it's taken me so long to get up here to see you, I've just been in another surgery and since then have been checking over your file and scans and so on.' She asks me what has happened and I explain as politely as I can, as plainly as possible because she does seem nice and I know it isn't her fault that I have to tell the story one-hundred times, it just infuriates me more each time I utter the words.

'Okay, I've had a look at your scans and I'm really sorry to say, the reason we are having to operate on you today is because you have something called Cauda Equina Syndrome. Have you ever heard of it?' Naturally I hadn't, she continued. 'Cauda Equina Syndrome is an extremely rare disorder, your L5 disk is compressing on the spinal nerve roots at the tail of your spine, hence the name Cauda Equina, it's latin for horses tail. If this goes un-operated for more than forty-eight hours you are likely to have permanent incontinence and permanent paralysis of your lower extremities. As you mentioned, this started at midnight on Wednesday evening so we really need to get you into theatre before midnight tonight to have any chance of salvaging your nerves. Also, full disclosure, we have a woman in surgery right now with a difficult labour...'

My eyes are staring directly in to hers as she talks, '...I am unable to proceed with your operation without a full surgical team as, obviously, this is a very complex surgery and we require all hands on deck, so the minute the surgeons working with her are free, we will be coming up to take you to theatre. For now, I just need you to read and sign the surgical consent form to state you understand the risks associated with having and not having the surgery and that you are happy for us to go ahead and the nurses will get you in a gown to prep you. Unfortunately, to minimise movement, we will have to cut through your clothes to get them off as the slightest movement at this stage could cause more serious damage... I am so sorry that this has happened to you, I am going to make sure we do absolutely everything we can to help you recover from this as best as possible and are comfortable. Does that all sound okay? Or as good as it can, I'm so sorry again.'

Fuck my life. Holy Moses. Jesus, Mary and Joseph. She said WHAT?! I hadn't noticed, but as she talked the room went quiet. I wasn't able to hear a word anyone else was saying, no machines beeping, wind blowing through the gap in the window, nothing. Simply, her soothing voice, carefully explaining to me what was about to happen to my body and what could have happened if my friends hadn't been there for me. The whole time she spoke to me she had one hand on her clipboard and one hand on my raised knee, her eyes pierced through mine continually. Not just a slipped disk, then. I read, briefly, the consent form that she handed to me, the front and back lines detailing all the horrible things that could happen to me within the next few hours. I couldn't care less what it says, my eyes were looking, but my mind wasn't paying attention to the words before me. If they don't operate I will be paralysed so why would I deny consent? It's not until I go to sign on the dotted line that I realise my hand is an earthquake, I'm not sure who's signature I just penned, but it certainly doesn't look like mine. Even the lines are trembling. Instinctively, I quip about signing my life away as I hand the clipboard back to her. The room remains quiet. I suppose this is the first time that I've ever signed for something where that could actually be true and nobody seems to find it funny.

Rachel leaves and the next time I see her will be when she takes me down for surgery. As she goes, the little nurse reappears and in her delicate hand is a whopping great pair of scissors and in the other, a gown and carrier bag, I can only assume that means it's time to make more of an ass of myself. It's not long after that mum and dad are politely asked to step behind the curtain, they haven't uttered a word to me since Rachel was here, I can only think that they're still processing everything she said. After all, it must be scary for them, too, knowing what the potential outcomes are from this. Cold scissors start to hack away at my polyester polo shirt, my work uniform is undeniably unflattering and this is actually an improvement! Taking an arm each, they slip on an equally unflattering gown to cover my dignity as they slide the remains of my shirt off underneath - i didn't have any left after the anal exam earlier so at this point I could've been butt naked banging on the bathroom floor without batting an eyelid. I appreciate the thought though. Next goes my leggings, but I, like every other girl I know, owns around nine pairs of exactly the same kind so this isn't much of a loss; they are Jack Wills though, so I'm aware of the fact I just lost £24.95 worth of fabric.

The growling under my gown right now is, borderline, Gruffalo under the bridge. Chiming in at the thought of food, must be where I get it from, mum starts grumbling about how she hasn't eaten since eleven this morning because she had to take the early lunch so one of her girls could leave to pick up her poorly kid from school.

'Never have children' she says. 'They ruin your life and ruin your income.' She says it in such a way that she has clearly forgotten where she is and who I am, I look to dad for reassurance that she doesn't mean it, but he's eyeing up the biscuits on the table of bed number six.

'There's a sandwich in my bag if you want it, mum?' I'm not exactly going to get to eat it and the longer it's there, the less I'm going to want it anyway. Without hesitating she unzips my bag and pulls it out, making sure, for the second time today, that the Cheesestring falls swiftly to the floor.

'I'll have that!' Dad grins, snatching it up off the unimaginable germy hospital floor, again, thankful it's in a wrapper. I watch as they chomp and demolish what was supposed to be my lunch, reflecting on how differently today was supposed to have gone. With half a mouth full of sandwich, she's a different woman when there's food in front of her, honestly, it clearly runs in the family. Mum asks me who else knows that I'm here and what's happened.

'I called Lily and Annie.'

Mum nods, eyes still on the last half of the sandwich she's about to pick up, then dad adds, 'What about Tom?'

My parents know of Tom, but they've never met him. We're not together and unless we ever were what would be the point? I obviously don't even want us to be an item in the first place, just IF we were I suppose they'd meet him. Mum continues to scoff.

'Uh, don't get me started on this again, I do not understand you two, you say you're not together, but you're basically together, what is it with your generation? Just be with each other or don't, how hard is that?' I, yet again, declare the fact we are not together, we are just friends and no dad, he doesn't know I'm here. But maybe I should tell him?

'Hey, so I don't really know if you need to know this or not, but I'm at the hospital in Leeds and I'm about to go in for an emergency spinal operation, just thought I should tell you, sorry if you didn't really need to know - I hope you're having a good day'

Next, I write to Lily.

'They've had to cut off my work uniform, I'm so sorry!

It's in a carrier bag if they really want to see it though... I'll let you know how the op goes, lots to explain. Also, thank you for not laughing at me when I cried earlier - such a state! Speak soon. X'

And, last but not least, one to Annie.

'I'm just about to go in for my op, I'll let you know when I make it out (if I make it out, mwhaha). Sorry, it's not funny, I know, but you know I can't help it, humour is my reflex, don't shout at me! Make sure you sleep, I'll be fine, I'll let you know the second I'm awake and kicking - literally! Love you XXX'

The clock ticks over 23:20 and it's finally time for me to go to theatre. Only forty minutes before the nerves sever.

Chapter Eight

03.45am. The weight of my eyelids feels impossible, five Dwayne Johnsons' weighing on either side - I wish. With every flicker I can only see my eyelashes masking a glowing yellow light, it seems far away, as if a street light, but my bed doesn't face the window? Where is it coming from? Hang slack, Noddy... I'm not at home. Suddenly fancying myself a weight lifter, my eyes spring open and it's like the events of the last forty-eight hours flash across my face. I'm actually in the hospital, I really had an actual operation and I'm super, really not dead; I don't think. I rummage for a nurses bell, feeling the bulky buzzer beneath one of my many cushions and press it hard, as if the harder I press it the quicker someone will appear. Like playing Mario Kart and leaning to the side when you want to turn a corner.

'We've been wondering how long it would take before you woke, it's been a long night for you!' It was the same nurse from before, 'everything went well, the surgeon will be around in the morning to check in on you. How are you feeling?'

'Can I have my phone please?' I didn't even realise that's what I was going to say, it just blurted out. Before I'd gone down for surgery they'd put it in a safe on the nurses station so I didn't have to leave it in the cupboard open for any one of these old ladies to steal. Now I realised I wanted to let my friends know I was okay and I was awake, see if maybe my parents had left me any messages. The blood pressure sleeve was unattached from my arm and she unclipped the heart rate monitor from my finger, making a note of my observations, then she slid away to get my Blackberry. Instantly, I felt like a co-dependant, phone addicted millennial and hated myself a little bit. Along with my phone, she'd brought me a jug of water and informed me to drink frequently because she was going to be back every hour to re-do my observations. No rest for the wicked millennial then.

Turning my phone on, I waited patiently for it to warm itself up and ping through any messages I might've received whilst I let it sleep. Shit, Tom. I had to put it on silent at the speed of light because I had messages and missed calls pinging out my ears!

'What?! What's going on?'

'Pip, which hospital are you in? What happened? I'm worried!'

'Please tell me you're not dead, tell me you're okay'

'I've tried calling the hospitals and no one will tell me anything, they just keep saying you're in surgery! Please let me know when you're awake, I'm so worried!'...

Along with the missed calls, I couldn't believe it, I didn't even know if he'd get my message with his work signal being so shite, I didn't even know if he'd have much more to say than, 'I hope you're okay', but apparently I was wrong. Well and truly. Before I have chance to press my buzzer again and ask if he'd called, Anan, the nurse, is pacing back towards me.

'Just so you know, I forgot to mention, we've had a Tom calling for you, LOTS! We couldn't tell him much, but the poor boy had called through the hospital for about an hour just trying to find you, then when he finally got through you were in surgery, we did tell him, but we couldn't tell him why or anything. He sounded a bit dodgy to be honest!' She half laughs and I can tell my face is making some interesting motions as she says it. Tom is so polite and well spoken, ever a gentleman and a total professional, I can't possibly see how he could sound dodgy!

So she explains, 'Well, we asked if he was family and he said not exactly, so we asked if he was your boyfriend and he took a long pause then said no, then yes, then no, then yes again! He explained your parents might not know about him. But that he needed to know you weren't dead and you were okay. Funny boy, he sounded all over the place, he was very worried so you'll probably have a few messages.'

I couldn't see my own face, but I could feel the Cheshire cat grin spread right across it, ear to ear. He was worried about me. My whole body went warm, my stomach was giddy (I hadn't eaten for a day, so that could easily have been it, but this was different), Anan could tell I was pleased by the idea of being cared for and patted my leg before leaving me to gush. I'm not usually the blushing type, people are unreliable and nobody should feel like they need someone else to care for them, you should be content caring for yourself. I am. Not wanting to dwell on it much more, I decided to try and call him. Sober minded Pip would never call someone after 4am, nothing good can come of it and at the very least it's completely anti-social, but I just wanted to hear his voice. My emotions are running high and I'm absolutely blaming the drugs.

Understandably, there was no answer, he was last active on WhatsApp merely an hour before, so he can't have been asleep for too long, he'd be off in dreamland right about now. Instead, I opt for replying to messages. I text Annie and Lily back, whom both have messaged to say "let me know when you're out" and to reassure me that I was going to be okay. I text them both the same copy and posted message to let them know I'm awake and I'm okay and we'll see how I feel in the morning. I debate texting my parents, but I'm unsure how well it will be received at this time of the morning so I decide to let the hospital inform them of my well-being instead. And finally, Tom.

'Hey you, I'm so sorry for my message, I wasn't sure if you needed to know or not, sorry if I worried you! The hospital said you'd called, I've just tried ringing back, but I hope you're getting some sleep. Just to let you know I'm out of surgery and I'm okay, I can wiggle my toes and everything! Call me when you're awake, I'll be up. X'

Actually, I don't even know if I can wiggle my toes, I've been awake for nearly an hour and not even checked to make sure I'm not bloody paralysed - nice one. Feeling like I'm in Kill Bill, I stare down at my feet and pull up the warm blanket, exposing myself to hospital airborne germs. I stare at it for a minute, wondering what I'll do if I can't move, if for some reason it didn't go as well as they thought and I can no longer walk or run or play badminton; I'm so badass. What if the only item on my bucket list was now an impossible dream? Why hadn't I done it when I had the chance, instead of always saying "one day", why do humans do that? It's not like I'd just decided to do it on a whim, I'd not seen a post on Facebook and thought, yeah, why not. Before I even reached secondary school I'd always told people that's what I was going to do. I had a ten step plan:

1. Go to uni
2. Gap year and volunteer in Tanzania
3. Climb Kilimanjaro
4. Move to the US
5. Get a job with the US Geographical Survey
6. Buy a house
7. Meet someone
8. Get married
9. Travel the world
10. Have a baby (maybe)

Okay, so number ten was tentative, but still an option, you just never know how you're going to feel about that until it happens. The rest of it, that was the absolute dream, straight from the heart of an eight year old girl. Although the entire dream has changed over the years and I haven't done everything eight year old me thought, climbing Kili was always the transferable goal, always the one I have continually said I would do and it's not until right now, staring down at my probably paralysed extremities, that I realise I should've done it. If I can't walk I will regret this for the rest of my life, and I don't believe in regrets. I take a deep breath, "3... 2...1..." Yes! Houston, we have lift off: all my little piggies can dance.

A wave of relief washed clean over me, I don't know how I had brushed past the small detail that things could easily have gone awry, but I press send on the message to Tom, knowing I'm not wrong and I can, in fact, wriggle my toes. I decide not to stop there, after all, what good to me are toes if I can't move my legs? One at a time, as I tense my core muscles (the few that I have anyway) I try to slide my leg up the bed towards my chest, bending at the knee. The right one goes first and it feels like I'm tugging at an eighteen-wheeler, but I manage to bend at a forty-five degree angle and judge that sufficient for almost two hours after surgery. Brava. The left leg can only just manage about the same before I feel the strain on my lower spine. It's a strange, unfamiliar, sensation considering, before Wednesday, I'd never suffered with back pain in my life, it's unpleasant to say the least and I honestly feel for people that have to live like this permanently, I can only imagine. Not only that, but the people who have to adapt to living without the ability to walk when they could so easily before, it's all so harrowing when your reality could've easily been fated that way, it really makes you think.

Right now, I am going to promise myself something, something important. I just need to make sure I can write it down because I currently have no clue as to how many drugs I'm on and I may forget if I get chance to doze off again. Paper and a pen, anyone? I don't really want to bother the staff again, I already feel like a nuisance with them having to come and check my blood pressure every hour, so instead I reach for my bag that mum left in the little cupboard. Thankfully it's just within reach otherwise I fear I'd have happily fallen from the bed as a sacrifice; the things a girl would do for stationary. I am absolutely sure there's a carrot shaped pen in here somewhere, it makes me feel just like Judy Hopes in Zootopia as I begin to write, my hand doesn't feel like it's attached to my wrist, it feels almost numb, like I've been sitting on it for too long and the words now don't look like my own.

'I, Pip Parker, hereby declare that I WILL climb Mount Kilimanjaro. I will complete the only real dream I ever had and the minute I am allowed to, I will go for the summit.'

Skimming it over, I realise I'm better off giving myself a date to do it by, just in case I need that extra push of motivation. Goal by 31st December, two years from now. That seems do-able, it's September 24th right now and so I have a whole fifteen months to recover, heal and train before heading up. Plenty of time, especially when the average time to train is only four months! Easy peasy, squeeze the lemon, as Ben from Horrible Histories would say. My mind feels much more at ease now I've got that off my brain and it's probably about time to grab some sleep, I want to be as fresh as I can for when the surgeon comes around in the morning. I check my phone one last time before tucking it away under my pillow, I want to be able to feel it if Tom decides to call.

Realising there would be no way for me to turn over and sleep comfortably tonight I reluctantly lay flat on my back, propped up by the cushions enough that my head can just see over the table at the foot of the bed. If bed number eight is the one opposite mine, I notice, that must mean I am number five... '5,6,7,8...' As I sing the rest of the tune to a popular Steps number, the last thing I remember is chuckling softly to myself at my genius realisation, my eyes closing tightly thinking of my boot scootin' baby.

Chapter Nine

Urgh Christ, it's bright in here. I can feel a cold breeze tickle my exposed shoulder so I burrow further into my blankets - and by that I mean I drag them further up to me, way over my head. It's still not very comfortable to move and I realise I haven't had any pain killers for a few hours so that's probably not much help. In the light of day the room looks completely different; smaller, maybe. There's more noticeable clutter when the sun is shining over every crevice, even the lady's wrinkles in bed eight seem more defined - no offence of course, just a touch of poly filler and I'm sure she'll look smooth as a baby's bum!

At the foot of bed seven, two ladies are chirping to each other over a trolley of tea, coffee and toast - it must be breakfast time. The woman from bed six is away from her bay, but they seem to know what it is she likes and leave some dry toast and a yoghurt on the end of her table. Suddenly my mind flashes back to the toilet troubles she was having yesterday, I can only hope this helps... move things along. I'm not actually very hungry, which, for anyone that knows me, knows this is quite a huge deal. I think I was born with the appetite of two, I like to think sometimes that maybe I absorbed my twin and kept their stomach. Not that I ever had a twin, I'm right handed for starters.

'Ooh, you're awake. What would you like for breakfast, love?' The pair make their way to the end of my bed, smiling like they've got hangers stuck in their mouths. Firstly, don't call me love, it's gross and I'm nobody's love. Secondly, I notice that it wasn't so much as a question, more of a statement of "you are going to eat something, but we have to pretend you have a choice". I am not happy with either of these things and my tone indicates it, morphine and pain seem to make it difficult for me to mask my feelings.

I press my nurses bell and wait for someone to come running, although, I think the movies may have lied to me because it takes ten minutes for someone to come sauntering down the hallway. In the meantime I made brief eye contact with my room mates, a morning smile and nod to indicate I wasn't a total bitch. That all felt like too much interaction for now though and I desperately wanted some privacy.

'Please can I go to the bathroom so I can have a wash?' I asked the care worker who was stretching behind my bed to turn off the beeping I'd created with the buzzer.

'Actually,' she replied, rather shyly. 'I've been told you're not allowed out of bed until the surgeon has come to see you and until you eat something, we don't want you falling over.'

Bloody snitches, grassing me up for not having breakfast! I don't know that many people that want to eat before 9am and since it's only 8.30 I thought I was well within my rights to refuse sustenance.

'Okay, well do you know when the surgeon is coming around? Will it be long?'

'Doctors rounds have started and I know he wanted to come to you first so hopefully it won't be long at all.'

'Smashing, well can you shut my curtain until then, please? And see what the crack is about getting me some more pain relief? Thanks.' She was pretty sweet, bless her, and promptly closed my curtains so I could be alone for a while. She said she would ask the nurse what painkillers I could have and told me if I wasn't going to eat breakfast I at least had to finish my jug of water. What is it with these people and water?

Out of nowhere, my bum started to vibrate quite violently. My phone. I shifted as quickly and as carefully as I could to pull it out from beneath me, it was Tom calling and I don't think I could've answered fast enough. His voice was deep and soothing, like a verbal version of a safe place and I instantly felt relaxed.

'I'd have picked you up from work and taken you straight to hospital on Wednesday night! Why didn't you tell me?!'

I refrained from explaining the reason I hadn't told him was because I didn't want to rely on him for anything, I didn't want him to think that I thought it was his responsibility to be there when I needed help. (This thinking business is hard work!) Instead, I told him I hadn't been worried and thought I would sleep it off, which wasn't entirely false. Again, he scolded me for being so silly and promised he'd be there to see me when he could, he had work in the afternoon until finish, but he would try and get here before. I naturally told him not to worry and that I hadn't even seen the elusive surgeon yet so I had no idea what was going on. I could be going home today as far as I knew. I said it with my fingers crossed as I tried to cross my legs at the same time for double the luck. It was so nice to be able to talk to him, to not have the sickly feeling in my chest any more that he somehow hated me for not answering his calls last night, even if I was having an operation, it didn't stop me feeling overwhelmingly guilty for making him worry.

We chatted for almost forty minutes, with him laughing about how he'd spent almost two hours on the phone calling into hospitals and how he was on the verge of just driving through to Leeds and seeing if he could find me before he'd managed to get in touch with my ward. I told him the story of how the staff here had thought he'd seemed dodgy and he reeled in pretend shock at the notion. Maybe I did have some smiles in me this morning, just not for people that were trying to force feed me.

It's almost 11am before the surgeon arrives, but I had another dose of morphine in that time, so thankfully, I had a bit of a trip to pass the time. It's not a trip like LSD or anything, it's not hallucinogenic, but it is strong stuff and I feel like a cartoon that's had far too much coffee for the first two hours; shaky, unstable and I find almost everything funny, especially myself - although that's not exactly new information, I am hilarious after all.

Mr Sant is the name of the man who operated on me, he is a specialist spinal surgeon and nothing like I imagined. His face is plump, but not in an alcoholic way where it's red and blotchy, he actually has great skin for a bloke. Weird thing to notice now I've noticed it. He wears little, dark, round framed glasses; you know, the kind that Arthur wears, the kind that never suit any one, yet, he absolutely pulls them off.

The light from where they pulled back my curtains is shining wonderfully off his bald head, I'm going for shaved bald, but who ever really knows. He comes straight towards me and holds out his hand, something I didn't expect, but appreciate nonetheless. He's kind. Bringing my legs to the side so he can take a seat, he chooses the arm chair instead and pulls it out to face me. Behind him, two others hover with piles of notes, I assume they're his prodigies or assistants and drown out their presence - only what he has to say is important to me right now.

'So, what a night!' He exclaims, smiling and raising his eyebrows so they get lost in his non-existent hairline.

'Late December, back in '63...' I can't help myself from singing a response to such an obvious, "there's a song in there somewhere" line. He laughs and dances with hands.

'I'm glad to know your voice still works, you're not a bad singer!' He chuckles again, just a few breaths, before putting his hand on mine. 'Really though, I am so sorry that this has happened to you, I cannot believe it.' I really believe in his apology and I am surprised at how much I already trust this man I just met, I feel instantly reassured by him. Removing his hand from mine and addressing his clipboard, he continues. 'Last night's surgery was a success by our makings, and everything inside looks great, I just want to double check how you're feeling, have a look at the incision and do some little tests on your nerves if that's okay?'

Duh. Of course it's okay, the man saved my legs as far as I'm concerned so I'll do whatever he needs. Step one is checking the wound, it is difficult to turn for him to see and I am so aware that my arse is in his face, but there's little I can do about it considering it's my lumbar spine. He saw it all last night anyway, at least this time I'm lucid! Not that I can see, but he says everything looks like it's going to heal nicely and moves on to the nerve tests. He tickles my feet with a stick, although I don't think stick is the medical term, and the wriggling from laughing makes me wince so he stops. He has enough to know my reflexes are working and that I can feel the sensations clearly. The more positive the results are becoming, the more giddy I get, I'm hoping I'll get to run home later at this rate.

It wasn't until he bent to the side of my bed that I'd even noticed the catheter bag. My face became quizzical and my heart started to beat in my ears. Why do I have that? I'm surprised that I hadn't noticed it at this point, who wouldn't feel the big tube sticking from their fanny - sorry, protruding out my urethra is more accurate, there's nothing in my vagina, I hope! Then I remember, I hadn't been able to wee yesterday. Now I understand why everyone is asking me to drink all the chuffin' water, my urine is bright orange and it's illuminated through the catheter bag. Apparently, the Cauda Equina nerves that they operated on, also connect to my bladder and bowel and so the reason I hadn't been unable to go for a wee was because the nerves were being compromised by the disk that was tangled up in there causing retention. That's why they had to put a catheter in, to drain my bladder to stop it from bursting. Now, there's hardly anything in there, apparently they had to drain it immediately after putting it in when I went into surgery. I had 800ml in there then; no wonder I was uncomfortable, apparently the average bladder only holds 600ml. Then, since coming to, I'd only drank a cup of water in defiance in the middle of the night so drainage was slow and the colour of Tigger - minus the stripes. I hope, on top of being able to walk, I can wee, I'd forgotten all about that somehow.

Before I had chance to open my mouth and ask the question I'd been dying to know the answer to, Mr Sant telepathically took it from my little brain and answered.

'Okay... so, we are going to keep you in overnight tonight, but don't be sad. I want to make sure you can go to the toilet on your own and that you can walk safely before we discharge you. If you promise to drink enough during the day today, I will ask a nurse to remove your catheter in the morning and if you can urinate successfully on your own, a sufficient amount of course not as little as this, you will be allowed to go home. Also, no getting out of bed on your own, call a nurse, or wait for physiotherapy to come and see you, I don't want any accidents - very detrimental to recovery.'

He smiles at me and asks if I'm okay with everything he just said. I am. Well, I'd rather be going home to Tom's bed tonight as planned, but if it means making sure I don't need this ruddy catheter in then I'm happy (ish) to stay.

I text Tom and let him know I'd be here over night and he replies saying he'd be there to take me home tomorrow as long as it was after 3pm. I told him not to bother trying to rush over today, I was going to get some sleep and I didn't want to risk him being late for work now it was lunch time. The tone in his response was reluctant and I liked it, I'm glad he wanted to see me, even when I have a bag full of wee attached to me.

Physio came and went and there was no stopping me. At first it took a few minutes to get me to sit up and then a few more to get me standing up, but, with the two of them, I managed to walk to the window and back to my bed twice in a row! Twelve hours after an operation on my spine and I was up and about, using the legs I never thought I'd be able to use again, my Kilimanjaro legs. Obviously, it goes without saying, my steps were little and delicate and a bit more wonky than normal, but that was just the pain and trying to be cautious; a little more painkiller and a smush of faith, I'd be fine. There's a Julia Roberts smile across my whole face, I'm so proud of myself. Proud enough I even ask the nice physio lady to take a picture of me standing up so I can send it to Annie and Lily, I've not checked in with them today, but I think they'd like to see this. I'll send it to mum and dad too.

I only perch on the armchair to send it. Mum replies alarmingly quickly for her, saying she and dad were going to come through to see me today, but they'd spoken to the nurse this morning and heard I would be going home tomorrow so they were going to keep their plans tonight and see me then instead. I didn't even expect a response, let alone an explanation. So I reply with, 'see you then, have fun!' There was no mention of my photo. I send the picture to Annie and Lily, then decide to call both of them.

It's visiting hours here now and all three ladies in my room have guests. Mostly family from what I can gather, daughters, sons, grandchildren, maybe a few friends have come to see the lady in number six, but nobody for me. I'm going home tomorrow though, so I try not to dwell on it, these women must've been here a while, at least I'm going and not coming back. Annie is out when I call her so I tell her to hang up the phone and enjoy herself, she's gushing down the phone about how great it is that I can stand up and she can't wait to squeeze the life out of me when she sees me. It's nice to hear her voice and to hear her sounding so happy, she works far too hard and I'm glad she's letting her hair down. We keep talking about going away together, after twenty years of friendship you'd think it's something we'd have done by now, but maybe it's about time we got something planned. We do both need to throw caution to the wind. I mention it to her briefly and tell her I'm going to check

Google for some deals and send her some links, it's about time I had a holiday. Her too. She agrees wholeheartedly and tells me she'll go wherever, as long as she has the chance to research the place before we set off; she can't even try and pretend to be spontaneous with me.

When I call Lily she's at work, but she doesn't mind talking because they're quiet.

'Someone else can do some work for a change anyway!' She comments loudly across the office, hoping another manager will hear her - not too loudly though, she doesn't want to make a scene after all. I ask how it's been and apologise a hundred times for not being able to work this weekend. Weekends are our busiest time, clearly, and so I feel doubly mean for not being there. She tells me off for being sorry and fills me in on the latest gossip. For two people who say we don't care for it, we're certainly masters.

'Eli and Adam have had a massive fight this morning in the office,' she laughs and asks me to guess why. I go through a couple of silly things, like forgetting to do tasks and who cooks the best chilli, but I'm wrong. 'It was about you!' She laughs, quieter this time, as if waiting for my response.

'You are joking?! What on earth about?!' I fold into creases, I know morphine makes everything seem a bit doo-laly, but this was surely a joke? Apparently, Adam had tried to say I should look after myself, then Eli had gone for him saying he had no right to talk about me like that, we weren't friends, Eli was my friend and he was allowed to be worried about me but Adam had to shut his mouth! I was totally gobsmacked considering I'd not actually heard from either of them since yesterday anyway. I told Lily this and she just laughed even harder, what is it with boys? She joked further about how they clearly both had crushes on me which I wholeheartedly denied.

'It's okay, I know it doesn't matter anyway because you already have a boyfriend!' Ooh she thinks she's so funny that one, constantly busting my balls.

'I do not have a boyfriend and you know this!' Clearly my response only made me more susceptible to ridicule so instead I opted for a subject change instead. We chatted more about what Mr Sant had said, I promised to keep her in the loop and she tried to make me promise not to do too much - naturally I obliged, only she couldn't see I had my fingers crossed.

Once I'd put the phone down, I'd decided I was famished. It would be tea time soon, but I'm not sure I could wait. Using the fact I hadn't had breakfast or lunch as leverage, apparently the person in the bed before me hadn't ordered anything over the lunch period so I hadn't been offered anything, I got the nurse to bring me a cheese sandwich from the kitchen. It wasn't anything special, but it did the trick in suppressing the overwhelming sick feeling from all the drugs and, washed down with a full jug of water, it sent me happily into a sleepy coma. I was zonked before I even had the chance to pull my blanket over me. I hope I wasn't flashing anything!

Chapter Ten

By the time I reached Harrogate on Sunday it was already past 6pm, discharge seems to take a full day in that place, but, I was buzzing. I may look like death warmed up and I can't seem to walk very fast yet, but that doesn't mean I don't feel so much better already. I CAN WALK. In fact, I can walk so well, I even opted to take my own sick note into work on the way home, not that I wanted everyone to see what a mess I am, I just wanted to prove I could, and even Tom couldn't stop me; with his manly arms and Disney Prince-esque features, he's such a Flynn Rider - oooft - any way... The hospital have signed me off for six weeks until I have chance to see the specialist again and get the all clear, then it's back to business.

'Surprise!' Annie is in my room when I arrived home and finally make it up all my stairs, it's a lot harder after spine surgery for some stupid reason. 'I got us a present!'

She's jumping on my bed holding some print out paper with a ragging vibrant smile on her face, it's almost bloody scary. I slide towards her, slipping my socks on the laminate like a forwards moon walk to try and eliminate some of the pain from taking steps. Luckily Tom is still behind me carrying my bags otherwise I may have fallen back down the stairs, one slide in and I was almost on my arse. Annie hopped down off the bed and came to give me a hand to sit down, sitting isn't as comfortable as it could be so I lie back instead, staring out my sky light whilst she flops down next to me, Tom gets in on the other side of me after he's dropped my bags - a Pip sandwich, I like it.

'So what's this surprise then?' Tom motions to Annie to spill the beans as I lay there watching the back of my eyelids. I'm just so tired.

'I've booked us a holiday, Pip!' she squeals, unable to mask her excitement.

'You what?!' NOW I'm awake. I try to sit up but forget physio have shown me a ridiculous way to do it now and I suddenly can't be bothered. Turn to your side, put your legs down then push up into the upright position, No thanks. Then, almost like he knows, Tom sits himself up and offers me his pillow as an extra head rest. I have loads of them, I'm a pillow hoarder, it seems, yet I somehow always end up with my head on the mattress, tucked under the armpit of Mr Bear or Mr Tom - armpit hats are the only way to get a good nights sleep - Pip approved.

Annie hands me the paper she's been hulk gripping since I got home, as I read it, she further explains the plans.

'So, it's nothing too glamorous, not like abroad or anything because I didn't know if you'd be allowed to fly, but you are allowed in the car, right?' She looks at Tom for confirmation that my journey home was okay and carries on. 'Even if we have to make stops it still shouldn't take us too long to get there, it's out by Scarborough, kind of, looks there's a map on the back, you can do the directions for me, geography girl!' She says that her and Alex have been there before; Alex is her boyfriend, they've been pretty solidly together for three years and it's not often they do anything without each other, I'm surprised he's not here, too. Apparently, he can't get the time off work this last minute so it's going to be purely a girls trip and she refers back to me talking about us going on holiday together - I have no clue what she's talking about, I must've been off my face on the drugs at the time. I don't disagree though, I'm absolutely ready for a trip.

Tom confirms all the details too, to make sure I'll be safe, of course, then says he'll get off and leave us to it. I won't see him before we go, since we leave in the morning, but he says he'll call. Annie heads off, too, after a while. She offered to help me pack, but stubbornly I refused and said I'd do it in the morning before we go, she wasn't coming to get me until 10am anyway so it's not like I didn't have time. We were going Monday to Friday because she and Alex had plans for her birthday on the Friday night, some big family gathering from what I'd heard, his family and hers. They were all very close and it made me gag just hearing about it, either grossed out by all the affection or completely jealous, but I refuse to believe the latter.

I made a vain effort to shout mum and dad up to see me, so I could tell them I was going to be away; no answer. Unsurprised, I turn on the TV with the remote that was hiding under one of the many cushions and I must've been asleep within the first fifteen minutes. Not forgetting the sleep timer beforehand.

I did, however, forget my alarm. I woke up at 8.15, groggy and confused, no longer hearing the sound of people's machines beeping and nurses chatter, I'd forgotten I wasn't still in the hospital. I'd also forgotten I was getting picked up at 10am until I checked my semi charged phone and read a text from Annie saying she was ahead of schedule and would be at my house for 9.30... Christ that woman is punctual. I'd been asleep for about twelve hours and had about as much energy as a dodo, but I still needed to pack, so I haul myself up and spend five minutes staring at the floor, trying to find the motivation to crack on.

I packed all sorts of things I'm sure I didn't need and the only thing I really did need I packed three of... Bikinis! We are staying in a log cabin, deep in the woods and on our deck is supposed to be a hot tub/jacuzzi thing - who actually knows the difference? Regardless, I think three bikinis will suffice as clothes.

All my tablets are packed in a separate bag to make sure I can keep them in the front seat with me at Annie's request. She understands me well enough to know that I will not be taking them unless absolutely necessary because I hate filling my body with medicine, but at least if I make the effort to seem as though I was going to, she might forget. Maybe. I've never heard of half this stuff before now, but I suppose I've also never suffered with anything like this either. I spend the next fifteen minutes of 'getting dressed' time, making a list so I know what I can have and when.

Tablet	
Paracetamol	2 tablets 4 x daily
Tramadol	2 tablets 4 x daily
Pregabalin 75mg	2 x morning 1 x night
Pregabalin 150mg	1 x lunch time
Oromorphe	5-10ml hourly or when required
Cyclizine	1 morning
Omeprazole	1 night (and as and when required)

Looking at that makes me feel like a heavy drug addict so I shove it in the medicine bag (a Princess Disney Store bag for life, of course!) and know Annie will at least be happy with what she thinks I'll be taking - sucker! With the remainder of my allocated dressing time, I throw on some leggings and a vest. Over the top of my super fashionable ensemble goes Tom's Adidas hoody that he may or may not (definitely 'may not') know I have. He's working all week this week so I wouldn't have had much chance to see him if I was here, it makes me feel a little better about leaving.

'*Outside XXX*' My phone beeps off the laminate scaring me half to death, it's Annie. I hear her opening the door with a slow creak so I snatch my bags, making it look like I was absolutely on my way out already. My yellow rain mac screams to be brought along for the ride.

'Where are you going?' I hear my dad ask from the front door, Annie is standing on the doorstep, car keys in hand.

'To stay in a woodland cabin for a week, she needs to relax and there's no better place. There's no stairs either so it's okay, it's safe, I called her specialist and asked.' Of course she did, I expect nothing less, she's such a goody two shoes! As I appear at the foot of the stairs she instantly reaches past my dad and grabs my bags from my hands. I forgot my parents didn't know I was going, but the reaction to me leaving was even less than I'd anticipated in the first place, so I wasn't sorry.

'Have a good time, Annie, drive carefully!' Any normal parents would be worried about their child being driven miles away into the middle of nowhere after such a serious operation, and I know I would've been plainly annoyed by their worrying, but that's what parents are for.

Having to stop for me to get out and stretch my legs every thirty minutes made an hour and a half journey just over three hours long... but we got there in the end. It was nice to be able to jam out together on the way, warm enough to have the windows down a bit and because Annie doesn't drive over the speed limit at the best of times, let alone with an injured me in the car, it was never too windy for it to start doing your head in so you'd put them up in a huff and blast the air con. I hate air con.

'H2O-O-O, It's something every time I know baby it's so true...' On road trips our inner chav usually comes out and singing along to H"two"O featuring Platinum is always how it starts. We go from British chav classics, to rock, 'Beverly Hills, that's where I wanna be... living in Beverly Hills...' in the space of about 4 songs, and not forgetting our Number 1 anthem. The one, the only, Defying Gravity! If you don't love musicals, then I'm afraid you're wrong. There's something about Annie and I that we constantly question how we ever got to becoming friends in the first place, we have just about nothing in common at all, until it comes to our mini road trips and we realise, if nothing else, we have always got the ability to dance out our differences together, and dancing it out solves everything.

Trees lined the road side for at least two miles from our last turn. Stretching back further than my horrible vision can see, creating forests full of wonder - or ghosts and paedophiles, depending how you look at things. It's a ruddy good thing Annie drives like an old lady sometimes otherwise we would've had a good chance of ruthlessly murdering a good couple of chickens we encountered crossing the road - and no, it's not a bad joke!

Past the chickens though, and around the bend, there was a light at the end of the woodland. On the left through the opening, over the road from the line of cabins, was an enormous field that rolled down a hill into more trees and a zip wire that spanned the entire length. Now that's something I want to play with!

Annie got us checked in and we drove around to our temporary home, zip-line facing cabin number five. This decor is something I could absolutely get used to. The deep wood and high ceilings, so much space and character it felt like standing in the middle of a roaring log fire, but without the heat and imminent death. We dropped our shoes in the hall-way and had a little explore of the place, it was huge for the two of us. Annie took the room upstairs, it wouldn't make any sense for me to have it considering half the reason physio let me come in the first place was due to the lack of climbing. My room was under hers at the end of the hall; two single beds and lots of cushions - perfect, she helped me squish them together and move the side table out of the way, and by help, obviously she did it all at my request - no denying she's a good egg. Whilst she was busy with the heavy lifting I decided to unpack the kitchen, she'd been to Asda on the way to my house and bought a shed full. I managed to fill all six cupboards and the fridge and I still had to use the table for storage of breakfast cereal and crumpets! I do love her for buying me crumpets. The woman's a feeder, there's no question about it.

Once we'd unpacked and she'd told me off sufficiently for lifting a finger, we opened the double glass patio doors on to the decking, ahh the hot tub. The staff had even turned it on in anticipation of our arrival so we only had another thirty minutes before it would be ready to use, plenty of time to browse the telly channels and have a glass of Prosecco to celebrate. Well, I thought I'd gotten away with the prosecco business, but she kindly reminded me I'm not allowed to drink on my tablet's, so Vimto cordial for me.

On the beautiful suede couch, we connect to the wi-fi so we can stay in touch with some of the outside world, there's no phone service all the way up here, so it's kind of vital we can at least Facebook chat an ambulance... I have a flick through the free movies we can get on the little smart TV in the living room, some good ones to my surprise and naturally I'm now more excited to finally watch "Get Hard" and "The Theory of Everything" than I am about to get semi-naked in a hot tub. Much to my surprise so is Annie. We decide on "Pitch Perfect 2" to get us going and share a box of Celebrations between us.

Chapter Eleven

I got bored during the film, it's not usually my cup of tea the whole girl-power movie thing, I like horror films much better, at least the bitchy girl usually dies at the end! I also only really like songs I can sing loudly along to, at the top of my lungs, hands in the air making dramatic gestures to whoever is closest to me, not acapella versions that make it impossible to figure the beat. Annie watched intensely, simultaneously telling me to stand up every twenty minutes as physio recommended - I didn't sign my life away on it or anything, but damn I forgot how bossy she can get when there's rules outlined. When I thought the film may never end, the credits finally started rolling and almost exactly as they did, I could feel the sun against the back of my neck - hot tub time I think! Annie went to change upstairs, not before asking if I needed any help changing, which of course I didn't - perve! I could hear her opening her bags through the ceiling in my room as I also tried to find my bikini - bingo! I decided to wear the first one I pulled out, nobody is going to see me other than Annie and she's seen me in much worse states than this I'm sure. I could feel the soft blue fabric and the luminescent pink lace fringe as I tugged it from the depths of my holdall, it twanged out of a pair of socks and the little pink bead hit me right in the forehead, bollocks that hurts! Annie heard me swear and it was seconds before she was taking the bag out of my hands.

'Give it to me, stop lifting things! What did you do?' This woman is relentless.

'It's fine, I just twatted myself with a bead off my bikini, it's fine, I'm fine, stop worrying woman!'

She goes to leave my room, hands in the air as if to say "I'm not fighting!" but she doesn't reach the door before I squeak, sheepishly, 'Actually, whilst you're here, I think I might need a hand getting this on? Sorrryyyyy' I know I don't have to be sorry though, she wants to help me and I really should let her, I know she feels bad that I don't have anyone to look after me at the best of times, let alone when I'm in this state.

All the lack of eating over the last few days must really be paying off, my stomach has never looked so flat and toned, I look like a different person in this mirror. When I turn around to grab my towel from the end of the bed, it's almost like I'd forgotten about the big bandage up my spine, from my arse crack right up to my waist, a sticky, white strip of bandage covers a scar I'm yet to see, a permanent mark on my body. I wonder if it's going to be big or if it's like a little keyhole thing? I suppose they don't do spine surgery through a keyhole.

Annie is already by the steps of the hot tub ready to help me in when we realise that I can't actually get in it at all, I'm not allowed to get my back wet. Reasoning that sitting on the side should be okay since it's only my fat arse that will get a little damp, she helps me swing my legs into the deliciously warm water, the ample bubbles making it look like I am being lowered into a boiling cauldron Hocus Pocus style. I drape my rainbow striped towel over my shoulders for upper body warmth and swirl my feet gleefully. There's something about being in or near water that completely soothes the crap out of me, showering isn't the same, neither is taking a bath, I like to be submerged with the space to move within no boundary and in this tub my feet can go wherever they please, provided they don't drag the rest of me in.

'Fancy going somewhere Thursday? It's the only day we've got no activities planned. Maybe to the beach if you're up for it?'

'Oh, good plan.' I reply, staring out to the sun which is now fading behind the zip line down behind the trees, 'I miss the sea.'

'Woman! You're mad, tell me you're joking?! It's bloody freezing!' She was right, it was colder than it had been the last few weeks and we were very obviously getting into late Autumn, not to mention the sea breeze was making the situation way more intense than if I was shielded by a bush or something, but it's not going to stop me. Perched on the edge of the wall, I roll my leggings down over my, already purple, knees and slide them off my sandy feet. Once they're neatly rolled into my left shoe, I shed myself of my winter coat, hoody, and my t-shirt. Soft gasps come from behind me and when I stand to rearrange my bikini bottoms that are gently being eaten by my bum, a little elderly couple laugh in my general direction - I'd love to see them doing this.

'Are you not worried you're going to fall over, because I am. The sand is uneven and the tide seems strong and you're not even supposed to be getting your back wet.' I flash her my back to show the splash-proof bandage cover I bought whilst I was waiting for her to have a wee in the public loos back in town. I've never in the last ten years of my life, come to the seaside without a bikini tucked away under my clothes, who knows what kind of shenanigans you can get up to, if you don't have one with you you'll never know and who's really got time to find somewhere to change? Better just to strip off right there and give strangers a show, what are the chances you've going to see them again, anyway? Not selling it to Annie at this point, but I'm happy for her just to watch, the sand in my feet feels too good to ignore so I gallop down to the water's edge, literally galloping like a chuffin' pony because I don't get to be at the beach as often as I like so I'm going to it enjoy it whilst I'm here. It's been almost a week since my operation, what's the worst that could happen?!

I waded in as far as I could allow myself before my splash proof cover felt maybe a tad more than splashed. The water was freezing, if I could've belly flopped in just to stop being able to tell the difference I would've done, my shins felt like they'd been removed from my body, just my thighs left, attached to my ankles! Even though I was in here on my own I could feel Annie laughing, she'd decided to video me frolicking about as if I was in a one woman show of Grease and so I behaved accordingly, splashing water out towards the sand at her, what a day.

It was almost midnight when I began tottering around the dining room with blu-tac in one hand, banners in the other, I was trying to be as quiet as a mouse, but with all the morphine in my system I could've been playing the drums and not noticed. I love birthdays, especially when I get to celebrate somebody else's, it's such a special thing to get excited about, the people you love having travelled around the sun one more time. Annie's birthday is two weeks from mine and so I get even more giddy when September comes because it's not just me, it's her, too. I'm hoping she's asleep, or at least talking to Alex so I can finish decorating the cabin ready for the morning, we're leaving at lunch time, but it isn't a birthday if you don't wake up to balloons and your presents stacked on the table!

This year I bought her: Prosecco, because she's not-so-secretly an alcoholic, a fancy new work pen with a unicorn head, because she's never out of the office and a framed picture of the two of us, like I get her every year. It's always a picture of an adventure we've had throughout the previous year and this years is a picture of when we went to the airfield so Alex could have a flying lesson and we took the opportunity to do cartwheels across the car park whilst we waited. The sky was clear that day and blue, we had gone up together with the intention of going for lunch afterward. Whilst Alex was in the sky, we set my phone to timer mode and snapped loads of pictures of us mid-air. It wasn't until the first few were taken that I realised every time we got our legs over our heads we flashed our bras, I kept those for our private gallery and framed the one of us laughing instead.

When I finally turned in for bed, with my cushions arranged like scaffolding to keep me from twisting the wrong way in my sleep, I pulled out my phone to text Tom.

'Home tomorrow, looking forward to seeing you - no worries if you're busy though!'

I know he had been so good to me at the weekend, surprisingly so, but I didn't want me being ill to change anything about us or how he treated me. I really don't want to become some basket case because I'm obviously quite capable of looking after myself. It was more of a courtesy text so he didn't feel like he had to be there the minute I got back, I'm absolutely not an obligation.

Chapter Twelve

Tom has stayed with me in my bed since I came home from the cabin in the woods and it's been the most adorable thing, I am so grateful. Much to my dismay though, he has to go to work this afternoon and I really don't want him to leave. However, I am also too stubborn to let myself admit that out loud, especially not to his face, that's not like me at all - I'm as outspoken as they come, so by way of defence, I'm practically shoving him off in an effort to disguise my disappointment of his looming absence. It's not his fault. And if I can't cope now, I especially don't know how I'm going to cope when he goes to South Africa for two weeks at the end of this month, I might have a mini melt-down if I think about it too much. In the meantime, I'm blaming the high dosage of medicine for all this mushy emotional feelings shite, it's not my style, at the end of the day the man can do as he pleases, he doesn't belong to me and I'm quite glad about it. As Holly Golightly would say "people don't belong to people" and she's quite right, I'll get a cat. (I don't actually like cats either!)

It feels like I haven't seen him for days even when he's only been gone for a few minutes, so when it's been days without a visit I feel I've grown years older. Especially when the last visitor I had was my mum bringing the Dominos I ordered up to my room and complaining about ordering food that I can't go downstairs to fetch myself quick enough... such a hardship for her, honestly. Lily and Mick's footsteps bound up my staircase and I'm so glad to hear it. I've lived off that Dominos and cookies deal since she brought it up here on Friday night and it's now Sunday evening; there's one slice left, but it's only dustbin worthy at this stage. I don't even like cold pizza.

I immediately grill them about work and all the juicy gossip I so evidently love hearing about. Who's sleeping with who, who's leaving, who's been getting into bitching contests, so on and so forth. When the topic inevitably turns to what to have for tea and where they're going to go, I realise I haven't left my house since Tom took me for dinner last week, we opted for Chinese and it was gorgeous, he was gorgeous too, come to think of it. I digress. Mick, Lily and I are constantly out to eat, or ordering in, it's practically our favourite past time so tonight I opt for joining them, it's been four weeks since my operation and I've only left my house twice. And Chinese does sound wonderful! At this point, four weeks post op, I think mum and dad expect I am back to normal. They don't even bat an eyelid about me going out. It's not an entirely neglectful thought because I am better at moving around; much less stiff and I don't take my painkillers constantly, only when I feel like it. So I AM getting better. In fact, I feel I'm getting better enough that I decided to email the Climb Kilimanjaro company yesterday about the conditions of whether or not I can climb with this new found illness. I got a response back from them super quick and now I can't wait to get planning!

Hi Pip,

Many thanks for your email.

Firstly, there's no rush in making a decision or committing to a challenge date, as we usually take sign ups 6 months out from departure.

The 7 day Rongai route is certainly the one to consider, as days tend to be shorter leading up to the summit attempt (compared with other routes). It's a beautiful route and the only one to approach Kilimanjaro from the north – hence, it's usually less busy and you're almost trekking in isolation!! You will have to be signed off by your GP/consultant before taking on such challenge - I have attached our medical form. Hence, you may want to wait until you have built strength in your spine!

If you have any questions, please don't hesitate to contact me.

Kind regards

Ollie

Obviously, I'm not going to book anything yet, I'm going to wait until I see Mr Sant in two weeks and show him the medical forms, but at least it means I CAN do it. He can fight me for it. I've already started writing a packing list based off some online templates and recommendations and I ordered some hiking socks so I can take them when I go to try on my new hiking boots, they're not due to arrive for four to six weeks since they're coming all the way from China but that doesn't matter because it's not like I'll have time to fit hiking boot shopping in for a while once I'm back to work.

Dinner was incredible and being out of the house was so liberating, I'd forgotten what it felt like not to be cooped up inside. This is the most moving I've done since the day at the beach with Annie and I must be making progress because climbing back up my stairs doesn't feel half as exhausting as climbing into bed did that day. I'm still not quite ready to sleep when I strip off for bed, something feels like it's missing and I think it must be Tom. I've been so accustomed to his being here, just me and him in a little getting better bubble, that now the smell of him has faded from my sheets I feel a pang of sadness at his absence. I clamber into bed, using Mr Bear as spinal support, he's not as sturdy as Tom, but he is squishier and he doesn't complain when my hair is up his nose.

'If you're feeling up to it, how do you fancy a picnic tomorrow? Might be nice to get out of the house and I leave for Africa on Wednesday so I might not get chance to see you beforehand?'

I immediately pressed to call him. Tom had text me when he finished work and I had the audacity to be asleep, I felt awful, even more awful that he might have changed his mind in the last twelve hours that I didn't respond and I might not get to see him before he goes away. I can't believe I've been asleep so long, I wasn't even tired. Unnecessary panic sets in when he hasn't answered my call, is he mad at me? Is he ignoring me like I ignored him? Suddenly, from the front door I hear, "Special delivery", someone is shouting through the letterbox, mum and dad are obviously at work so I chuck on last nights clothes and do a little jog down the stairs.

'Ta-Da!' Upon opening the door, Tom is stood, carrier bag in one hand and flowers in the other.

'I didn't know if maybe you were feeling bad today because you didn't reply so I thought I could bring the picnic to you?'

I take the flowers from him, mostly to hide the giant smile pinned all over my face, I imagine it looks a bit like the joker since I just got out of bed with yesterday's make up on.

'The weather looks really nice, let's take it outside somewhere - I know the perfect place, just give me five minutes to sort myself out so I don't look a total dog!'

He laughed and made a "Woof!" as he followed me up the stairs and I flapped my arm back at him to give him what for, the damn cheek. He mocks me for just getting out of bed, and I let him, throwing on a pair of leggings and my most favoured t-shirt, Friends style font with Princess Consuela Bananahammock across the front. He always says I'm just like Phoebe so I like to call him Crap Bag when he winds me up. Two can play at that game, mister.

'Are you sure you should be doing all this walking, it seems pretty far?' He sounds so cute when he's worried, I'd never noticed until now. 'Are we any closer?'

I'd brought him down to one of my favourite spots as a kid, I was constantly wandering off on adventures and expeditions, the little geography explorer that I was. If you followed my street right to the end and crossed over at the bridge, there was an old railway line turned walking path, at the end of which there was a field and through the field was a wooded walkway leading down by the Gorge, the Nidd Gorge. One of the best places to have an adventure in the whole of Harrogate, it goes on for miles and you can follow it as far as you like; come off in Knaresborough or Bilton or Ripley. Where I was taking Tom was my favourite part of the entire walk, the little beach between Bilton and Knaresborough, a fifty minute walk away from my house and you felt like you weren't even in the same town.

Like a proper gent and everything, he cleared the space in the sand where he was going to sit and, since I still can't quite get down on the floor without getting stuck, he found a broken tree log for me to sit on next to him. Unpacking the carrier bag it was a typical British picnic: Sausage rolls, mini scotch eggs, coronation chicken sandwich filler (hot dog buns to make sandwiches with), cheese strings, pepperami's - the spicy ones, and some cream cakes for afterwards, a proper little feast for two. We spent the afternoon munching away, him more than me because he has the appetite of a blue whale, we ended up in a cream cake fight somehow, both with fresh cream our noses trying to lick it off the other. It was like something icky and childishly romantic from a bad film, think 'The Notebook' only less depressing. At that exact moment a dog walker came by and I can imagine that it must've looked highly suspicious, two grown adults licking each other's faces, but that only made us laugh more. Embarrassingly, I ended up admitting I was shit at skimming pebbles after one failed attempt and so that was it, he was such a show-off getting eight to nine bounces off the surface whilst I stood there chucking rocks in like a toddler, giggling at the poo-like plopping sounds and trying to kick his concentration. We are just a couple of kids, I tell you.

We talked more than we ever have, down at my little beach, about when we were younger. He told me about his family and what he was like in school, and although I already knew about his many, many siblings and his ginormous extended relative list, somehow it was different this time. When it was finally time to leave, the sun was shining gold through the surrounding trees and across the river. So strangely unusual for this time in October, it doesn't feel like it's the middle of Autumn at all, everything is still so green. We hiked the path back to my house where he got in his car and sped home to get ready for work, his shift started at six and we didn't make it to my house until just gone five. I tried not to make the goodbye seem too drawn out, he was only going to be away for two weeks, ten days actually and that's not very long at all, he'd be back before I knew it. He made me promise to take it steady and not to push myself too hard and I am under very strict instruction not to do any running - he knows me too well. We kissed as if we had done it one-hundred times before, which we had of course, but this felt so natural I almost didn't notice until his tyres pulled away and the breeze drifted over the imprint he'd left on my lips.

Chapter Thirteen

All day Tuesday, thus far, has been spent wandering around town, on my own. Quite brave of me I think, considering the circumstances, but I haven't fallen to my death yet and I'm taking very little fairy steps so I should be fine. I'm on the hunt for a rucksack for my Kilimanjaro climb and I don't want to buy one online because I want to make sure it's fitted to me properly, especially now. The main problem seems to be that I live in Harrogate, just about the smallest, most useless town ever when it comes to needing something specific, the only outdoor shop we have is Blacks and they don't exactly hire specialists in climbing Mount Kilimanjaro, so it seems. It looks like I'll have to go further afield, maybe get Annie psyched for a shopping trip to the White Rose centre or Metrocentre on one of her half-days, as long as there's going to be a stationary shop nearby she's sold.

Waterstones is last on my list, it's just about one of the best shops in the world and it makes me obscenely happy whenever I see one, especially if I'm not in Harrogate. Ours is three floors tall, elegant and modern, very natural woods and cream walls. My favourite place is the third floor, it's the travel section and it's isolated from the noise of the cafe below and the cashiers on the ground floor. Pages and pages of travel books line the walls, Lonely Planets', Rough Guides', they've got just about everything you could ever think to need. Apart from for me. Jesus Christ today isn't my day at all... I wanted to get the Rough Guide to Tanzania, I'd been thinking about how there's nothing stopping me, after my climb, staying in Tanzania and volunteering and travelling around the country. Alas, today was not the day to plan this trip so I made a hasty exit, before I could let it convince me it was a bad omen or something.

I was going to get the bus home, I left the shop and made for the station, but something stopped me and instead I trailed my feet across the other way, to work. I haven't been in since I'd dropped my sick note off and I am sure I'm starting to get withdrawals, Mick and Lily are both in today I'm sure of it so it would be rude not to say hello.

'Crazy Lady! Are you supposed to be out wandering on your own?' Of course Lily was infuriated by my stubbornness and demanded an explanation, Mick was more forgiving of the fact I was clearly going stir crazy on my own at home. One of the many things I love about this job is that even though I'm not at work I can happily sit on a spinney chair in the office and chat shit with the people that are supposed to be working. A small luxury I'm very grateful for.

The office isn't exactly a nice hang out room, it's narrowly better than the staff room, but it has a cleaner fridge and less mess on the floor. Mick always has his iPod on and Lily is usually looking at holidays, I'm a bit of an encourager there. Today's offers are Disney deals and I'm loving them, I think being let down by Waterstones has only heightened my want for a holiday and realistically Tanzania and Kili are over a year away so I'm going to need something to tide me over in the meantime, who wouldn't? I'm usually on at least three holidays a year, this year was New York, Ibiza and Germany so maybe next year can be Disney and then Tanzania at the end of the year. Two big holidays equal three little ones, right? Not only have I talked myself into it, I think I'm talking Lily and Mick into it, too, ever a bad influence and all that. Happy that business is quiet on a Tuesday tea time, we scour the internet for a good enough offer we can all agree on, Disney is our thing after all and so it's only right we go. We're all smiling nervously as if we're waiting for someone to convince us not to do it, like one of us is going to say "but come on, we can't REALLY just book a holiday", but none of us are showing any signs of faltering. Mick takes control of the mouse whilst Lily pulls up our holidays sheets, we can easily all have two weeks it just depends when we take it. Another good sign.

'Oooh look, here...' Mick uses the curser to highlight a deal and we all say "Yes" in unison. Two weeks, full meal plan, Disneyworld Florida September, it feels like a long way away now, but it's only eleven months, it gives us time to pay it off and gives me time to book and save for Kili, too. I run it all through my brain; if I'm anticipating being back at work by November, I can pay my deposit for Disney today, pay it all off by January and then book and pay for Kili by June (six months before my intended trek) then, finally, I can save from then for Tanzania travel money until December when I go - SOLD! Before I have chance to second guess, Mick is on the phone making the booking and I'm transferring him the £200.00 deposit, it's a good thing I'll be back at work next month because being off is making me so skint! Balance now: £176.20 - urgh! Worth it though, I'm going on holiday! Can I get a WOOP WOOP?! (Fairy Godmother - Shrek 2 - legend!)

It's nice to finally feel like I have a plan, something to look forward to and work towards, being off sick really can make you feel worthless. It makes you feel unnerved by the uncertainty of when you can continue with your life, like nothing is real, time doesn't mean anything when you've got nothing meaningful to fill it with so you lull through your days, sometimes hazy from pain and sometimes hazy from your medication, constantly with a question mark on your head. I know I thought that Waterstones lack of Tanzania books was a bad omen, but maybe it was just a change of course, it's put me back on track, I'm getting (and going) somewhere.

I hang around the office for another hour just chatting about all the things we're going to do whilst we're away then, when the evening starts to pick up, I make a quick exit to walk home. It only took me thirty minutes to get to my front door from the office and I can consider it impressive, it's almost back to my standard twenty minutes. After all the Disney excitement I'm in a lull, I feel exhausted and empty, like all the energy I had to give has been used up like a kid high on sugar, and now I'm crashing. Flopping into bed sounds beyond perfect and I can practically feel the covers closing round me as I trudge up the stairs.

What in the hells bells is that? Next to my bed is a relatively large white box that I've never seen before in my life, it doesn't look like a parcel, there's no sticker or wrapping? I inspect all sides and there's nothing, but it is plugged in to the wall for some reason... a door? Oh my goodness! Stuck with tape to the shelf when I open the front, is a note in familiar handwriting:

'Hello little one, I decided to let you borrow my mini fridge for the time that I'm away (you're always saying how much you wish you had a kitchen up here!) It's just bits for you to pick at with your tiny fingers, I know you don't have

a big appetite on all your drugs so I hope these things will be okay.'

There's a little arrow pointing to the backside of the note, but before I turn it over, I have a brief look at the contents of my new found mini-fridge, I give my best smile to the twelve-pack of cheese strings on the top shelf - this boy knows me far too well and I love it. He continues on the turned sheet of paper that I notice has been ripped from my Disney pad from my table - mickey mouse is smiling in the corner...

'Don't do anything silly whilst I'm away, it won't be long before I'm home.
Be strong little one, I will see you soon.
Tom XX'

Without hesitating I reach for my phone and call him. Whilst it's ringing I notice the time is almost 21:00 and suddenly hope he isn't already in bed, he leaves for the airport in the early hours.

While staring at the red "end call" button, deciding to just text him instead, he answers and sounds particularly flappy.

'What's the matter?' I ask instinctively before any hello has been uttered.

'I can't find my passport, I don't even know where I last had it and it's the only thing left to pissing pack!' His voice is strained, I know he doesn't like getting frustrated, but for some reason I find it so wonderful when people can be themselves around me (despite my inability to always reciprocate) I always push to know these things and then to subsequently fix them. Part one of Pip Parker, what is your biggest flaw? It's easily fixing people, or at least trying to.

On this occasion, thankfully, I can come to the rescue.

'Don't worry, it will turn up. Have you checked on the side table in the lounge? It was there last time I saw it and if it isn't on top then look to make sure it hasn't fallen down the side?' My voice is calm and annoyingly girlish, and according to dad, it's my "hostage situation diffusing voice", he always says that whenever I use the same tone on mum, she's prone to flapping fits too.

'Nope, not there...'

'Oh, right...' I pause for thought as to where else the damn thing might be, but he jumps in.

'Ah-ha you believed me! I'm only joking, you're a clever one aren't you? It was on the table. Thank you.'

Now he had released the stress with a terrible prank and I could hear him zipping his bag, I let my thanks for the fridge burst through the phone. He loves to be helpful, he's such a superman, Henry Cavill ALMOST could have a run for his money - very almost.

When we come off the phone half an hour later, we leave on one of those super elongated "Goodbye's". You know, the ones where you can tell the other person doesn't want to go and the more you say bye the quieter your voices get, but you somehow feel so much closer, like instead of drawing the conversation to a close you now strangely feel like you're in a secret world of just the two of you and you can't possibly hang up. After a while you just stare at the screen in silence waiting for the other to cut you off. This time I was the one to cut it off, it was my ridiculous way of trying to show him that I'm not going to even miss him that much anyway, why would I? I have everything I need, Mr Bear, snacks and telly... he can enjoy his holiday!

Chapter Fourteen

'This is fancy!' I expressed to dad whilst mum was in the toilets. He'd brought us out for a family meal to celebrate mum's fiftieth birthday and it was already uncomfortable. The restaurant is deathly quiet, but it is a Thursday so I can forgive them for not being rammed, also, looking at the prices on the menu it's clearly not somewhere you bring the kids for a slap up tea after school. They'd spent the day at The Spa, since I ruined their first attempt at an experience, then they came home to change and pick me up. I'd given mum her present this morning, nothing fancy, I'd asked Annie to grab it for me when she was in town last week; a gorgeous Yankee candle, the large kind, in her favourite linen scent, and a voucher for a beauty experience photo-shoot day. It's the kind of thing I thought she would like to do to keep as a reminder of how she looked when she was fifty, a compliment because she certainly doesn't look it! In response I got a thank you, an awkward hug and I got to watch her put the voucher back in its envelope and leave it on the pile of post in the kitchen. Always so grateful and charming, my mother.

Dad has bought her a trip to Portugal that's leaving tomorrow for a week and she is clearly over the moon about it even though they've been to Portugal a million times. Once she'd finished telling the poor waiter about her holiday plans, even though he only asked for our orders, the conversation turned dry and so I attempted to do my best to rectify it.

'Mum? If you could have anything for your birthday what

would you have, if money were no object? Also, whatever you pick is the only thing you are allowed to receive on your birthday for the rest of your life... go!' She glances across to my dad and laughs, an Yzma from The Emperors New Groove, laugh.

'I'd have you moved out!' She laughs again and clearly thinks she's hilarious, but I don't seem to find it funny and my face gives it away. Dad smiled at her cruel comment, I was trying to be nice and I was trying to have a fun conversation with my parents and yet again, I'm always the butt of their joke, the butt of their happy life. I could find it funny if I knew deep down she didn't really mean it. I reached for my glass of juice in order to keep my face from being too distractingly offended, but mum saw my eyes roll back in my head.

'Oh for god's sake, here we go, you've just got to ruin my birthday haven't you with your stupid questions. Why ask if you are not prepared to hear the answer?'

'Mum, please don't start, I know you think it's funny, and fine, it's your birthday so it IS funny, just let me drink my juice.' My tone was dry, my hostage voice, and it made dad sit more quietly than the waiter watching from the corner.

'Don't you dare tell me not to start with you, you are MY daughter and I will talk to you how I like, you know it was just a fucking joke Philippa, learn how to take a joke- jesus.'

I continue to sit in silence, like the rest of the restaurant, thinking, stupidly, that if I stop responding she'll stop having anything to say...

'You know, you're twenty-two years old, why don't you start acting like it, me and your dad would love some space, they say when you're eighteen you're supposed to be living your own life, not still living at home. So what's wrong with you? Just because you failed at going to university and work in a cinema doesn't mean that you can't move out you know?' I'm waiting for dad to chip in and say something, but he doesn't, nor does the waiter come over and attempt to break the ice, or hurry our food out as a way of intervening. 'What have you actually got planned for your life at this point? Because at this rate the only thing you're doing is not even working at the minute and seeing Tom.'

'I'm not working because I just had a major operation, you know this. I'm due to see the specialist next week and so hopefully I'll be back at work immediately. And actually, I'm going to Disney World with Lily and Mick next year and after that I'll be going to climb Mount Kilimanjaro in Tanzania, then I'm thinking of doing some travelling following on from that. I'll work until that point and if I'm not going to go travelling I'll work another year and save for a deposit on a house, then that way I'll be out of your hair as soon as possible. Okay? And Tom and I are just friends, he has nothing to do with this, you know that, too.' Dad decides now is the time to step in whilst mum looks at me, bewildered that I no longer have my insufferable monotone sound and it's more like I'm "answering her back".

'That all sounds great, let's just hope you can actually stick to it and finish what you say you're going to start, this time.' I thought he might have been saving the day at first, but instead, another backhanded insult and right as the waiter starts bringing the plates - last word for dad this round.

I think our family seriously suffer from the "hangry" gene. Once mum has had her fill of lasagna, and ordered a coffee, conversation is back to them going to Portugal, I nod at the right times and keep a neutral face so as not to cause more trauma, mostly for myself.

I was beyond glad they were gone when I woke up the next morning, I wasn't surprised they hadn't woken me to say goodbye, but I was tempted to see if they'd even left a note. Now if only I could get out of bed, it's so cold! Definitely November weather upon us, which makes sense with it actually being November. I gingerly check my phone, trying to keep as much of my body within the warm blankets as possible, and there's a message from Tom.

'Only one week left to go until I'm home! The weather is unusually miserable for Africa at this time of year, but it's still like 23 degrees so I'm happy enough. Send me a picture of something good to keep me going, little one, and tell me... how are you feeling?'

He'd sent me it in the early hours of the morning so I imagine he was very drunk and he would now be asleep. Surprisingly I'm glad for the knowledge of him being in dreamland, it gives me more time to not have to lie to him about how I'm feeling, because this morning I've woken up more uncomfortable than I like to admit. Let's walk it off. Down the stairs, there's no note left from the parents, but there's something much better... SNOW! And a shit tonne of it. I hadn't noticed upstairs with my sky light blind down for a change, but looking out the kitchen window the garden was Narnia and I didn't hesitate in sending a picture straight to Tom.

'Look at what you're missing!' I typed beneath it. I knew

how happy it would make him to see, we love the snow.

I decide to take some morphine, just to edge on the side of caution, after all, building a snowman might only end up causing more strain by the time I'm finished. Then, with my favourite wellies on (they're pink and have little blue tortoise on them. I worship them!) I step out in the front garden to build a snowman. Usually, I'd also like to do a snow angel. I did one on a roof top in New York in my pyjamas, it was freezing and probably absolutely filthy, but a thousand times worth it, I never fail to pass up the opportunity. Today, however, is probably not the day to attempt to get on the ground, especially when I'm home alone. We have a little bench at the end of our garden, like a love seat under the tree, so to avoid further bending than necessary I start taking snow from the branches to form the snowman's bum. Building from the bench seat so I don't have to try and reach the floor every few seconds with more snow, I only have to move less than forty-five degrees and everything seems to be going along very smoothly, I'm impressed. I'm also really thankful that mum has left her car parked on the drive way instead of in the garage, it must've been done to make it seem like someone is always home whilst they're away so we don't get robbed - but for me, it's ideal for swiping the snow off and trudging over to shape the rest of my snow man. If they were here now I'd be in trouble for making shoe prints in the foot of snow across the grass. Whoops.

Once I believe he's finished I stand at the other side of the garden to admire my work from afar, and to take a picture to send to Tom later. He looks like a Gordon and I think that's what I'll call him until he's nothing but a little pile of ice, for some reason it always makes me sad knowing they don't stay around forever, even though I know he'd look completely shit without a snowy white backdrop in the summer. Putting my phone back in my pocket, I turn to head back inside, happy with my morning frolic in the snow and ready for a hot bath before a day in bed watching Gilmore Girls (again!) I get one foot on the step to the front door before my entire body freezes to the spot. A hot rod of iron is slammed through the right side of my body disabling any motion without feeling as if I'm going to be torn in half and my face scrunches up into a raisin. Stay calm, is the only thing I can think to tell myself as I stand there halfway to warmth, knowing full well what is happening.

'For fucks sake,' I groan out loud in such a way that it sounds comical when I play it back in my head, my body is so done with this shit and yet my brain is still trying to convince me not to think the worst. 'It's not what you think it is, it can't be, just get inside and it will wear off.' I'm not convinced, but I can see the logic. When I left the hospital they told me there was only a five-percent chance that this would ever happen again in my life. Cauda Equina syndrome is not something that usually happens to women my age and so the chances of it happening again, a week before I'm due for my follow up appointment with my specialist, six weeks after the first time, just feel too slim. I'm being paranoid, definitely. I think.

The amount of tears it takes for me to get in the front door is equivalent to Alice drowning in hers when she gets to Wonderland, there's very possibly a white rabbit knocking around too, but that could be the morphine kicking it. I wish it would work for getting rid of the pain, it just makes me smushed in the head. Although, I do appreciate it giving me a sense of false confidence, suddenly I'm convinced if I move quicker it will be less painful so I take four large steps to the arm of the couch and let out a huge scream into my hands once I'm perched. My eyes are swollen into puff pastry and I'm in so much pain that I don't even consider how much, normally, thinking that would make me hungry. I've still got my wellies on and there's snow melted on the laminate in the hallway and into the carpet beneath me in the lounge. Everything is wet and everything else is pain and I'm home alone.

Chapter Fifteen

Once I'm as used to the intensity of the searing agony racing through my little body as I possibly can be, I pull my phone out of my pocket to dial my GP. I've been sitting here for half an hour and there's been no change, only my bum feels wet and I can't recall sitting on any snow, it must be running off my jacket and wetting the sofa, too. Thank god it's only water. After listening to the monotone recording of a receptionist talking for two whole minutes about how you shouldn't call the doctor for a common cold, I finally get through to reception who, as usual, were useless. Apparently she's going to get a doctor to call me back within the hour, but her tone of voice said it would be an hour before she even raised the flag. I prop myself up as best I can, I'll be damned if I'm going to spend the afternoon on the arm of this sofa, my body, however, disagrees and so I fall back on to the couch, angrily screaming my way through the motion. If the neighbours don't call the police thinking I'm being murdered at this point, then frankly they're not very good neighbours, it certainly feels like murder. Or is it suicide when it's my own body doing it?!

"Hello Pip. Doctor Parker here, what can I help you with?"

I love doctor Parker, not only because he has the same name as me, but he is the only doctor that's ever given half a shit in that place. It's proven when I don't even have to finish to explain what's happened before he tells me he's coming to see me, he can't understand why they suggested I needed a phone call when I very clearly need to be checked over in person. Just short of cursing the receptionist out himself, he tells me he'll be with me soon and hangs up.

At the sound of his sports car pulling up my driveway I have to question whether or not I left the door off the latch? I did. He comes quietly into the living room, pulling up a dining chair to perch on. He's a rather tall man, especially when I'm laying down, his shoulders stoop and his hair is almost a spike on top. He has soft features though, kind doctor-y eyes that make you want to empty your soul in front of him, pour your heart out and feel completely fine about it. I'm not that kind of person though and as much as he's wonderful, he can only get a heartfelt emotion from me as much as anyone else, which is never.

'Pip, do you feel like you're sitting in a damp spot?' His eyes are quizzically going from the end of the couch and back to mine again.

'Well, I thought the snow had started melting off my jacket maybe, why?' He does his best not to look worried, but I'd know that face anywhere. "My bladder has gone hasn't it? Is it everywhere?' I groan, unsurprised. Of course it is. Luckily my sofa is leather and so mum and dad will never have to know, but I'm slightly mortified. My jeans have doubled in colour, they're thick and chafing against each other with every slight flinch of my thighs, urine has pooled to the back pockets. I try to move so I can get cleaned up, but it sets the tears in motion again and all of a sudden I can't see any reason why I should even try and get out of my piss soaked pants. Sod it. Doctor Parker reaches in the linen cupboard for a spare towel (not the good ones, of course) I suggest a Disney one just to be safe, they're very obviously mine and I can always buy a new one, if I'm still even allowed to go to Florida. Naturally he doesn't need to do any physical examination of me now he's here, instead, he has to go back to the surgery to call me an ambulance, it will get here quicker if he can make the referral from his computer apparently.

His kind heart doesn't want to leave me on my own, but I insist and say I'll call someone, although, if I'm being honest, I hadn't even thought about bothering anyone until he mentioned it. I check my phone; Tom hasn't replied, I haven't heard from mum and dad to say they've landed, even though they should've done by now, and otherwise my phone is completely dry of notifications, so I don't bother to reach out, I don't want to be a nuisance and if I haven't heard from anyone it means they're busy any way. It's not long at all before Dr Parker calls me to tell me an ambulance is on its way and he'll wait for word from the hospital about what is going to happen, he seems pretty confident I'll be going straight to Leeds for surgery. Round 2, DING DING DING.

Upon arrival at the LGI I'm sent straight back to my previous ward, but, thankfully, this time I'm in a window bay so I can shut out the rest of the ward whilst keeping the view - suckers! Honestly, I'm not paying very much attention to what's going on outside regardless, I'm too busy thinking about going in for further surgery. This time I know what it's all about and it suddenly seems much scarier than it did the first time around, maybe because I was ignorant of the actual complications for so long before, maybe because this time I'm alone.

Whilst I wait for the doctor to come and see me I decide to check my phone, I'd got the ambulance guys to pack me a little bag of shit; phone charger, laptop and charger, jumper, crossword book, just stuff that I had lying around, I didn't fancy them going in my drawers to get my pants, I'm not that easy! Tom has replied to my message from earlier and it makes my heart stop for a brief moment, it's a good thing I'm not hooked up to a monitor or else I'd be beeping.

'The snow isn't the only thing I'm missing... send me a picture and one of you, too!'

I don't think he's ever admitted to missing me before, to actually enjoying my presence that much that he's felt the need to say it and I feel completely loved for just a second. An entire second of zoo animals in my stomach and flushed cheeks and dorky smiles, until I realise that we're not together and it doesn't matter what he says or what he means. I send him the picture of my fabulous snowman anyway, and the selfie I took of me in my winter woollies in the snow, too, patting myself (figuratively) on the back for taking them so I don't have to send him the reality of me being in a hospital bed. I do contemplate telling him, but I can't see how that would benefit anyone. One of two things would happen; either he'd not care so much and that would upset me because as much as I pretend, I do want him to. Or, he'd be worried sick and it would ruin the rest of his holiday and I think I like this option less, I want him to have the time of his life, I didn't even need him to message me whilst he's been gone, but he has done.

I don't ask for much and I always thought that was my biggest downfall, not demanding what I need and being too unconditional in my affections, but I only consider it a strength with age. The right guy will respect me without me having to ask or demand. If there even is such a thing, I'm still pretty certain they're all twats in tinfoil at this point. Maybe not Tom, but we'll see.

'Hi Pip, my name is Dr Rizzoli. Firstly, I'm so sorry about your wait, we've just been looking at your file and scans...'

Oooh, we have an Italian in the ranks, lucky me! Dr Rizzoli looks just the part with his jet black hair and olive skin and Disney Prince eyes, I'm surprised that I never met him on my last visit and I make a mental note to tell Annie about him; she's always had a thing for Italians and I know she's got Alex now, but looking never hurt! He even has glasses, and boy does she love a smart looking man!

'So it seems your MRI that was just taken at Harrogate might be inconclusive so we're ordering another with our out of hours team, we're just waiting on him to get here and set up for you, so it could still be a couple of hours, just hang tight, we are getting on!'

'What do you mean my MRI is inconclusive? Is it not cauda equina?' The confusion spread across my face could be seen for miles, I'm sure. My eyebrows furrowed into one and tears pricked my empty eyes. Everyone always asks me if my eyes are black because they're such deep a blue, it's one of the first things strangers ask me and people always jump to them being brown because they're not poetically the colour of the day time sky. Usually this winds me up, I'll get right in the persons face, eyes wide and shout blue until they shut the hell up, but right now I think it's helping my look of fury and befuddlement sink in.

'Well, it's just that the scans were blurry so we can't see if anything is lodged in your nerves and we won't do surgery out of hours unless it's seriously necessary. We have time to do another scan with you only starting with symptoms twelve hours ago, we get up to forty-eight remember so don't worry, I'm not even sure it's anything to panic about.'

Coolly and calmly the Italian stallion left and I thought maybe I wouldn't tell Annie about him after all, his arrogance radiates, his lack of concern has become a real turn off and even though she'd probably still find him handsome, I don't think he's worth the conversation. How can he dismiss what my body knows to be true? Am I not the one who was in this position exactly six weeks ago? I understand the need for confirmation, but Christ on a bicycle it's safe to say I'm unimpressed already and I've only been here four hours. Speaking of being unimpressed, even the nurses have been shitty with me, just generally rude like they're having a bad night or something, but it's not my fault and I'm not exactly having a good time either! It could just be me if I'm totally honest, I'm well aware of the fact I have had another day of not eating, the idea of having another operation looming over me, they've kept me fasting for it! I could murder some cheese, what's new?

When I get down to the MRI scanner (again) it's 1am. One o'clock in the chuffin' morning, they may as well have just left it until it reopened at eight. The first thing I do is apologise over and over to the worlds loveliest technician, he's such a darling coming all this way to put me in a big magnet and he still can do it with a smile on his face, half the staff in this place could really do with taking a leaf out of his book. I think the morphine makes me far more blunt and honest than normal, as it happens I said those things out loud and I'm not even embarrassed when he laughs at me and asks if that's true. He also apologies on behalf of the other staff, saying he's just clearly better than everyone else - I like his style! Also, for the first time in what has been like, four MRI's or something daft, this wonderful human has given me a choice of music to be played through the headphones, with the promise of turning it up.

'What kind of genre are you into? I have rap, pop, rock, country, classical...'

'Oooh, do you have any old stuff? Like Blue Eyes or Dean Martin or Frankie Valli? I could listen to them all day! I do sometimes...' He starts to hum 'Volare' and I laugh excitedly enough that I end up 'ow-ing'.

'Okay don't hurt yourself, I'll play you some Deano. Just so you know, you're the first person to hear this album in here and the last person I'd expect to ask for it, no offence of course.' For the first time all day, other than the Tom text, I am smiling. Although, the great thing about this smile is it's not dependant on this mad man's feelings towards me and so in that sense it's, very almost, better.

I definitely dozed off in the machine, there's something about all the booming sounds and Deano's ridiculously soothing voice that send me happily to dreamland. My mind was still heavily focused on playing his entire record when I got back to my ward and realised I'd been gone for over an hour. Not only that, my little nap in the scanner had made me more alert than ever, I was no longer ready for bed, I wanted to do something exciting. First though, I was in dire need of some anti-sickness. That's the thing about morphine, if and when it isn't sending your brain doolally, it's sending your stomach into theme park mode. I call the nurse and she writes me up for my next dose of tramadol, another shot of the morphine and some anti-sickness I'd never heard of, that's all I'm allowed until morning so it better bloody last. Before she goes I ask her when the doctor is expected back with my scan results and, as usual, her response is inconclusive and she tells me to get some sleep. On all these tablets?! Sleep, my arse!

Chapter Sixteen

The sun is rising behind the buildings beyond my window and the sky is a deep orange, not something that we are lucky enough to witness this time of year, usually it's cloudy as balls, but this is really gorgeous to see. The light illuminates the face of the elderly woman in the bed across from me, her wrinkles don't seem so harsh in this glow and her hair could easily be blonde if she wanted it to be. Not the same platinum as mine, but softer and more like a golden sand. I think about my hair and how it must look now after not being washed in forever and just as I start to run my fingers through it Dr Rizzoli waltzes in, pulling my curtain to before he stands in the window and squirts his alcohol hand gel into his palms - I bet those curtains are filthy.

'I hope you've slept well, I didn't want to disturb you so I thought I'd wait until more sociable hours to come and talk with you.'

I could've told him I haven't slept since the MRI, but I couldn't be bothered, I just wanted to know what was going on and he was the man that could tell me.

'The MRI is still not really very conclusive, it might be because you've not long had an operation and the scar tissue could be in the way, we can't be sure. So, I've requested an X-Ray from the team today and hopefully that will tell us what's going on, in the meantime, we'll keep you on the painkillers and get you one of our larger catheter bags put on, the one from Harrogate was only temporary so it will need changing today, a nurse will do it for you this morning. Finally, I'm requesting that your bloods are done too to make sure there's no infection going on, we're also testing your urine so I have to ask...'

'No doctor, there's no chance I could be pregnant.' I am so tired of being asked this it comes across far too noticeably in my tone and he almost looks taken a back. They can check that I'm not when they take my urine sample anyway so why bother asking? What if I'm the Virgin Mary, how would I know I was with child if the Angel had forgotten to visit... honest to God. It appears I also had that rant out loud too and my eyes fill then overflow with tears.

'I'm so sorry, I am the most horrible person, I am so sorry!' The more I talk the worse it gets and I'm snotting into the blanket. 'I just know that this is the cauda equina again, I-I can tell and I just want to be able to move! I'm so uncomfortable, I want to be able to wee on my own and move, you know I'm only twenty-two! And I know it isn't your fault, but I have hardly slept and I'm still fasting in case I need an operation and I understand I really do, I don't mean to be so mean, I'm so sorry!' I even surprised myself as I listened to the blubbering of the emotional wreck I'd become. I don't ever have outbursts like this and it just makes me cry harder knowing what a tit of myself I'm making. Truth is, I hadn't even realised how much this was affecting me. I've been relatively sound the last six weeks and I've been so excited I just want to know that everything will be fine, so I can climb my mountain and go and meet the Mouse. Dr Rizzoli sits in the armchair next to my bed and hands me a box of tissues, waiting for me to finish my flood.

'I understand and I'm really very sorry, I wish I knew why this was happening, you're very unlucky and I'm so very sorry. You, on the other hand, don't have to be sorry, you've every right to be upset, I promise I'll push things through as soon as I can for you." He glances at the Rolex on his oddly-thin wrist, "It's eight o'clock now… If I can get down to x-ray I'll see if I can get you on the first half of the list. How does that sound?" It sounded reasonable, unlike me, and I thanked him. Profusely.

It's probably time to call someone. Annie is the only person I want to tell for now, until I know what's going on, and she's the only other person who's seen me in pieces before so I know she wouldn't be unhelpful if I had another meltdown. Naturally, her initial reaction was to shout at me for not calling sooner, I knew I'd be in trouble, but it's only because she cares and the feeling of being cared for right now was overwhelming. Within five minutes she had a list of things I needed and she was a woman on a mission to Leeds.

Alex was biking with all his mates anyway so she was just sitting at home doing some paperwork, it was no trouble, she'd insisted. I'd made it very clear on the phone that I needed some Cheese strings bringing because I was famished, but Annie being Annie knew better than to help me break the rules and subsequently arrived food and drink-less. It was one of the many reasons I had to love her. She also made me tell my parents I was back in hospital. I know she's right, if I don't tell them I'll only be in trouble for keeping them in the dark, at least this way if I let them know they don't have to pretend to be angry, loving parents and they can dismiss me from the get go. As I predicted, I received a text reply once I'd returned from my x-ray saying that I was just to let them know where I was expected to be on the day they get home. After an angry rant about their selfishness and lack of love for their only child, I made Annie add her contact details as my "in case of emergency" at the nurses station, she's easily more reliable.

I let her stay in my curtain when the nurse came to change my catheter. By 'let her', I mean I heavily encouraged her to, it's not like she's not seen me naked before and as long as she stayed by my head she couldn't see the interior design any way. Having a catheter removed and replaced is a strange thing. Apparently, with my suspected bout of cauda equina it's normal to have no sensation in the "saddle area", even in my bum. The cauda equina nerves are vital for it all to work properly and when the nerves are tampered with or compromised by disk, this is supposedly a telling sign that they need to operate. I hold back from bitching about why they haven't yet, which can only mean I must be due some more morphine if I finally have some control of the motormouth. She says I'm supposed to be able to feel a bit uncomfortable when the catheter reaches my bladder, but I still don't feel a thing. Annie is squeezing my hand, for her benefit more than mine I think, as it's taken four different tubes to actually get one in the right place. Apparently my urethra is inflamed because of the nerve damage and so it's making things super difficult. "It's probably just me, I'm a real jinx. Let's not give the probable caudal equina ALL the credit!" I jest to the nurse trying to feel her way inside me, eurgh. Annie sighs at my poor attempt of getting some laughs, but the nurse commends me for still being able to keep a sense of humour throughout it all, well, what does she want me to do? If I don't laugh I'll cry and I've always preferred laughing.

We spend the afternoon watching Horrible Histories on

my laptop and singing all the songs with actions, one of our favourite pastimes that never seems to get old - even though it is history, ba-dum-tsss! Every now and then she will pause the screen and ask if I need anything or want anything, she's such a mother. She bought me some slippers and made sure they didn't have any metal on so I could wear them for my x-ray and my other scans without having to take them off. I adored her for staying with me all day, so when the man came to take my blood I told her that I was fine and she should go outside to call Alex - I know not speaking to him every hour puts her on edge, like me she likes to know everyone is okay. When she excused herself, I took a minute to be quiet. I know she wouldn't want me to be putting a face on for her, but I didn't want to seem like I was too upset all the time, it gets boring when someone is constantly complaining and I don't like to whinge at the best of times, even when I can't move.

'Why didn't you tell me you were back in the hospital?! Have you had an operation? Are you having one? I can't call you my phone doesn't work here unless I'm on wi-fi, I've just got Annie's message! Little one, you should've told me! I'm so worried please let me know what they say about your operation, I'll be home before you know it, keep strong X'

When she returns from her, no doubt gushy, call, she apologies for being so long and asks if I've heard from Tom. She thinks so sly honestly! My eyes are squinting in a 'mhmmm, you know I know' sort of way with my eyebrows raised as much as they can be, but i quickly soften and thank her for letting him know I was here. 'You're too stubborn for your own good you know, that boy cares about you and you won't even admit it.'

'Yeah well where do you think I get it from? Mrs "always right!"' It's funny how well someone can know you when you don't even know yourself. I press the play button again on the laptop as Annie climbs on the bed with me... 'Terrible tudors, gorgeous Georgians, slimy Stuarts, vile Victorians...'

Chapter Seventeen

'I fucking told them! I have been telling them since I got here that I know my own body and I know that this it's the cauda equina again so why not just listen to me?!'

Less than an hour of Horrible Histories watching with Annie something had felt wrong and so I'd sent her to get a nurse. I told her that I thought my catheter had been leaking and when she checked there was bright red blood seeping into the bag, and even worse than that. My bowel had gone. I wasn't sure what they meant exactly when they told me about the nerves and how they had the potential to make me lose my bladder and bowel. Lose them how? My bladder was in severe retention and stretched beyond the norm by 500ml, I'm lucky I didn't go into renal failure before they put the catheter in and now it was just causing me grief. Up until now the bowel thing hadn't made much sense, did it mean I was going to be constipated all the time? Apparently not. When the nurse went to remove my catheter, I had... shit myself, to put it delicately.

I hadn't even felt it, I was just concerned that my catheter was uncomfortable and that was the least of my worries. Twenty hours ago i'd arrived here and i've had an MRI, an x-ray, bloods and urine tested and I still don't know what is wrong with me. This can't be right. The humiliation of crapping my pants at twenty-two years old sets the tears in motion, but I find they're coming more from the anger of not knowing. It isn't the nurses fault, but I cry at her anyway. Annie is sitting by my bed, going red from the neck up the more upset I become, she's mad for me and she'll be seething until it's just her and I and then she'll hit the ceiling - possibly literally, at 5ft 10inches she's a giant compared to me.

'I will have to let the doctors know that this has happened and I'll see if they've had your x-ray results yet, hopefully it's nothing, but we'll soon find out. You're all clean now!' She'd had to pull all the bedding out from under me as I still can't stand and the shuffling around to help her get it back on only made me even more furious with pain.

'How can she tell me it's hopefully nothing when I've just done THAT?!' I sob uncontrollably to Annie for a brief moment before rubbing my eyes and holding my face in a stern glance through the window. I refuse to let them see me this upset about their lack of concern, my body knows what's wrong with it because it can feel it and I'm sure they will see that if they could just read a scan properly. In the back of my mind though, I can't help but worry about what could happen if they find out it's not the cauda equina, I could almost feel myself praying to God through the fluffy white clouds that this won't be permanent.

'Going in for surgery now, they're idiots! I'll tell you about it when you're home, I don't want to ruin your holiday! I'm fine, don't worry, just enjoy yourself! Sorry Annie messaged you and not me, I didn't want you to panic! I'll let you know when I'm out, send me a picture of something good! X'

Annie had to go by the time they'd come to tell me I was right. I was, obviously, absolutely correct in thinking it was cauda equina and they now had to operate immediately because my bowel was compromised. After I'd sent Tom a text I also tapped one to Annie to let her now I would be going in and that I'd let her know when I was out. I wasn't going to let them lock my phone away this time, I wanted to be able to call her the minute I came around to bitch about how shit they were. I also felt a bit guilty for not letting Lily and Mick know I was back in, I hadn't wanted to bother anyone, but now an operation was going to happen I felt I probably should say something...

'Guess who's going in for Cauda Equina round two?! Yes, that would be me!'

It came out far more casual than I felt but it was good to know I could still fake it. I'm not even sure the operation is actually scaring me at all, I think it's more the prospect of what would happen if they don't operate and the way they've come around to doing it that's making me irritable. Thankfully though, the minute they told me it would be Mr Sant doing the procedure itself I had every faith - at least someone in this place isn't a total monkey's uncle.

Coming round off the anaesthetic is always so strange, you have just been asleep for hours and you don't feel refreshed at all, you feel groggy and dreamlike, as though you've just woken up in a foreign country and don't know who you are anymore. The best comparison I can make is it's a little box of time just missing from your life, you go under and within the same minute you could be brought back to and you'd have no clue. Apparently, this time, I was under the knife for six hours, a couple of hours more than last time, something about it being more difficult to remove. I can't say I was listening, I was too hungry to care in that second. They kept me in recovery so I could eat a little bit of a sandwich and make sure I wasn't sick and they made me finish a whole jug of water to get my blood pressure back up, too. I was the only patient down there and there were four members of staff sitting chatting about their respective holidays for the winter period, I tried to fight a battle on why snow is worth staying for, but I don't think I was making proper sentences because of all the drugs. They weren't listening anyway. Placed in my hand was a morphine pump, unfortunately it was capped so I could only pump it once an hour, probably a wise move in my practically drunken state, or I could easily have started sweating the stuff.

Finally parked back in my bay by the window, it was beautifully dark outside, the clock on my phone said it was 1am, maybe too late to call Annie. I opted for a copy and paste text to Tom, Annie, Lily and my parents instead of individual ones, I'm surprised I even knew how to type:

'Ou of surgeriee, ifind out how if it went in the morrow. Loveeeeeeee XXXXX'

It was coherent enough to me, but it wasn't until I read it back the next day I realised none of it had made much sense, lucky for me my friends know me well enough to code break.

Nobody came to visit the day after my op, Annie and Alex had family plans, mum and dad were still away, Tom ditto and Mick and Lily were working. Instead, the only faces I got to see were physio. I'm not complaining though, they were both lovely, they had a good dynamic so I guessed they'd been working together for a little while and they didn't bully me too much. Rachel was tall and Alice was small, I imagined that's what Annie and I looked like, my short, fat arse next to her Kendall Jenner. The first step on their agenda was to get me to take a step. When they'd first arrived, late morning, they had to schedule to come back later because I hadn't been given my pain killers at the right time so any activity would have caused unnecessary pain. I insisted I would manage and I was happy to give it a try, but they just gave each other a knowing look, that I was strangely left out of, and whispered to the nurse about returning mid-afternoon. Something felt off and I couldn't put my finger on it, physio were being timid about touching me and I still hadn't had the standard surgeon visit to check everything was working okay, what do they know that I don't?

I tried not to worry and just put it down to lack of decent communication between staff, the poor NHS being run into the ground and I'm laying here flat on my back, not exactly helping. I napped the afternoon away, in and out of REM, having drugged up nightmares. I purposefully slept through lunch because even though I'd been starved for days my stomach wasn't in the mood. I was woken about 15:30 to take my meds because physio had called to say they were on their way up to see me, I'd started nodding off again by the time they were at my bedside.

'Come on Pip, both feet on the floor, you can do it just shuffle a little further.' Alice was vocally encouraging me whilst Rachel did the man power simultaneously trying to salvage any dignity I had left by covering the gaping hole in the back of my gown.

'You can do it!'

It takes so much energy to focus on forcing yourself up onto your feet, I'd forgotten what it felt like until I tried. My right side screamed with pain all the way up from my toes, swirling through every inch of flesh through my spine. The intensity clouded all thoughts about what was happening to the left side of me, which turns out wasn't very much at all.

'You're doing so well, just a little bit more and you're standing!'

I pushed through the pain, tears rolling down my face and dripping onto the floor beneath me, thinking that I would look brave, like a fighter. They would be proud of me and tell me I'd worked hard enough for today and I could go back to bed. As I forced the strength through my hips and thrusted out, I reached with my left hand for Alice's, hoping that I could step forward onto my left foot releasing the tension and agony in my right.

'Can we get another hand in here please?!' Rachel reached across the bed from where she was kneeling and pressed the nurses bell. I had fallen. No, not fallen, I'd collapsed heavily beneath the weight of myself, as I thought my left leg was stable enough to hold me, it wasn't even stable enough to hold a fly. Within minutes, a care support worker came in, switched off the bell and helped physio get me back onto the bed. It felt like it took hours, the whole time Rachel and Alice were giving each other that same 'knowing' look, and if I hadn't been in so much shock and so worried about the minutes events, I might realise how much it was starting to piss me off.

Falling had only made the pain worse, and there was something new that was happening to my bladder that I hadn't felt before. The cauda equina leaves very little sensation at all in that particular area, but suddenly everything was heightened and I wanted nothing more than to rip the tubes right out of me, it was burning and rubbing and I felt hysterical. Lost in my own mind of what felt like torture, I didn't even care that my curtain had been open the whole time, that the visitors for the elderly ladies in my room could witness this from whatever angle they could see - probably directly up-gown, but I truly didn't care. Not in that moment. When a nurse came she pulled the curtains to and spoke to physio about what had happened, she let them go and sat by my bed, holding my hand until I had calmed down.

'I just want it out, please take it out, I can't have it in there any more, please.' I was begging and she remained quiet until the tears had slowed.

'Pip, I'm waiting for the surgeon to come and see you, I can't do anything apart from give you painkillers until he's been, I'm so sorry, but the catheter has to stay.'

My face crumpled back into a soggy piece of A4 and she waited again for me to compose myself, I don't remember ever feeling this emotional and exhausted. 'The reason it hurts so much now is because when you fell, you very likely irritated your surgery nerves and the scar tissue which could have temporarily caused hypersensitivity to your bladder. The pain will soon fade, I'm going to get you some more Tramadol and your morphine should be ready to pump again, if not I'll get you some more from the cupboard to ease it for you.'

Her face was so incredibly sad for me that her eyes melted into mine. This woman genuinely cared about what was happening to me, or she was a bloody good actress, and I appreciated her for trying to help me understand.

'When I can get hold of the surgeon again I'll try and let you know how long it's going to be, make sure you have something to eat too, because I'm well aware you've skipped breakfast AND lunch today madam!'

She made me smile, talking to me as if I'm an "up-to-no-good-er" as if I was trying to cheat the system, which, I suppose, I was. When she was satisfied that I'd stopped crying, she helped as best as she could to get me into the jammies that Annie had brought me. I could only get the top on, it had a picture of platform nine and three quarters on it - I think she was hoping they'd bring me some magic, too. The trousers were dotted with wands and broomsticks, a Primark special, but they felt so soft I was gutted when we couldn't get them over my catheter, but instead, the nurse, Dot, brought me some old man hospital trousers that would be wide enough to fit over.

In all my life I've never met another woman called Dot who could pull it off so well, it was certainly meant for her. Short grey hair, soft and white in parts, her small, slight frame hung her nurses tunic ever so delicately. She's definitely a Dot. As ridiculous I felt about the trousers, she reassured me it didn't matter if they didn't fit around my middle because I didn't have to worry about standing up and them falling down. At first I saw she had a point and laughed a little, but then... I don't have to worry about standing up? What is she trying to say?

I slept horrendously that night, the surgeon hadn't come to see me which had pissed me off so much I thought I might say so, but instead I'd slept, hoping that it would make time go faster and therefore I would see him sooner, that didn't seem to be the case at all. Rather, I was out of it until midnight then wide awake again. Tonight, I'd already been told off for being awake, then I was scolded for not drinking enough, which I am tired of explaining is impossible. On a standard day I only drink about 600ml, so drinking over two litres is incredible progress, I feel like they're constantly trying to drown me. It's not my fault my blood pressure is naturally low.

I contemplate lying in silence and waiting for the sweet release of unconsciousness, but my mind is overtaken with loud thoughts about Christmas. It's a month away after all and here I am, stuck in a hospital bed. Usually, at this time, I've finished my shopping and then the 1st of December is dedicated to watching Arthur Christmas and wrapping gifts, filling the paper with glitter for a touch of frustrating sparkle. My other favourite thing to do at this time of year, is to wrap every corner/inch with tape so when it's torn open in a fit of rage after minutes of struggling, it only sends the glitter further across the room, into their hair and up their noses. That's the real joy, right there.

This year, I'm stuck in bed. I can't stand. I can't walk. I can only hope tomorrow physio come with extra reinforcements and I can be on the move and home again before December starts. That's the plan. If I can be home before December I can be back at work in the New Year and that's keeping me on target with being able to climb Kili in December. Easy. For now, it's drastic measures and ordering Christmas presents online. I pull the glittery cased Macbook from my table and open up Google. "Best gifts for best friends", I think if I start generically I'll be inspired, but nothing stands out, they're nothing like what my friends would want; I think I knew that would be the case before I started. Countless photo frames and candles and engraved prosecco glasses, everything only "personal" because you can put their name on it. Disney is a much better way to go. For Lily and Mick, anyway. Horrible Histories for Annie, and some stationary, of course, she is an addict. Mum and Dad are always hard work because I never like getting joint presents as it seems cheap, but they do everything together so getting separate things seems a waste. I go for a book each, and the DVD to match, that should keep them busy for at least a few days and they can swap books then watch the films together - genius.

Buying Christmas presents can be stressful when you don't know if you've bought enough for the right people, and do you really need to buy for your third cousin and their child? Thankfully, I'm lucky my circle is small and I only have to buy for a select few, I think that's part of why I enjoy it so much. In the process of clicking 'checkout' more times than I can count for my nearest and dearest (mostly), I order myself a gorgeous bikini to take to Walt Disney World, retail therapy is a blessing when you don't have to confront crowded shops and your frumpy body in a changing room mirror.

I tell you, it's a good thing you get emails of your orders sent as confirmation because when I woke up again that morning, after nodding off mid browse, I had basically zero recollection of even opening the laptop, let alone spending a great deal of money.

Chapter Eighteen

'Hi Pip, I think we need to have a chat?' Mr Sant nodded towards physio to indicate they could, or should, leave us be and he pulled the curtain behind him. It was three in the afternoon by the time he'd come to see me, a whole twenty-four hours after we thought he might arrive, but I was too anxious to see him to let him know I was miffed.

'I'm sorry I didn't come to see you yesterday, I've been dealing with a number of specialists and teams regarding your case, you're pretty famous here now. I didn't want to discuss things with you until I could be sure what was going on.'

There was something about the way he spoke and his facial expressions that caused me some concern, I trusted him infinitely, but I knew there was something he needed to say.

'Before we chat I just want to do a couple of neuro tests if that's okay? I'll need your legs if you don't mind removing the blanket?'

I did as requested and removed the blanket from my legs, pulling it up towards my chest so i didn't feel cold whilst I watched him put his papers down and pull out his 'hitty stick' (and no, that's not a euphemism! Ya filthy animal, it's one of the many instruments used to test sensation.) He started on my right side and the aim of the game was to just let him know when I could feel him touching me. I closed my eyes so I didn't feel like I was cheating. First he ran the stick above my knee, check. Then down my calf, check. Then down either side of my foot, check. Finally, he pulled it up the sole of my foot from my heel and I nearly kicked him the face. Oops! Before moving on to my left leg, he took out a smaller stick which had a sharp and a dull end, I was to indicate which side he was touching me with. Again, he started from my thigh and moved to my toes; sharp, dull, dull, sharp. Pretty standard, until it came to my left leg.

'Can you feel that?'

Upper thigh. 'Yep.'

'Here?'

Right side above the knee.

'M-hm.'

'Now?'

'Now, what?'

'Okay, what about here?'

'Here?'

I could feel my face warming up, going pink with confusion and not sure if I'm having a joke played on me or if I should be worried. I open my eyes and Mr Sant is running the stick up my left foot from the heel, I realise I don't feel like kicking him. I can't seem to ask any questions, I don't really know what to say. How have I not realised that I can't feel my leg? Why is it only now I've noticed I can't bend my toes or wiggle my ankle? I'd spent the last few days in this exact position, only moving on my right side with the help of the bars on the bed and cushions for support, surely I'd have realised before this very second that I had no feeling, surely someone else should've noticed, what have physio been messing around at? Before I have chance to reel in anger, panic and utter confusion, Mr Sant sits facing me on the edge of my bed and picks up his papers. Usually this is a man who shakes your hand and sits in a chair, very professional, but this felt different, he felt less rigid and his face was sunken.

'Pip, I'm really very sorry to have to tell you that I need to do another operation.' I remain silent, but smile to encourage him to continue - I didn't even know I could smile.

'The cauda equina this last time hit very quickly and your symptoms started much sooner than they did the first time. Even though we operated with more time to spare, we almost didn't, because it escalated so much faster. This is the reason you now have paralysis in your left side.'

'What...'

'The teams and specialists I have been in discussion with the last day have all vigilantly read your scans and notes and other symptoms; your MRI's and your X-rays show the same, unfortunate problem. I wanted to come and do the neuro exams yesterday, but we wanted to investigate first to see if this was a physical problem, which it is.'

'So does that mean you've got to do the operation AGAIN? For a third time? Aren't I lucky?' I laugh and hope I'm understanding him correctly, he's basically saying they need to repeat my operation because they couldn't fix it all in one go last time? Right? He doesn't laugh with me, instead he carries on with his explanation.

'The operation we have to do is not a small procedure, neither is it the same as you've had twice before. This is very much larger and comes with serious risk. But I need you to understand this is, after much deliberation, the only way we will be able to try and save your left leg from its current paralysis. Pip you need to understand if we don't do this operation, and soon, you may not be able to walk again. Not like before, and that's just your leg, there's no saying how this could affect your bladder for the rest of your life, too. Or your bowel.'

I'm surprised that I can't feel tears swelling behind my eyes, I don' feel sad or distraught or scared, I just feel like laughing.

'Okay, so what is this operation? What do you have to do? How long will it take?' I've turned into the responsible Pip, who solves problems and stands like a rock in a gale.

'It's called a spinal fusion, I've never seen someone your age have to have this done in all my years in this job, like I say, you're unfortunately, some kind of phenomenon in this place, I'm so sorry about that. What we do, is we open your spine and remove as much of the fragmented disc as we possibly can from your cauda equina nerves, this is the most important part for ensuring you get sensation back in your leg. Next, we will have to remove your L5 and S1 and the bone in-between, which will be crushed and mixed with synthetic bone in a pestle and mortar.' He's using his hands to indicate what they're be doing, as if he's holding up a faux skeleton and operating in front of me. 'Whilst that's being made I will be inserting a metal cage where your disc used to be and screwing two screws into the plate above and below to secure it. The cage will be filled with the mixture and then we will coat the framework with the rest and close you back up. The operation can take up to eight hours and I have to stress it is not easy. There are risks.'

'If you know me by now, you should know I'm pretty bad luck - lay 'em on me!' He smiles with one side of his face.

'Well, obviously there's infection of the wound, blood clots, severe pain, there's a 5% chance that it won't work at all, in that, it won't fuse together, but that's only 5%.'

'You say that, but 5% is the reason I'm back in this bed to start with...' I say it with a smile and a roll of my eyes, but in all seriousness, he could've said 1% and I'd still think it more than likely. He does laugh when I say that, he seems more comfortable with the fact I've not had a melt down and we spend a minute making jokes at my misfortune, well, I do. He just laughs.

'Not forgetting, they are just the risks of the lumbar fusion itself. We also may not be able to recover the use of your bladder or your leg, the removing of bone fragments may end up being superficial at best so you have to be prepared to know that this may be your quality of life from now on.' He pauses and looks me dead in the eyes, sincerely. 'I really am so sorry, I wish I had better news, but we are going to do everything we can to put you in the best state possible. I've brought the consent forms with me so once you've signed them I will go and book you in, it won't be today, we need to make sure everyone is available and that might mean swapping shifts to get this done as soon as possible with the best experts. I will let you know when it will be, I'm hoping by the end of the week to give us the best chance of rectifying everything. In the meantime, you are going to have another MRI and another x-ray just so we can compare and make sure nothing else has changed since the last ones. Do you have any questions or anything you want to know before I book you in?'

'Nope, I'll just sign it and trust you. Worst thing is I don't recover from this, it's not going to be worse than where I'm at now when you're done and that's all I can ask for.' I felt like those words were coming out of my mouth forever. They dragged through the air like a slow motion boomerang and when Mr Sant had left, they smacked me in the face. I may never recover from this. I may never have my leg back, or my bladder, or my life. Oh my god.

It's not very often that I'm lost for words, but now feels like as good a time as any. I don't know if I need to call anyone or if I should just let it sink in on my own first, after all, I don't actually have a date yet. My fear gets the better of me though and my sweaty palms pick up my phone to call Tom, he might be in South Africa, but they're only two hours ahead. I know I wouldn't usually want to bother him, I just don't know what else to do. It's instinct. The phone rings that stupid foreign dialling tone only twice before cutting out 'd-d-d-deee'. Maybe he hasn't got a signal? I try to call via Facebook messenger instead, but he doesn't answer. Same again via WhatsApp. As I start to try him again, he messages me on Facebook to let me know that his phone isn't letting him answer calls, but he's going to try and call me. Rather than ringing through, I just get a missed call notification, twice. The frustration starts getting the better of me and my blood pumps faster, my heart feels like it might burst out my chest and run to Africa on its own.

'What's the matter? I can't seem to call it keeps cutting out?'

'I didn't want to tell you on the phone, but it can't wait, I need you to know what's going on before you get home to a shock at the weekend, but I have to have another operation...'

I write in that message everything that Mr Sant has just said, all about the bladder and paralysis and the risks and the operation itself and I tell him that I'm scared and what if I never get better and that I miss him and I want him home. My fingers ran with the keyboard and there was little I could do. My emotions had taken over and I suddenly realised I was on my own and I did miss Tom, he was the only person I wanted with me and I would never usually tell him that, but it was too late, I'd hit send and I couldn't take it back so I just watched the dots in the bottom left of the screen.

'I just want to talk to you! I can't stand this! Stupid fucking phones!'

Another messaged followed.

'I will be home before you know it, please don't be upset, I will be there soon I promise. I will bring you whatever you need, you can do this, you are so strong and I am so proud of you, please stay strong mighty one'

Another one.

'XXXXXXX', just kisses.

Seeing a bunch of kisses made my eyes sting, he never sends kisses and right now I needed a real one more than ever and a big squishy cuddle to go with it, the kind that engulfs you into a Bermuda triangle of safety. I needed him and I resented admitting it even just to myself. I didn't want to reach out to anyone else, I didn't want to tell mum or dad or Annie or Lily or Mick. I didn't even want to talk to the nurse about it, I just wanted Tom and he wasn't here, so I covered myself in the blanket, head to toe, and sobbed.

It wasn't until the next day that I let everyone else know. I wasn't due any visitors, it was a working week again. The only person who came was Mr Sant to tell me my operation was booked for Friday morning at 8.40 and I'd see him them. Collectively I text, saying my next operation was on Friday and hopefully it would be my last and I'd keep them up to date. Nothing fancy, I couldn't be arsed to explain it all again, I could have copied and pasted my message to Tom, but I didn't feel so emotional about it by then and I couldn't be bothered to edit it. Short and simple would do. Any questions, they could ring the ward if needed, I just wanted to turn my phone off. I couldn't actually turn my phone off, of course, just in case of emergencies, but for some peace I put it on silent and blocked anyone that wasn't important. It remained tucked under my pillow until Thursday when I was feeling just freaked out enough to need it.

Lily and Mick came to visit Thursday, too. The benefits of working in a cinema mean you get at least one day off mid-week and they used theirs to come and see me, daft bastards. They brought me a box full of wonderful little goodies to keep me occupied and clean. There were sprays and dry shampoo (which I've never been in more dire need of in my life!), colouring pens and a sketch book, socks and a nighty with a tortoise plastered on the front - to let people know that's the only speed I can go at for a while, they said. Fingers crossed I can even go at all. My favourite thing in this box, however, was a little goals diary. It was a Paperchase purchase which automatically makes it wonderful, but on every page was a place for the date, your goal, how to achieve it, if you achieve it and when, and how to celebrate completing it. In the back, was a few pages of bigger goals. The first thing I did was go to the last page and write, "Climb Kilimanjaro". Then on the first page I wrote, "Stand up". Although it wasn't more than a few minutes before I changed that to, "Stand up - with support" - let's be realistic.

Chapter Nineteen

'Pip? Pip? Can you hear me? You need to wake up for us.'

Urgh, whoever that is can fuck right off, my head is banging, my eyes aren't willing to cooperate, I don't even know where I am and I couldn't care less, let me sleep! I listen as the voice keeps telling me to move my feet and I feel strangely like I'm in a film, but which one? My eyelashes flicker up and down, but the light in the room is blinding and so they squeeze shut in protest.

'We're going to sit you up a little bit.'

Oh are you now? Stupid voice lady... Although, it must've worked, because once upright, it's like my body hits wide-awake mode and my eyes swing open. I'm sure if anyone was watching they would've been able to see my pupils dilate to the size of a lead pencil dot, so much lighting. But wait, I'm in recovery, I'm out of theatre, they've done the operation. Suddenly my mouth is on speed.

'What time is it? Did it work? Can I go upstairs now? What's my stats? Good enough to go back to the ward or shall I drink more? Can I have some water? I feel sick, please don't make me drink that, I don't have to eat too do I? I just want to go upstairs I hate it down here! I cannot stand listening to that person in the corner throwing up, it's making me feel worse PLEASE let me go back to my own bed! Pretty please? With cherries on top?'

My ramblings must've either been annoying or convincing (I'm going with the latter) because there's four people surrounding my temporary bed right now ready to wheel me back upstairs. Winner.

'She's in bed number fourteen by the window'.

'Is this her? Is she back?' I know that voice... I try and turn to strain my neck around as they push me backwards into my bed space.

'You're here?!' I squeal, ever so quietly, my eyes full to the brim with tears and there's a grin so big across my face I don't look like I have any other features, just a big, wet smile. Tom grabs my hand over the metal rail as they secure my bed against the wall and I practically pull his arm off dragging it further across to me, squeezing it with both arms across my chest and kissing every inch of it, simultaneously making him have to stand off his chair from the force. Who knew I could be so strong?

'Looks like someone is happy to see you, we'll leave you to it and come back and check on you soon okay?'

I don't even care who's there or who saw or what they said, they could've told me I only have minutes to live and I don't think I'd have heard them. He's here, he's not hundreds of miles away on another continent or even just less than thirty miles away at home, he's right here next to me and I couldn't be happier. Even though I don't have a complete spine, a functional bladder or a working leg - yet. Right this second I have never felt more content.

'What are you doing here? I thought you'd be flying back tonight? Weren't you supposed to get in in the early hours? I'm sure that's what you said...' Despite the confused tone, my face was still glowing. Of course, verbally I apologised for the state of me and wished I'd had known he was coming so I could've taken my makeup bag to recovery!

'You look beautiful, don't be silly.'

No need for blusher, my cheeks flushed.

'I was booked on a flight tonight, but I wanted to be here for you. I didn't know if anyone else would be, I know your parents aren't home until tomorrow, not that I imagined they'd be here anyway.'

I needed him at that moment to climb onto the bed with me, I couldn't stand, but I needed to give him the biggest squish of his life, so I made him drop the bedside bar and help me shuffle across so he could fit in, too.

Physically moving was impossible if it hadn't been for Tom. I felt as though someone had chopped out my middle and it was no longer there. I couldn't use my feet to push because I couldn't feel them either so I just had to force Tom to slide me across on the sheet and then I could semi-curl into his armpit - my favourite place, even if he had been travelling for hours. He told me all about how he managed to get a seat on a flight early evening last night so he landed in Manchester at 10.05 this morning. Instead of going home he drove from the airport, two hours, to see me here thinking I'd be out of my operation mid-afternoon, it's now 18.00. The apologies kept coming, I felt horrendous that he'd been waiting almost six hours just to see me. But he assured me it was unnecessary to say sorry, the nurses had been nice to him, fed him, and he'd managed to get some sleep in the chair while waiting - he'd also made friends with the woman in the bed opposite me for a while - Jill she's called, apparently.

'Thank you so much for being here, I am so glad you're here and I am so grateful to you being here.' I'm sure everything I just said was meaningful and lovely, but it seems the drugs are kicking in and I'm just waffling on saying the same shit in more than one way. He is laughing at me and kissing my head and I just want to lay here forever, no matter how off my face I am. As if right on cue, Dot appeared with a magic trolley of even more tablets. Her and Tom had already been acquainted whilst I was under the knife, and it's because of this that she let him stay on my bed with me in my fragile state. Usually, she says, they don't let visitors on the bed at all, but she's willing to keep shtum and pull the curtain around just for us. What a gem.

'So I know you've been given your morphine intravenously downstairs already, but I still need to give you everything else. Here's the tramadol and the paracetamol, I've just got to go and unlock the Pregabalin...'

'The what?' My stomach is in stitches, with every exasperated laugh is a cry of pain, but I can't seem to stop. Tom and Dot were giving each other a "what's going on" glance when I started again. 'You're going to feed me GOBLINS?!' I seemed to think it was the best thing since sliced bread, and when Tom got the gist he started laughing too, but at me and not with me.

'I think the morphine is kicking in,' he chuckled, reaching for my flailing hand and kissing it.

'What is she like, honestly! Although, I can kind of hear it now she's said it Pregabalin - Pre-goblin bless her, I'll be back with it in just a minute.'

Dot dashed off to find my meds and Tom informed me he had a surprise. Oooh, now isn't that a good tactic to get me to focus. He pulled off a bunch of flowers from the chair he'd been perched on and a card, followed by a little box. The flowers were gorgeous, bright yellow with a sunflower in the middle, my favourite. He sat them on my thighs but I pulled them into my face and hid behind them imitating Bambi, or a bee. He put the card on my desk next to the little box and put me under strict instruction not to open them until he's gone, bless him.

Once Dot had returned with my goblin tablets and a sandwich that we all knew I wasn't going to eat, it was knocking on seven o'clock and I thought I should probably let everyone know I was out of my operation and alive, but I let Tom do it because I couldn't guarantee what I was going to type would make an awful lot of sense. Mum and dad said they would come and see me tomorrow, I had Annie booked in for tomorrow too so that should be nice, then Lily and Mick were going to come again next week, I've never felt more popular in my life, it's funny what having an operation can do.

Tom tried many a time to convince me to eat that sandwich, but even he knows that that isn't what I'm hungry for. The morphine might make me feel sick as a dog, but there's one thing I'm always in the mood for... cheese! With the permission of Dot we order a Pizza Hut 'four cheese' pizza with a cheese stuffed crust and suddenly I'm salivating, so's Tom! The nurses let him stay an extra hour after visiting hours are over so we can finish our pizza and I make him tell me all about South Africa and the filthy things they get up to on boys holidays. He tells me about the animals he saw and puts on his best David Attenborough voice to do it, much to my amusement. I cling on tightly to him whilst he's in my bed with me, thinking if I grip hard enough he might not have to go, my little arms barely reaching around his entire chest. He's a giant beside me and I'm not complaining. When it was time for him to leave I couldn't help but cry. It made me remember how seemingly cold this place is, with the big windows and clinical decor, the big white beds and hygiene alcohol gel on every corner. Every blanket is blue or white and it smells, god does it smell. It's a mixture of poorly people's diarrhoea, vomit and cleaning products, like there's no lemon disinfectant strong enough to withstand the sickness. It doesn't smell like Tom, or like my room or anything remotely welcoming and it's cold. Colder now without someone to cuddle.

'Let me know when you get home.' I declare as he's walking away. It isn't a question, but he always answers the same.

'I won't!' And he runs out of the door before I can tell him off. Of course, he always does let me know, I know he's just saying it to wind me up, boys will be boys. The only good thing about him leaving is that I can finally open my present and my card, I really love cards, there's something so personal about them, I am constantly buying random ones to give to people, not for any occasion, just because. This one is beautifully hand-crafted, the card is wonderful quality, burnt orange with a safari Jeep etched out of the front and when I open it there's a 3D lion popping out, as if walking across the page. The detail is so intricate, every line is smooth and I'm scared to touch it in case I rip right through.

'To my little mighty warrior,
I am so proud of you, keep smiling.
The worst things happen to the best people.
All my love,
Tom
XXX'

There's a little smiley face drawn at the bottom, the

corners of the smile reaching right below the eyes, I imagine that's how my face looks right now. I don't know how many times I read it and ran my fingers over the words, but I almost forgot to open the box. With the card against my chest, I lift the lid, it's small enough to fit in my palm, but it feels quite heavy. Inside is the most gorgeous golden tortoise ornament and when I pull it out to get a better look, a piece of paper drops out with it.

'This is called a homopus signatus tortoise - it is the smallest tortoise on the planet and this is a true to size replica. It reminded me of you, little one, small but strong.'

I am almost one hundred percent sure that this is the best thing I've ever received and I sit staring at him in my hand for what feels like forever.

'Thank you a gazzzillion times for my present (and my card)) I lovee themAnd thank you for being with me today and for beingYOU. You are bloody very chuffing wonderful and I am never not greatful X'

Okay, so my typing might not be all that great, but it's pretty hard to type when you can barely read the keys. The fresh dose of morphine has my head heavy and it's like constantly fighting the urge to fall asleep even though you're not tired. I can hardly tell my hands from someone else's, but I think it's clear enough that it will make sense to him, I hope.

'I'm glad you like it, you don't have to thank me. I'm home now, please try to sleep I will call you tomorrow - sweet dreams.'

Chapter Twenty

Jill is actually a pretty nice woman now I've gotten to know her, well, as good as you can get to know someone in the space of about forty-five minutes; she's the woman who is currently residing in the bed opposite mine, and the woman who was chatting to Tom yesterday whilst I was down in surgery. She was the one who initiated conversation by asking me how I was feeling when I was trying to sit up in bed after a difficult nights 'sleep'. She proceeded to talk about how lovely my boyfriend was and how nice it was of him to turn up for me like that.

Naturally I tried to let her know we weren't together and of course her only response was, 'you should be'.

Her short brown hair hung on her shoulders, genetically curled from her mother's side, apparently. Complaining of the need for a serious trip to the hairdressers I worried that I didn't care enough about my appearance for a brief moment, but my hair is too thin to manage anyway, whatever I do it just looks greasy and gross. Professedly, she admitted to being jealous of my dry shampoo for, like me, she wasn't allowed to shower just yet. Looking at her hair was making her want to buy a wig for the sake of a few more days, although I'm sure she could afford it.

'Have you got any visitors today? Is Tom coming back?'

'No, not today, he's back at work unfortunately, the boy never stops!'

It's true, he doesn't stop, he's always so busy working or doing things for people; Superman is real because it's him. I don't say it out loud, I don't want to give Jill more of the wrong idea. 'I think mum and dad are coming, they got back from their holiday last night and then maybe my friend Annie will come, too. What about you?'

'My husband, Andrew, comes every day to visit me, he's the man with the flat cap and glasses, you've probably seen him?'

Honestly, I hadn't even noticed, I'd been so caught up in watching without thinking I could've spent all day staring at Johnny Depp's face and not have had a clue, the very thought depresses me.

'Oh yes,' I lie, 'have you been married long?'

'It will be thirty years next year, that's a long time, I'm just hoping I'll be better so we can go on our trip we had planned to Greece. I only hope I'll be able to cope with the walking.'

Obviously the weather had been lovely in Portugal, my dad had clearly had too much to drink, his beer belly was sticking to his crisp, white shirt. I let them tell me about their travels, it's the most we ever converse when they're gloating about something fabulous they've done. Mum never made any effort to pretend to apologise for the disagreement on her birthday and neither did dad, nor I. In typical fashion we were putting it behind us as if it never happened. Classic Parker style. They were only half way through their extended story about the man on the boat trip who very blatantly fancied mum, when my physio came over to try the first attempt of getting me out of bed after my op. Mum and dad were asked if they wanted to stay and see the results, but they opted for grabbing a coffee from downstairs instead. Physio looked a bit taken a back that they didn't want to see the progress, but I let them go without a fight, who cares anyway? It's only going to give us an idea of if I will ever be able to walk again, but sure, it's nothing.

Admittedly, I was scared. What if it didn't work? In my head I was willing to give it a couple of days before deciding I was forever doomed, but it doesn't mean you don't hope to Tony the Tiger that it will work first time. It was Rachel and Alice again so I felt a bit better already that they knew how I struggled before, I'd also taken all my tablets only about an hour before their arrival so hopefully that would help too. The first step was getting me from the semi-laying position I was only just comfortable in, all the way to the edge of the bed with my feet on the floor. If you've never struggled moving before it's a debilitating, heart-breaking realisation when you can't just hop off your bed or shimmy down the covers; it took both of them and all the strength I could muster just to get me from my back to my side. Once on my side, on my left, facing the side of the bed I wanted to step out of, I had to use the mattress to push myself up on to my bum. That's the physio friendly way to do it, supposedly. Unfortunately, as it turns out, I wasn't quite ready for that yet so we used the less technical system of dragging me up as quickly and painlessly as possible. Oh so glamorous with the yelping, the deep breathing and waterworks erupting, not really helping either with their grunting from lifting a dead weight, too. I bet Jill was wishing the curtains were open so she could get a good look at the circus.

Once they'd got me to the sitting position with my legs dangling over the edge of the bed, they lowered it so my toes could touch the floor and put my slippers on for me - don't need to be creating a law suit if I slip and die now do we? Again, the technical way of getting up is to push off the bed with my hands - really healthy people are supposed to just use their leg muscles, but, again, I wasn't quite there yet. With one arm under each one of mine and all the power my legs could muster, we yanked me up into a stand. Well, Holy baby Jesus. I was standing up. I wasn't on top of anyone on the floor, I wasn't collapsing (pretty much), I was standing on my own two feet. I may have been shaking like a back door in a hurricane, but this is already almost a step closer than I was last week, to being able to live.

It didn't last long, though. The pain, although not completely traumatic, was enough to cause my knees to bend without instruction and make me keel over slightly, and the more I bent, the worse it got so they sat me back down again.

'That's more than enough for today I'd say, Pip! Well done!'

'You stood up! How do you feel?'

I didn't need to answer how I felt because my body answered for me. My hands were shaking and my face had drained to white. Within seconds my body had slumped forwards and my eyes had closed.

'Go and get a nurse.' I heard someone say, one of the physios to the other I imagined. It seems as though I'd mildly fainted, as excited as I was to have stood up there was no denying it was a hell of a strain on my body and we clearly needed a reboot. A nurse I didn't recognise came by and checked my blood pressure and my heart rate, then suddenly I found myself being scolded, yet again, for having a low blood pressure and needing to drink more fluid. Lucky me though, this time, my urine was on my side and it wasn't because I hadn't drunk enough, my wee was a fabulously hydrated pale yellow.

'Still, you need to make sure you're drinking.' She'd reiterated before sticking my chart back on the end of my bed and flunking off. Some help she was.

Physio commended me for my efforts and said they'd be back again tomorrow, I was, however, under strict instruction not to even think about moving or getting out of bed without the help of a nurse. It was their job to look after me and if I dared attempt to do a thing without them I'd have hell to pay. It's beside the point any way because at this early stage, physio are the only people allowed to help me push further than I have before, the nurses can only assist with what physio know I can do safely. So in a few words, the only thing I am allowed to do right now is stay in bed until they return.

Mum and dad weren't very enthusiastic about my standing capabilities, but that's not exactly something they know much about anyway. I don't even know if they know the real severity of the situation, although I did see dad chatting with someone at the nurses station before they came back from their coffee break so who knows.

'I knew you'd be okay!' Annie came bounding through the doors, flowers in hand.

'Hello Mr and Mrs Parker, I hope you had a good holiday. It looks like it!'

I tried hard not to giggle when she said that, so it came out as an overly toothy smile, it was clear she was making a point about their changed skin tones, but they just said thank you out of politeness, looks of confusion plastered across their faces. Whatever could she mean? Annie had known my parents since we were tiny, but the formalities always stuck.

'Oh, Annie, we didn't realise you'd be coming today,

we'll get off so you two can spend some time together, we have an early start tomorrow anyway.'

Annie smiled courteously and insisted they stay a while, knowing full well they wouldn't otherwise she wouldn't have said anything about it.

'We'll be back again soon, just not sure when exactly, obviously being away we have a lot of work to get back to. Dad will keep calling the ward for updates and they've said they'll let us know if there's any need-to-know information. Be good, don't do anything we wouldn't do. Get well.'

'Get well? Do they not realise that it's not as bloody easy as that? Honestly their ignorance astounds me. How do you put up with it?!' She gets so passionate, does Annie, about my parents. She has had to watch me grow up with them and in a way I feel like she was my secret sister.

'Distract me,' I say. 'Tell me all about what's going on with you and Alex.' She had text me saying they'd had a bit of a barney, but she explains it turns out he just wanted pizza for dinner and she wanted a Chinese... honestly, the two of them make me sick, how can you possibly fight over that and it end in tears? I'd expected some blow out about him talking to another girl or cheating or something scandalous, not what they're going to have for tea!

'I love talking to you, you always put things in perspective and make me feel so much better. I just wish I could do the same for you.' Her words make me smile and I remind her of the irony of my singleton status and my stellar agony aunt relationship advice.

'Well, you're not single because you've got Tom. If only the two of you would just give up pretending and get it together.'

'Don't start with me, woman. You know it's not like that.' But it's too late, she's seen the card and she's off on one about how we're perfect for each other and he gets me and he's cute and it's been over a year, most normal people have sealed the deal by now... 'You already sleep together and see each other more than twice a week, he looks after you, you celebrate occasions together, what is actually left apart from asking the question? I always thought you had more balls than that when it came to boys!'

Whilst she was wittering on about my failed love life and its potential, I had struggled to sit on the end of my bed and told her to hold my nurses bell, just in case, she'd not even noticed she'd just taken it off me and carried on. I had zoned out from listening and was focusing on my breathing and steadying myself. This will shut her up, I thought. 1, 2, 3... 4, 5, 6... It's okay to need a little extra time... I pushed myself off the bed and held on to the bottom railing for dear life.

'What are you doing?' she squealed, jumping off the end of my bed and running to my side to hold me.

I know what physio had said about not doing anything without them, but don't challenge a fool. Annie was gobsmacked and I told her to close my curtain so I didn't get into trouble, thankfully Jill was too busy gazing into Andrew's eyes to notice. How nice they are still so in love after all this time. Either that or they're plotting each other's demise. With the curtain shut, I lifted my left leg slowly off the ground, I thought that if I used it to balance there was a greater chance I'd fall again so instead if I just stepped it forward it could be another accomplishment. I didn't lift it very high, every movement was causing agony and motion sickness, but squeezing the bed rail and Annie's hand I managed to step one foot forward. Just one and not really moving away anywhere, but it still counts and Annie wholeheartedly agreed.

Not only am I a rule-breaking scallywag, I am a woman determined to focus on fixing the important things in life; my health and my happiness and following my dreams. Not focusing on my non-relationship with a boy.

Chapter Twenty-One

I love it when Mr Sant comes to visit, it always makes me smile, he's such a positive presence and he's so calm. Honestly, I trust the man with my life (which is pretty convenient because he seems to be in control of it anyway!) He has a way of speaking to me like I'm the only person that exists, I don't really know how to properly explain it, but it's not meant in the "he looked at me like I was the only person in the room" sort of way - not romantic in the slightest, just personal, impeccable bedside manner for a surgeon.

That's the good thing about a Mr Sant visit, too, I can get my questions answered about all of the things I miss and all of my plans for recovery. This morning I wrote down all the questions I needed to in the notepad Mick and Lily had brought me, making sure I didn't make any mistakes and I wrote slowly so the first page of my pad would be pristine. Annie would understand the importance of a well presented writing book, some things from Primary school really stick.

I let him ask me all the things he needed to know first, before I bombarded the poor man with questions I imagine he'd think were ridiculous at this point in my recovery. It has only been three days since my op, but I'm not great at the patience thing. He started by getting the nurse to help turn me on my side so he could have a look at the wound and make sure everything was still in place - stitches and stuff. Moving is still agony; I had to hold back tears as I held onto the bed rail, I cracked jokes about how he's seen more of me than any man.

'Well, for that I am sorry,' he chuckled as he unpeeled

the bandages from my lower spine. After inspection, he also wanted to remove my handbag of blood.

'This is going to sound totally gross and millennial of me, but please could you take a picture once you've removed it - I hate not being able to see what it all looks like back there.'

'Well, that is a first, but yes, once I've removed the blood tube, make sure your phone is on camera and I'll get a quick picture before I cover it all back up, I've just got to get the bits I need to take it out and some new dressings, won't be a minute. Try not to move.'

Totally gross I know, but I'm fascinated by all of this, it's still so new to me and it's hard to explain to people what's going on when you can't see. I haven't told him at this point I also have a shit ton of questions I want to ask him; I'm sure he won't mind. The nurse who's assisting makes light conversation about if I'm having any visitors today and as far as I know I'm not. It can get really depressing when nobody comes for you and everyone else in the room has chairs full of people.

'Right, this might feel a bit strange, but it shouldn't hurt so let me know if it does, okay?'

I had learned by now not to brace myself, just to breathe deeply and 'relax', i felt like a yoga instructor or a midwife "ten deep breaths!" He was right though. It didn't really hurt, obviously I can't see where it's coming out, but it felt as though a snake was exiting my body, it was smooth and almost made me equally wriggle. I laughed at the sensation, Mr Sant rolled his eyes as I swivelled my head back as far as I could to have a look.

'Okay, okay, I'll have your phone now, don't move!'

I really like how we get on, I think me being here constantly and being such a nightmare, medical marvel patient helps, the consistency is nice.

'Oh my god why did you draw a dick on my back?' I am creasing with laughter and also saying 'ow' with every ab-movement, you can easily forget how everything is attached.

'I'm sorry?'

He is dressing my wound and so I show the nurse the picture, she chuckles and agrees. The iodine marks from where they cover the area before they cut have stained in a rather phallic shape right over my stitches and the head of said penis forms right at the top. Once I'm re-dressed and rolled back onto my spine with a cushion under my knees for support, I hand the phone to Mr Sant. He has to sit down from laughing and insists it absolutely wasn't purposeful, I joke that he was very obviously trying to call me names thinking I would never find out and he has now been caught!

'You, Pip, are the least of my patients to resemble this, not that I would ever call my patients such a thing!'

'Don't try and rectify it now, the damage is done.'

We're both smiling and just as he stands up I say, 'Actually, I know how you can make it up to me... my questions?' He sits back down and I get him to pass me the note pad off my desk, instead he pushes it over to me so I can get it myself. Funny how a man who's been inside of me isn't comfortable touching my belongings. I begin... 'Firstly, how long until i'm back at work?

'You're really not in any place to even be thinking about that right now, I know you want to, but we'll be able to discuss that when you're in your recovery, you just had an operation three days ago - a big one! Relax for now.'

'2. How long does a lumbar fusion take to heal?'

'Really it's anywhere between six to twelve months for a standard fusion, but yours is different because of the cauda equina and the decompressions we had to do, it could be more likely twelve to eighteen months for a full fusion.'

'3. How long roughly until I fully recover? (a.k.a. back to 'normal')'

'Like I say, the fusion could be eighteen months, but we need to see if we can get you to be walking again first, I can't really say, but we will have a better idea by the spring. Don't forget, you might not ever be back to exactly like you were which is what you might consider normal but we just want you to be functional'

'4. Will I be going home soon and what's the different plans depending on the outcomes?'

'You won't be allowed home until we know you will be able to manage and that's mostly due to phsyio. Obviously your wound looks good for now, but we will have to monitor and keep an eye. The catheter is not something we have any control over any more, that will have to get better on its own if it does, it might not, but you know that.'

'5. Will I be able to function normally if it works? Like, can I still use the gym etc?'

'What would you want to go to the gym for? No lifting weights, no skydiving or rollercoasters or anything that might cause potential cracking of a fused spine because we do not want to have to do this again. You have to be careful.'

'6. Do you know if I will be okay to go to Florida in September or not?'

'Right now I can't say. I will know more in the Spring,

hopefully yes, but I won't make any promises, that goes for most things.'

'7. What's the deal with rollercoasters if I CAN go to Disney?'

'... no rollercoasters. At all. I'm not kidding. If you go on a rollercoaster and you snap the fused bone it will all have to be removed, we cannot just plaster it back up like a crack in a ceiling and then you will have to go through all of this again. No rollercoasters.'

'8. What are the chances of my Cauda Equina striking again?'

'You have already had this twice. This should not have happened once and I cannot tell you why, the fact you had it twice is such bad luck and although I cannot say for sure it will not happen again, it's maybe 2% and I am still then not sure it will ever occur.'

'9. Can I do anything to speed up the fusion? Or to help my recovery?'

'Not a thing. No drinking milk or lying in bed or exercises or tablets will make this process quicker. It will happen in its own time. If it hasn't started to happen by twelve months, then maybe we will have to have another look, but there is nothing you can do, just don't do anything to jeopardise the recovery.'

How can he say those things? How inconclusive could he possibly be? "I don't know?" "I couldn't say" how is that supposed to make me feel better? I try not to show how utterly disappointed and deflated I am, but it's hard to hide and I think he gets that.

'We will know more when you start improving, but Pip, it's been three days... relax, rest, stop planning for the next three years right now, we need to keep you strong, that's more important than being a weightlifting champion. We'll talk again in a few days, I'll be back to check on you and the ward will take great care of you. If you need anything you know where I am.'

Almost on queue physio turn up. Not my usual girls, this time a girl and a guy I'd seen wandering the ward visiting other people before. I wasn't in the mood to try. I was agitated and infuriated and generally pissed off, I wanted to cry and lock myself away to deal with it for a while. Besides, what's the point in trying if I'm never going to be the same again anyway. Why not just lie here and wait for nothing to come? I hate feeling this way, I know it's not productive or helpful, but I can't help it and I really don't want to take it out on physio.

'Hey, I'm sorry, please could you come back a bit later? I don't think I can possibly do anything right now. I've just had my blood bag removed and I haven't had any painkillers yet, can I have half an hour, is that okay?' I never would've asked, but I really couldn't face taking half a step when I already feel atrocious about my lack of ability.

They graciously accept and say they'll visit someone else down the corridor first and whilst they're gone I embrace the shitty monster that's eating me alive. It might not be favourable to sit and dwell on feeling like the most unlucky human on the planet and usually I would have no time for such indulgent behaviour, but being here, alone, it feels like I should at least be allowed this. My face is thunder, I can feel the heat in my cheeks and my chest, my entire body is tense, every muscle holding itself inside a cage of denial. It might look like I'm holding in a gigantic fart, but I'm actually trying to contain the want of a scream. Physio left the curtains open so I don't want to completely erupt all over the place. When they're ready, my tears tumble down my flushed cheeks, dripping on to my gown.

If I call someone, everyone in here will overhear my frustrations and Jill and Andrew will try and talk to me about something good, pass on some wisdom that I'm not in the right frame of mind to appreciate. The bitch next to me will tut and sigh as she usually does and I worry if she does so one more time I may leap from my bed and punch her lights out - I am not a violent person, but just one more disapproving noise in my direction I'll have her. There's not much scarier than a tiny angry girl who would break her wrist from socking you.

I can't call anyone anyway, it's a Monday and so everyone is working and have other things to be doing, I'll just let the tears roll and keep as much of my hair in front of my face as possible, if I make it look like I'm on my phone I have a good reason to keep my head down. Dot appears as if my magic with a syringe of morphine for me and kindly ignores the mess I've become.

'You're doing so well you know, we're all really proud of you.' She says it quietly and with a little corner smile, 'if you need anything just press your bell.' Funny how such a small gesture can change your mind from despair to hope.

I am doing okay, she's right really. It has only been seventy-two hours since I couldn't walk, I couldn't stand or sit up, but now, only three days after a major spinal operation, I can stand and move my feet. All my toes move, if somewhat unsteadily, but they move and although I cannot feel some of them, they're still there and they still work. I still work. This is only the beginning, as long as I do what I'm told I will get better, I can get better, all those uncertain responses to my many questions will be certain when I prove them to be so. I have to start somewhere and I suppose, for now, all I can do is make sure I'm thinking the right things. I pull out my goals diary and write on the back page of generic goals, "To always remember I am resilient and I can do it".

When physio return they bring with them a Zimmer frame... brill. It's not even disguised as a nice one, if there is such a thing. It's old and made from dull, grey metal, it has four grey rubber feet and a grey handle across the top, my first thought is "surely that's not for me, this can't be happening," but I re-jig my brain into the positives "this will help me walk and if I can walk I can climb, it will also be good to decorate with such a bland base colour, I'm thinking rainbow colours..."

'Okay Pip, so we're not expecting you to be able to use this just yet, but we wanted you to get accustomed to how it feels and understand how it works so we can gradually do a bit more. The end game is to get you walking freely of course, but from standing to being able to use this frame unsupervised is a great initial goal.'

We get me standing and the morphine starts kicking in, when it does I always end up with verbal diarrhoea, making stupid jokes and asking way too personal questions to people I've only just met.

'You two look like a couple, are you a couple? Romance is gross or at least that's what I tell people.'

Through all the wittering, I haven't even realised I've made it to the end of my bed using the old people frame until Jill starts cheering for me.

'Well done, I knew you could do it!'

I've actually walked a good couple of steps, five according to phsyio; feel like I'm on top of the world. Again, I ask them to get my phone and take a picture, I'm really turning into an old woman with all this "capturing moments" business and Zimmer frame walking. I am so proud of myself and I know exactly who I want to share it with. Instead of letting me have my way and trying to make it to the door, physio know better and make me go back to bed, that's a lot of moving for one day and by the time they've lifted my legs back into the bed for me, I agree. I'm wiped out. Before I even think to shut my eyes, I attach the image of me, grinning from ear to ear and sporting white knuckles from clinging on to the frame, in a WhatsApp message to Tom.

I did it! I don't care if I'm not a classified pensioner, I can stand up!

What a feeling, I can do this!"

Chapter Twenty-Two

Just when you start to truly believe you can do something is always the time when life knocks you back. Today is that day. I feel disgusting and I am absolutely the furthest from myself I can be to a point even Jill has noticed. Something is really wrong. Since ending yesterday on such a high I can't quite figure out why it is turning out to be so awful. My heart is pounding, my head is pounding, I can feel every cell in my bladder and I want nothing more than to rip out this catheter, I just don't have the energy. I slept through lunch, again, but this time it wasn't because the drugs knocked me out, I couldn't bear to even smell it when it came, I wanted to be sick, I still want to be sick. Something is wrong.

'Are you okay, Pip? You don't look very well?' Jill had tottered over and sat next to my bed, I must've looked bad enough she could see it across the room and that didn't fill me with hope.

'I don't feel well, something is wrong I'm sure.' She felt my head and I was sweating despite my insistent chill. Without even asking she pressed my bell for me and waited for a nurse to come. Unfortunately, as luck had it, the bell doesn't always summon a nurse and a care support worker comes instead. Jill expressed her concern, looking to me for some kind of support in her claim, but I was hardly capable of obliging. She asked for a doctor or nurse to come and see me as soon as possible as I was clearly struggling, but that's all I heard before falling back into restless slumber. I must've been feverish because I had horrifying dreams, strange and too real for my liking, the kind that wake you up in a panic thinking you're still there. I'd murdered my parents twice before a nurse came, Jill was back in the chair next to her bed and doing all the talking for me, I felt that if I opened my mouth I may well throw up.

There was no concern, no tests, no discussion, just a "you're fine" and off he went. I was too weary to put up a fight or think much about it. Physio had been and gone when I woke up next, Jill had informed me she'd been keeping a watchful eye as I slept and I had looked uncomfortable. Usually I don't respond well to being mothered, must be something I'm not completely used to, but I didn't have the fight in me to refuse so I let her keep feeling my head to decide how warm I was. It didn't sound strange to me in all honesty, we had a little thing going where she was always cold and I was always warm, so her window stayed closed as did the one in the middle of us, but I kept mine open and my curtain round as much as possible to avoid giving her a breeze. Today I didn't feel hot though, I felt cold, I had my dressing gown and my blankets and my cushions and I burrowed my head deep beneath it all. I didn't even care for visitors. If I don't have to speak to any one for the rest of forever, at this point, I don't give a rats bum.

'Are you hiding?' I don't respond.

'Pip, is everything okay?' I open my eyes and peer out from the many sheets without a word.

'Oh bless you, you look awful, what's the matter?' Tom's voice is higher pitched and his eyes are wide, instinctively he climbs onto my bed with me and I curl into him and cry. I tell him how awful I'm feeling and that nobody seems to care, Jill joins in expressing her concerns and I find that she's actually called for a nurse three times for me now and nobody else is remotely worried. That just makes me cry harder.

'Why is nobody doing anything she's obviously not right? I'm going to go and say something!'

Again, on a good day, I would protest, let's not make a scene or upset anyone, but frankly I am upset and nobody seems to give a damn so I let him go.

'He's a good one that boy, isn't he?' I don't answer Jill, i just continue to weep.

It feels like forever before Tom returns, someone is supposedly on their way to talk to me, but they weren't very cooperative Tom says.

'Hello Pippi, so what seems to be the matter exactly? I have been before, but you were asleep?' The tone used is incredibly cold, she makes it sound as though it's my fault I was sleeping and that she could do absolutely nothing because of it.

'Something is wrong, I don't feel well at all, that's why I was asleep. I feel sick, I'm freezing and sweating and my bladder doesn't feel right.' I try and use the same tone that she did, but it's more of a whimper until Tom follows on for me. He wins this round and she decides to check my temperature, it's over by two whole degrees and yet she still doesn't think to check anything further without a fight.

'Well why don't you take off all those blankets, that's not helping is it, clearly.' Tom argues again that I'm obviously shivering and it's not that simple, but she refuses to do anything further until I've "made an effort".

I make Tom talk about random nonsense to console me, I make him tell me about work and about all the things he's been up to whilst I've been here. I haven't seen him since Friday and four days feels like a lifetime when he's not around and I'm trapped in this hell-hole. It's about an hour before Dot appears to check in and says that a doctor has requested blood and urine samples, and it's not until that point that anybody realises there's blood in my catheter. It looks oddly like when you pour blackcurrant juice into orange, they mix in the middle and the red drops are falling into the bag, running all the way up the tube. I told them my bladder wasn't right, but obviously it's nothing. Poor Dot's face.

'Why has nobody been to check this before now?' She's scanning my chart for some indication of observation, but Jill confirms nobody has even glanced in its direction all day. She offers Tom to leave whilst she has a look, but he wants to stay with me if I don't mind and in my state I have no modesty left - he's seen it all before anyway. He pulls the curtain to, whilst I get into position - feet together, knees apart. Thankfully I've not got trousers on today so there's no faffing about trying to get them off, I'm in enough pain as it is and really don't fancy untangling the meters of plastic tubing from my legs. Tom is seated on the chair next to my bed, head end like i'm in labour or something. It's not exactly a pretty sight down there when you can't bend down to shave and you're still not allowed a shower, bed baths only go so far! I resent it. Even my legs are hairy and I know I'm blonde, but I hate the feeling, the tickly Sasquatch leg rub whenever you move, I'd not even thought about my armpits until now and I'm mortified at what I look like. How has nobody told me I'm disgusting yet?

The catheter seems to be in fine and Dot isn't allowed to remove it without replacing it so she goes off to find another one and to call for a doctor again. Pulling a catheter out when you can't feel your saddle is honestly not so bad, but when you're in pain from the inside and the balloon is getting deflated it feels obscurely uncomfortable, it's a strange kind of pressure and then it scratches as it leaves my bladder, after that I don't feel a thing, but it's not very nice.

Putting the next one in always seems to be a difficult job for whoever is trying. It takes Dot three attempts this time and I'm grateful for my lack of sensation, similar to coming out, the only feeling I get is the scratching when it reaches my bladder, otherwise it's like I'm dead inside. Really, I feel a bit like I am dead inside most of the time, today especially. She reckons a doctor has been called and someone should be on their way then she leaves with my blood, wee and the old catheter. I ask that the curtain stays shut until he gets here, not because I don't want to see Jill, but I don't want her to feel the need to ask about me every couple of minutes if I go pale or throw up. And, I want to get out of bed without getting in trouble.

'Come on then, whilst you're here.'

Tom looks confused as I start trying to get myself up.

'What are you doing? You need to stay in bed, the doctor is coming to see you!'

I think we both know he isn't exactly on his way and I want to show off to Tom whilst he's here that I'm not a complete disaster of a person. My bladder might not work properly and my body is clearly having some sort of issue otherwise, but I know my legs are trying to be better at the least. I just feel like I need something to make him proud of me.

Physio had left my Zimmer frame in the corner under

the window near all my cards and flowers and I got Tom to put it in front of me as if to show him how I can stand up with it now... but I didn't. Instead, I didn't even know that's what I was going to do until I felt my hands on the side of the mattress and my knees engage. I pushed myself forwards and groaned heavily, insisting Tom stays seated, wobbling slightly as my thigh muscles struggled to understand what they were doing. I'd only gone and stood up unsupported and without medical supervision, it's funny that I feel infinitely safer with Tom there instead of anyone else.

Today probably was not the day for this. My head felt as heavy as my torso and my muscles couldn't play along for too long before I collapsed down onto the bed again. If it had been a harder mattress I think I'd have snapped in two, but I didn't cry. It was the first time I'd smiled all day.

'See, I told you - that was all for you!' I was exasperated and asked for his help getting my legs back on the bed again before any one sees - still not a task I can manage alone.

'You're mad, but well done, you did a great job, thank you for showing me.'

I love how polite and wonderful he is, that he doesn't mind holding my wee handbag when I want to stand up and that he doesn't mind watching someone put a tube up my hairy lady garden, he really is a saint.

It's lucky I got back into bed when I did because a doctor appeared, pulling my curtain back so I could see Jill entranced by her hospital telly. We are moving apparently. Both of us, together, going next door to ward twenty-four - the acute spinal ward. I wasn't exactly happy with the last minute decision, but I was quietly glad Jill was coming too if I couldn't take Dot with me and also glad Tom was there to help move my things. I'd collected an abundance of trinkets and bits to do and wouldn't want to risk losing any of it, especially not my lucky tortoise. Whilst we were packing, the doctor informed us we were moving because we needed to be on a more specialist ward - it was looking like I had an infection (which is what we'd been trying to tell them all day!) and Jill might have to have another operation. Tom set all my belongings into their own places in cupboards and on my desk, making sure my tortoise was close to me. Jill was bunking next to me this time, which I was happy about, too.

Once we got settled, Tom was once again back in bed with me and I felt so much more content. I'd managed to stand up without any help today, that was a giant step (pardon the pun) and even on my worst day so far, I did it. I surprised myself, and Tom, and it felt really great, even more great to hear how proud of me he is, little compares these days. To top it all off he reminded me that we still hadn't caught up on David Attenborough's Planet Earth II that had started whilst he was away, we had three episodes to watch so I pulled out my laptop and immediately downloaded the series to iTunes. Now it was going to notify me of every episode as it was aired and download it straight here to us, what more could a nature lover need? It gave us both something to look forward to every week now and even more so, it gave him a reason to visit.

Before I could press play on the first episode, the doctor came around again and told me about this potential infection. My body had all the infection markers, but they couldn't pin point the exact positioning of it so it wasn't going to be treatable for now. Tomorrow they would request more bloods and more urine now my new catheter was in place to see if it made any difference, he would keep me informed as they searched.

'There's no chance you could be pregnant is there?'

I felt Tom's eyes on me when I laughed, 'You've got to be getting some first doctor! It's a solid no on the baby front!' He smiled awkwardly and left us to it. Tom relaxed into me and kissed my forehead.

'She's quick this one,' he smiled and we heard Jill laughing too. 'Now, who's ready to get lost in some islands with David?' he pressed play on the episode and we oo-ed and ahh-ed all the way through.

Chapter Twenty-Three

I forgot where I was this morning, the sun was on my face and it was warm and it felt like waking up on a beach in the middle of summer. It wasn't until I properly adjusted my eyes and saw the hospital flowers in the window..."it's such a lovely day, and I'm glad you feel the same"... that I remembered I was still in the LGI, but I'd moved rooms. It wasn't until I sat up that I realised how shitty I felt with this potential infection, not nearly as bad as yesterday, but my body ached and I felt pretty sickly. The smell of hospital breakfast trays making their rounds wasn't exactly helping either.

It had taken me long enough to convince the people on the last ward that I don't eat breakfast and now I had to start all over again with this side, and, apparently, skipping breakfast on the acute ward isn't just heavily frowned up, it's unacceptable. I settled for half a slice of toast, but the minute I bit into the semi cold, condensation covered bread, my gag reflex kicked in and I had to let it fall out of my mouth into my palm. The entire slice went into my carrier bag that was doubling as a bin and nobody questioned when I blatantly lied and said it was actually very lovely. They must know it's rank.

Hospitals have a habit of waking everyone up before 8am, ready for tablets and doctors rounds, but forget that visiting hours don't start until twelve and so filling that time is extremely tedious, especially if you don't sleep well through the night. They discourage day time sleeping unless there's a half decent excuse, but nobody actually seems to care too much.

Whilst breakfast is making the rounds, the care support workers follow suit and bring a warm bed pan style bowl of water, a mini circle of soap and a separate bowl to use for brushing my teeth.

'Would you like your bed sheets changing today?' The answer was no, of course, I'd only been there one night and I didn't fancy trying to get out of bed and getting caught out by physio. I said that it wasn't necessary as they were clean on yesterday, but thanked her anyway and started with my bed bath. It wasn't an easy job really, but I didn't like the idea of having someone help me and so I struggled alone. I was stuck here with semi-warm water and dry shampoo for almost two weeks. Even my deodorant was running low, I'd been using it on every potential sweat area to be as fresh as possible.

Lily and Mick had put a few perfume samples from Debenhams in my box so I could spritz if I knew I had visitors, this morning I sprayed the Chanel Allure sample even though I didn't actually think anyone other than physio would be coming.

They had impeccable timing. When I thought it was the care support coming to take all my bowls away, I was as ready as I could be, it was actually Rachel and Alice again - they'd found me! Today's challenge wasn't going to be very strenuous as they knew I had some kind of infection and they didn't want to overly stress my body. They were going to show me how to properly get in and out of bed without help. It sounded mostly like stationary work so I hadn't thought of adding it to my goals diary, such a measly goal anyway. But, after one try of engaging my muscles, I knew how wrong I was.

'Hold your stomach muscles in when you lift your legs, it should help engage your core and make it easier.' Alice sounded pretty positive on the matter, but I don't believe I have abdominals at this stage. It's not like I'd put on loads of weight rapidly, but going from being fit and active and a frequent gym go-er, to a bed bound bum, really took its toll on any kind of definition I may have had. We took a break after a few tries so I could update my goals diary with my new objective and fill in the last few: standing with support; standing without support; making it to the end of the bed with my Zimmer frame and now this. Seeing it all written down with successful dates of achievement made me feel much more accomplished, even if I couldn't quite manage it yet, I would be able to if I just practiced engaging my muscles like they said. That was all that was really on my agenda for the rest of the day. It's pretty important not to need someone to lift your legs up for you when you intend on climbing the highest mountain in Africa. Kind of vital, actually.

The conversation turned to my going home criteria as we continued to practice the correct technique for getting me up and down.

'So, basically, you need to be able to climb the stairs - there are stairs in your house aren't there?'

'Yeah, my room and bathroom are upstairs and my parents live downstairs. I'm kind of in the attic of a bungalow, the kitchen is downstairs though.'

'Okay, if there's no way of you being able to stay downstairs you'll have to prepare for a couple more weeks here, hopefully not too many though. If your infection clears up and you can master the Zimmer frame quickly, and you're on crutches, you're out of here. As long as you're comfortable of course, but we have the final say so it's us you need to impress.'

I was pretty happy with that, if I did as Rachel and Alice told me I could be out of here soon. I asked if maybe they would consider coming back in the afternoon to do a bit more with me, now I knew it was them I had to prove myself to, there was little I would let get in my way, especially not an infection they won't treat. They agreed to come back later even if we didn't do anything further, just to check in and like clockwork, as they left the room, the doctors appeared. The big man leading the pack, his secretary behind with notes upon notes and the novices following quietly watching everything intently.

'Philippa, hello nice to meet you.' He didn't hold out his hand or move closer than the foot of my bed. 'Today we're going to get more blood tests from her so if you will do that for us...' He motioned at another doctor behind him, 'We're also going to re-sample the urine to make sure it's not infected now that there's a new catheter in place, otherwise, she's seeing physio and will hopefully be on the mend soon. We just need to get on with finding out if there's anything we can do about this infection. Thank you.' I think that thank you was aimed towards me, but it was hard to tell, it's not very nice being talked about when you're right there, but it's interesting to listen to the medical jargon and watch the faces of the confused interns. It's also fun knowing you know more about your condition than they do, depending on the day.

'Eeeeeeek!' I'd squealed when I saw Annie bound

through the door, and I held my arms out for a big squishy cuddle. It had been another lonely morning after being talked at and I was overly excited to see her face.

'Don't you spend Wednesday afternoons with Alex?' I'd asked when she'd made herself comfortable on the chair. Her hair was still tied up from work and she was wearing red lipstick, but she'd changed into more comfortable clothes on the train across - a pair of checked leggings and a black jumper, her Dr Martens loosely fit on her foot as she was a shoelace "tuck-er in-er" as opposed to my "loop swoop and pull-ing" I don't like shoes that feel as if they might come off at any second, she didn't seem to mind. There's also that thing where the shoelace finds its way to your baby toe and turns into a python trying to constrict it to death, at the very least causing a blister. Annie's style was pretty punk-y naturally, but whenever she had work or was with Alex and his family, it was like she became a professional woman with skirts and a blouse in every pastel colour you could imagine.

'Yeah, usually we do, but he says he's got to work over-time this month...' She sounds flat and I know what she's getting at.

'What do you mean "he says", do you not believe that's what he is doing?'

'Oh I don't know, it's just weird. Since we've been together he's never worked over-time, he doesn't need to, we have the house and we do just fine. But he's been really sketchy lately and turned his phone off or told me he'd talk to me later if I'm out with the girls from work. He never encourages me to not see him or not speak to him, I don't understand. It all makes me feel really suspicious.'

Annie's voice is quiet and her face quizzical. She really is frustrated by this and there's not exactly much I can say to comfort her, I don't know Alex all that well and although we do things together as a trio I wouldn't see him without Annie. He seems like a good man, and I really don't think he'd cheat on her, I know that's what she's getting at so I reassure her that I sincerely doubt he would do that and she should talk to him instead.

I'm a big talker. Can't stand "iffing and butting", if there's something you want to know you should ask. If there's something you need to say, then you should say it. Mostly.

'I hate that you're right,' she continues. 'I know he wouldn't, it's been four years, I think I'd know, I just can't figure it out and it's one of those gut feelings you can't shake off. Enough about me, I can't think about it anymore or I'll be sick. What about you? What have they said? You don't look great? Sorry!'

I don't really want to talk about me, I'm too fed up being here generally and not knowing things, I want to talk about good things instead. And just like that we got lost in an existential crisis kind of conversation, that begins all fun and games, talking about if we got married where we'd do it, or if we had kids what we'd call them and where we'd send them to school. We talk about where we want our honeymoons to be and where we think we might buy houses when we get to that point, then all of a sudden we come crashing down from our high into the harsh reality that we are not yet close to having all the things we can dream of. I remind her that she at least has Alex so she's one step ahead of me, she brushes it off and says I have Tom, I consequently brush that off and we sit in silence for a while before sighing and she declares she has to leave to catch her train.

It always feels good putting the world to rights, even if it ends on a bit of a bum note, it's all off our chests so we don't have to dwell on it subconsciously until next time. I think about what I told her about talking to Alex, "just ask him" I'd said... Should I just ask Tom what we're doing? Is that a wise idea? Does it even matter? I toy with the idea for a while, listening to Jill and Andrew have their daily conversation about where they're going to book to go on their next holiday. Jill still hasn't had her operation and Andrew is going berserk about how his wonderful wife has had to starve all day to end up not having the operation they promised. It's so lovely he has her back (almost literally) when she can't herself. It reminds me of Tom again and I decide to make him a present to say thank you for being here for me, thank you for being my back bone.

In my magical box of bits and pieces from Mick and Lily, who I really need to call, I haven't seen them in almost a week and I've been a terrible text-er in this place, there is a little tub of salt dough. I'd seen that Lily was making a Christmas ornament with some last month and I had mentioned how I wanted to play, so she'd sent me a miniature tub of the stuff in my box. I knew just what I wanted to make, too. I spent almost an hour trying to sculpt the perfect circle and making its underside flat, it's hard with no tools and just a desk, especially when every second your nose itches from the morphine and it ends up all over your face just to start again. I got there eventually though, a perfect little tortoise body had formed and I stuck some half-arsed feet on the underside to protect it from any dirty surfaces. His head was slightly crooked, but with such shaky hands from all the drugs it was the best I could do. I would colour him with pens once he'd dried. Jill had been watching and she came across to set it on the radiator for me with a little note for the cleaners "Please do not move. This belongs to bed twenty-three. Thanks".

Chapter Twenty-Four

I tried to spend as much time as possible out of bed this morning, it felt too good not to. I'd filled out my goals diary and I'd coloured in Tom's tortoise present. I'd even had enough time to make him a card with some doubled up art paper I'd managed to snag from the crafts room via one of the nurses.

I expressed my thanks and, again, how grateful I was for him being there for me even though he didn't have to be. I even told him I was surprised he'd kept showing up for me when I never thought he would - back handed compliment - but it was just about the most honest I'd been with him in terms of kind words. I sent a draft copy to Lily first, she was just glad I was finally saying something - her and Mick always laughed when I'd talk about him "You're so smitten, just admit it".

Today he arrived in the middle of the afternoon. We didn't have long. The Infirmary has notoriously awful parking and he'd spent forty-five minutes trying to find somewhere to get in, cutting into our visiting time so we only had a little over an hour together. As sad as I was I tried not to show it, I didn't want him blaming himself for not being able to park, it's not his fault. We got to watch the third episode of Planet Earth II that we hadn't seen, skipping the behind the scenes ending and swapping it out for a crossword and a catch up of our respective weeks so far. He said I was looking better than I had done when they first moved me, I didn't have the heart to tell him I could've been drowning in bronzer that day. I really want him to think I'm okay, I'd hate if he was this far away and miserable.

I didn't want to give him his present until he was leaving because I was embarrassed. I don't really remember the last time I'd felt like that about a boy. I'd signed the bottom of his tortoise with "I love you" in a foreign language. Not for any other reason than I was too scared to do it in English and I didn't think he'd ever care to look, even though I hoped. I'd chosen to do it in Chinese because there's no way he could just go to the internet and Google it in an easy translation unless he cared to find the individual symbols first. I also chose Chinese because in China they have a "Black Tortoise" which is a turtle/snake combo and it's one of the four Chinese constellations called "Black Warrior". I made it to look after him the same way mine is looking after me, and although I wasn't telling him that's why, I'd always know, until he figured it out, too.

I had to try not to cry when he left because even though I was feeling positive and I'd loved seeing him, it never felt like long enough. I felt so overwhelmed and didn't want him to leave me alone with the thought, but he said if I cried he couldn't come and see me anymore because it would upset him too. That sobered me up a bit and I managed to watch him walk away.

'Let me know when you get home...' I'd said.

'I won't.'

He was due in work at six, so that's why he had to get back, I was just so appreciative he'd come at all, especially on a work day. Even more thankful that he'd come here dressed for work - such a sucker for a grown man in a suit and tie, it was the first time I'd felt remotely turned on in weeks thanks to those well fitted trousers.

Mum and dad were the next on the visiting train. I was actually kind of looking forward to seeing them, it had been a few days and the meds must've been acting over time. They'd even texted me ahead of time to ask if I needed anything bringing which was a nice change. I asked for any parcels that might have been delivered for me; I couldn't wait to wrap all the Christmas presents I'd bought, I also asked for a packet of cheese strings and my 5ft teddy bear... that was a straight no, but they brought me the rest. Dad even picked up a little bear from the hospital gift shop, he was pretty soft considering he was only a fiver and he fills up a little space so I'm not quite so lonely.

'The nurses said you had an infection, what's that all about? Are you better?' Of course mum is straight on to me being fixed and sorted, she gets bored, I think, very easily and once I've been ill for a couple of days she expects me to be over it. Even with dad. He was once off work for a whole week because of a chest infection, but the second he was two days in, she was complaining he hadn't been polishing the silverware in all this new found "free time". I don't think she understands it, or she just doesn't want to deal with it, it feels like the latter. 'Any way, we brought you everything you needed, how much stuff have you been buying?'

The carrier bag didn't seem very full compared to what I'd ordered, but I know there were things coming from China and the likes, so I wasn't anticipating all of it.

'I can't open them whilst you're here in case it's your presents'. I insist as they place the bag on my knees, 'I will have a peep in some of them though then if it's not yours I can show you if you'd like?'

'Might as well,' she retorted, 'there's nothing much else

to do here, is there?' I let her comment fly right over my head. She wasn't going to be the one to bring me down today, nobody was, I'd decided this morning and pretty much stuck to my word since. Instead, I dove right to the bottom of the carrier and picked out the ones I was sure were mum and dads, they went in my cupboard. It's pretty easy to guess when you know you've only ordered two books and two DVD's and they all come from the same place - trusty, HMV. In all honesty, I had no clue what else might be in there, trying to recall my memories from the night I ordered it all wasn't exactly easy, it was equally exciting to find out what I'd decided on and play who's who.

There was a few tops for Disney that I'd forgotten all about, they went back in the carrier bag to take home with mum and dad, there was also a set of Disney Chewbacca Pj's for Mick, a Horrible Histories t-shirt for Annie, she had some funky highlighters from paper chase, too, and a new diary.

Every year I bought her a diary and wrote in one thing we were going to do together the following year, our little tradition. God knows what I'd say this year, I didn't even know when I'd be getting out of hospital, let alone what kind of things we might be able to do. I'd think of something I'm sure.

At the bottom, in a groove in the plastic, was a super tiny box and inside were a set of silver engraved cuff-links I'd bought for Tom, they had his initials on the front T.O.M. I always thought his parents must've been kidding. Apparently not. (I'd checked his passport to prove it.) Thomas Osmond Michaels, It made me laugh, but also ever more aware of the fact my parents gave me a name within a name too, so I didn't really have a leg to stand on- obviously.

I take a break from opening parcels to have my meds and and ask mum and dad where they might stand on the whole "me living downstairs" scenario.

'It would mean I could leave here sooner that's all, with me not having to get up and down the stairs, this place is slowly taking my will to live, I'd much rather be home. It wouldn't be for long I should think and it would mean you wouldn't have to keep coming all the way to Leeds to visit.' My protest is heartfelt and I don't raise my voice once, it's precise and I honestly feel hopeful until mum cuts in, dad has hardly said a word since he got here.

'If you think I'd really give up downstairs you've got another thing coming! No chance! If you can't get in your room you're not coming home, because you're not staying in the living room either, we don't have a telly in our room so we wouldn't be able to watch our films if you were in there all the time.' My body stiffens and my jaw clenches as I turn to dad.

'What do you think?' There's no point in even trying to ask because he always sides with mum and he just says, rather diplomatically, 'You'll have to learn to walk upstairs eventually any way so just do it here and get it out the way.'

'But I can learn to it at home where I'm more comfortable, surely that's preferable?'

'You're not coming home until you can do the stairs and I'll be making a point of it to the nurses on my way out now you're fighting me on it Pip. No way.' Mum again, she was really pushing my buttons, but I knew it was a waste of time asking before I opened my mouth. I shouldn't have bothered.

I told myself it was my own fault for asking, not hers and

I shouldn't let it get to me.

'Okay.' I smiled a toothless smile, mostly just motioning my upper lip into a curl in a vain attempt of a white flag. You win. 'Let's see what this is...' My tone of voice changing to 'moving swiftly on', as I push my hand into the bag to feel something squishy. I expect it's more t-shirts for next year, but when I pulled it out of its cellophane packet I could read the label "SmartWool trekking heavy socks". My Kilimanjaro socks.

You know when something awful happens or you see something you shouldn't have done and your heart beats through your ears and you can't speak, you can only feel the eruption of tears swirling through your body. Then, before you have time to stop it, they're hurling out of your eyes like a flood, you can't see and you feel broken? That's what holding those socks felt like. It felt like my dreams had shattered into a million fibres and I was clutching on to them for dear life, hoping if I hold them they'll be fixed and real.

'Oh don't start, I'm not out to get you I just don't want you in my bed, how hard is that?' I couldn't even breathe let alone start telling my mother that was not the reason my heart was broken.

My lip was quivering and I could feel the other people in the room turn to me, the nurse was still doing meds on the last bed and she came across to make sure I was okay.

'We're going to go now that's all, she's getting emotional and probably just needs a good sleep.' Mum uttered as she pulled her coat zip up to her chin.

My dad put his hand on my arm as he rose from his chair and I thrust the bag of things at him to take away, muttering, 'that's not why I'm crying, just please take this stuff home.'

Once they'd gone I was left to sob on my own for a while, until my eyes had become sunken and all the scratching from my morphine had become more of a wet slide across my face, dragging any remains of makeup off into my hair line and down my neck. I wasn't going to cry today, I was going to have a good, positive day, and I couldn't even do that. I am full of infection that they can't rectify and I can only just make it to the bathroom door using a bloody old peoples walking frame. I can't possibly climb a mountain, how would they ever let someone so useless and broken do something so extraordinary? I am not extraordinary, I am not even average. I am not worth having on this planet at all, not on what is now considered a good day and how often do I have one of those.

I wished they'd never come, I wished that I'd never ordered the stupid things or thought for one minute that I might be able to do something I said I would. I'm a flake, a failure and I don't think I've ever succeeded in anything worthwhile in my life so why start now? I'm going to be here forever at this rate, it's already been two weeks and I'm getting nowhere so why not just make sure I go nowhere on purpose. There's plenty of medicine here for me to play with. Nobody would miss me, mum and dad would be happier, they make that pretty obvious. Annie has Alex, Mick and Lily have loads of other friends at work and they have each other and, Tom? What does it even matter, nobody is going to want someone that can't even wee by herself or shower. He has plenty of opportunity and we're not even together anyway. No. Point.

Chapter Twenty-Five

'I want to break free, I want to break free...' Four days of serious infection and throwing up can leave a girl wanting to jail break out of hospital and never look back. Supposedly, the spinal pathology was showing an infection, but they still couldn't figure out exactly where so there were talks of another operation, but no action because they didn't know what they would be doing if they went back in and I wasn't allowed any antibiotics in case they were the wrong ones and fuelled the fire. I've just had to ride out the most awful illness I've had in ages and hardly anybody batted a bloody eyelid... If I wasn't already on the verge of a breakdown, the last four days have been a literal hell.

As long as I don't reflect too much on it, I actually do feel better today, mentally and physically - if I think too much I tend to get a bit wound up and emotionally frustrated so instead I've been singing to me and Jill most of the morning. I've tried to stick to stuff she'd know, which makes me laugh when she looks completely shocked at my Rat Pack and 70's lyrics knowledge, nothing like some good oldies to get you going (not in THAT way!)

I'd also spent a bit of time reading about people's adventures on the wondrous mountain that is Kilimanjaro, I was feeling empowered and motivated and reading about all these climbs completed by able bodied men only made me more determined as a not-so-able-bodied woman. If I didn't stop myself who else was going to? I had made a note in my writing pad to email the company again and check I would still be able to go with the spinal fusion, that it didn't disqualify me from their criteria, and opened my laptop. CESUK - The Cauda Equina Syndrome charity. I didn't really expect there to be a charity already in place for my condition, I'd never even heard of it until it threatened to ruin my life and yet here it is, a real life issue that people, not just me, have experienced. The website was informative and clear, easy to navigate and, by the time I'd finished reading every last line on the screen, I wish I'd seen it sooner.

That's what I was going to do. It was settled. People need to understand this illness and know the warning signs before it's too late, look at the state of me. I worked an entire shift having no clue this was something I should be worried about. I'm sure there are plenty of people left worse off due to the same reasons. Not only would raising money for the cause benefit people in my position and help spread awareness to others, it would be a huge driving factor to get me up that mountain, if not for me, for them.

'That's such a great idea! It will give you something bigger to work toward!' Jill had gushed. Sometimes, even when you're not feeling like it, positive things can happen.

Mick and Lily were also impressed with my idea and Mick was straight on with figuring out costs and part payments and how much I could raise and how I could raise it, so on and so forth. He has a brilliant mind and I really appreciated his enthusiasm, the pair of them were like my surrogate parents despite them only being two years older than me. I can't wait for them to have little babies of their own. It's good to see them, not just because I miss them, they're going to be so wonderful at it and if they don't teach them supercalifragilisticexpialidocious as their first word I'll be shocked, Disney is in their blood - Mick could be short for Mickey Mouse and Lillian was the name of Walt Disney's wife, they're absolutely made for each other.

It is good to see them, not just because I miss them and they make me laugh, and especially not just because they bring me Disney pyjamas and adorable slippers (Max from The Secret Life of Pets and I look fabulous!), but it's good to feel like a normal person, chatting about work and the possibility of going back and, of course, all the gossip! Hopefully I'll be back by January, even though I know that isn't even close to what Mr Sant has said, that's the goal if I want to climb Kilimanjaro by next December and pay off Disney. Lily has put in a request that I can come back to do light office duties to start instead of running around up and down the stairs, cleaning etc, that would all be hard on my back to begin with until it started to fuse I think. It's good to know there's such a supportive team awaiting my return and that I don't have to worry about work whilst I'm away. It motivates me more being able to think about all the things I'm going to do once I'm out of here, they keep telling me not to push it or get too excited and do too much too soon, but really, I have a good feeling. Everything will be okay.

'What happened with your card to Tom? Did you give it to him?' I had given it to him and he'd called me to say his thanks and ask what it said under the tortoise I'd made. Of course I didn't tell him and said he'd have to figure it out for himself. He told me to stop thanking him for being there for me when I was always doing so much more for him than he could ever do in return. That he wasn't any good really and I deserved more than he could give.

'What is that supposed to mean?' Lily asked, she pulled a face almost in disgust.

'Honestly I've no idea, I didn't question it. I was feeling shite and I was just glad he'd called, but the more I think about it now, the more I think of all the things he could possibly be trying to say.'

'Honestly Pip, I think you just need to talk to him, it's been going on so long and things are obviously getting more intense, you like him don't you?' Mick was right and I knew it, but hearing it made me embarrassed with myself. I felt stupid for even being hung up on something so trivial when I should be thinking of getting better and raising money for a greater good, how self-absorbed must I have sounded talking about boys.

'Screw boys, I'm better off without anyone any way... done with the lot of them.' That was a lie. 'I've got bigger fish to fry! Anyway, I'm pretty sure Gaston is going to fall madly in love with me when we get to Disney so I need to save myself. Maybe Flynn Rider, too!'

The topic turned to Disney from there and our excitement for the trip, we'd all been before, but not together and I'd not been for a hell of a long time. We talked about all the food we were going to eat and ended up watching YouTube reviews of restaurants on my laptop until they had to leave. Just in time for my, no doubt, gross hospital meal of twice baked mush. It's funny how quickly you can go off something when you have no choice but to eat it every day, I was never big into sandwiches, but they were up for consideration after tonight. I must've started nodding off, which happens quite a lot on morphine as I lose muscle tension, because I dropped a plastic cup full of cordial all over myself.

Bollocks. I pressed my nurses bell, hoping it would still work after being caught in the splash back, and waited for someone to come and help. It was clear nobody was in a great hurry to assist so I made the attempt of getting out of bed to my chair on my own. That way they could change my sheets then help me get re-dressed in to a fresh nighty without wasting time waiting for me to get up.

'Is everything okay?' It was a care support worker I'd never seen before.

'Well, I spilt my juice and I'm soaked and I just wondered if I could have a bowl to get clean and re-dressed and a new blanket? I'm really sorry! I'm such an idiot! I'm seated on the edge of my bed trying to reach for my Zimmer frame when she passes it to me and turns my bell off.

'Well why don't we get you to the bathroom and try you in the shower? Are you able to make it to the bathroom?'

'I can get there, but I'm not sure I'm supposed to shower yet until my wound has healed more'.

'I'll help. We can get you on the shower chair and use the shower head to give your front side a good clean at least. I can get some splash proof bandages to cover your back and then that way you at least can feel fresh? You must be desperate for a good wash!' I do not know who this girl is or where she came from, but she's an angel. The idea of getting to use actual running water was practically a turn on!

I felt like I was running to the bathroom, I was so ecstatic, but then when we were inside and the door was locked I realised I would now have to get naked in front of this stranger, who I'm sure was only my age, and I was more than mortified. She assured me not to be at all embarrassed, it was her job after all and dealing with me would be a walk in the park compared with half the older people she has to see. Not that she should say that, but I appreciated the gesture and I tried to see it as a compliment. In the forefront of my mind I could only think , "I'm not even sure what my body looks like fully naked anymore, so I can't promise it won't be worse".

She closed the shower curtain so I could sit down and get as undressed as possible, then she stuck the splash proof covers over my other bandages. I stared down at my body, being seated is never the most flattering view, even in clothes, but somehow I only felt impressed. Impressed with how well my muscles and my bones and my skin were coping with all of this change and how without them I couldn't be here. I'm grateful to have the facilities to keep as clean as possible and the food to be able to stay a relatively decent weight - maybe too decent judging by the third tyre on my hips, but that's all part of the healing. I didn't have dry skin or many spots considering my cleansing routine was way out of whack, overall, it really could be much worse.

The hot water started to pour from the shower and I asked for it to be turned up. Hotter please. Using mildly warm water from a cardboard bowl is easily not the same, mixed with cucumber wet wipes and a prickly dry towel, this was heavenly by comparison. The soap covered my rolls and I looked like the bubbly Lenor man from the adverts. We had to leave my hair because we could not risk getting any more wet than I had to, but I still had some dry shampoo left so at that point I wasn't too bothered. By now I had become used to the hobo look.

The only other thing I'd have liked is to have been able to shave. Seeing my stupid bush and being able to actually see the blonde leg hairs from a metre away was driving me insane. I've always kept it all off, I don't like to feel the stuff it makes me cringe! Clean and smooth all the way! Even when I'm not getting any, it's just for me, it makes me feel better! I apologised for the abominable snowman look and was presented with a razor.

'I can do your lower legs for you if you like then you can do your knees and your armpits. At least that will be some of it gone?' Honestly, this girl was changing my life, alongside Jill, easily my favourite person on ward twenty-four so far!

Getting into bed, with clean sheets that had been changed whilst I was showering, was a dream: A fresh nighty, clean bedding, no hairy legs rubbing against each other causing a fire hazard, no smelly, jungle armpits, I practically felt like a new woman. Even my catheter bag had had a bit of a wash, it accidentally got wet in the shower stream and now was cleaner than me.

Tucked in under the sheets with Horrible Histories on my laptop and my headphones in I was ready for bed, just one more round of meds and I could go to sleep, hopefully. I was in my nighty from Mick and Lily with my hair in a bun on top of my head like a Mulan and I felt like an absolute warrior.

Woman power to the hippy bush, too!

Chapter Twenty-Six

Dear Ollie,

Really sorry to email again, circumstances have changed and I'm just wondering if I'm still going to be allowed to do the climb - so sorry for asking again!

I've had a spinal fusion a couple of weeks ago and they say it could take up to eighteen months to heal, I'm confident when it does I will be back in full working order, I just was wondering if there was any rules that say I can't climb with a certain 'injury' so to speak?

If it's just the same as getting my specialist to sign me off then that's great, if not please let me know!

Thanks in advance,

Pip

I'm almost annoyed with myself for being on top of my to-do list today, it would give me something to be thinking about other than the agonising pain I'm in. In the last week I managed to nearly end up having another operation (again!) And fighting with any doctor that came near me to take my stupid catheter out. Being on all this morphine isn't great for your body, other than the itchy face it gives me and the sickness feeling when it starts to wear off, it also causes pretty shitty - pardon the pun- constipation. Mix each two hourly dose of the stuff with only potatoes and cheese, pretty much, everything is bound to go a bit skew-whiff.

If it wasn't for Jill's husband bringing me in a box of blueberries I don't think I'd have made it out without surgery, but my god did it take some doing! Not only that,

I'd never been constipated before in my life so I had no idea what kind of pain it could cause and, according to the nurses, it was ten times worse due to the pressure it was putting on my spine, meaning that I couldn't force anything without potentially popping a screw in my fusion. Talk about drama! I demolished the blueberries within twenty minutes, it was a large box from the Tesco on the corner opposite the hospital, and then I moved on to fluids for a bit before going back in on the pears. By 2am I thought I was good to at least try and with the assistance of three nurses it was like going into labour, I've never seen three happier faces looking at poo in my life.

It did send me into a collapsed state though and I promptly fell off the toilet on to all three of them, sweating buckets and weak at the knees, I had to be wheeled back to bed and given intravenous therapy. By the next morning I was on a roll, the surgeons were happy and everything had seemed much better, for all of a day and a half. Then my catheter started giving me hell. It was like I had overwhelming sensation and there seemed to be blood in every drop of urine so I requested we removed it and try me without, just to see if I could manage or not. That request took over a day to be discussed and executed, but by the following evening they were going to do a trial over night to see if I could manage in the morning. I was under strict instruction to drink plenty and if I managed to empty my bladder to 200ml (the medically acceptable amount to retain) I would be allowed to have it removed, hopefully permanently. Hopefully, my bladder was on the mend.

Or not. The next morning I managed to go for a wee, but it practically dripped out, there was only 250ml in the bowl and still 1000ml in my bladder according to the little machine! That's insane! The nurse who measured it was concerned and put a catheter right back in, but nobody continued to check the output, they just kept the valve open and emptied it straight out.

Now today, days after all that kerfuffle, I am once again in shocking agony with my bladder, there is blood coming out of the tube, the bright red kind that looks like the start of season five Supernatural episode title card. And nobody seemed to really give a damn, I think I'm going stir crazy , if they don't remove it I'm going to take it out myself, that's it! Once again I press my nurses bell to tell them of my supreme discomfort.

'Look, please, last week I had my catheter removed and I was in nowhere near this much pain, please just let me try again, I need it taking out!' I don't think I've ever spoken to any of the staff so curtly, but I was getting absolutely nothing done and I felt as though my bladder was being ripped into little pieces. 'At least just call Mr Sant and ask him to come and see me, please!'

'We'll do what we can, I'll get someone to call him, but your output was weak and you're retaining so much it wouldn't be safe just to take it out, you could go into renal failure.'

'Okay well see how much is in there now and we'll have another go! Just speak to Mr Sant and ask him, please!'

With the catheter removed almost an hour later, a care support worker come to carry out my scan. I'd been drinking a tonne of water in the meantime so I could get the best results possible to prove my point. The bladder scanning machines were like getting an ultrasound but without the picture. They squeeze cold jelly onto your lower abdomen and use a little hand-held scanner to rub over your bladder and find the highest point of volume. She found a clear reading and she went off to tell the nurse.

Writhing in pain on my bed felt like second nature to me at this point; the back pain I could pretty much breathe through most of the time with the morphine to soften the blow, but nothing seemed to help the massacre going on in my bladder. Tears were rolling down my cheeks and I couldn't decide how much was anger considering the lack of support I felt I was getting, I couldn't even sleep through it to pass the time. Frustrated and sore I just wanted to be anywhere else. I tried all the tricks, I imagined laying on a beach somewhere listening to the sea, I thought about mentally covering my bladder in aloe vera to sooth the burning, I moved on to envisioning ripping the bloody thing out altogether before Mr Sant appeared. I'm surprised he came at all, the man is so difficult to pin down.

'What seems to be the matter, Pip? I hear you would like you catheter removed again?'

We went through the whole conversation a few times before he said I was to have another bladder scan and to go and empty my bladder naturally whilst he was still here. I was surprised at his commitment, but I honestly felt as though he was just trying to prove to me I was wrong so I'd stop hassling them. The chances of my bladder rectifying the damage done on their own weren't exactly high and I don't think anyone believed it would ever get better. With 700ml to try and get rid of, I Zimmered into the bathroom. They offered me a commode, but they will never get me on one of those things as long as I live, no hope in hell, I don't want everyone listening behind the curtain, I'm a nervous go-er as it is.

Tom arrived during my giant sob-fest on the toilet.

'But I can feel that I need to go so why can't I go?!' My cries from the toilet could be heard back in my room in the hall and I felt so stupid for even trying to convince them, again, I could manage. I had passed only 250ml, again so they had no choice, but to replace my catheter. All this going in and out could be causing infections and they were adamant they didn't want to do it anymore, but I was gutted. Why could I suddenly feel the need to go and still not be able to do it? I couldn't feel anything before so surely things were improving?

'Pip, it's me, I'm really sorry. Can I come in?' Tom was behind the door and I motioned for the nurse to let him in, she left us alone for a few minutes. Even though I was still seated on the toilet, a watery emotional mess, he knelt before me on both knees and kissed my hands that were shielding my face and my sobs.

'You will be able to do it one day, I know you will, but your body is going through so much it's not all going to be fixed this fast. You are doing so well, I'm so proud of you, you're strong, little one. Please don't cry.' His hands were pulling mine away from my face and he held them in his a moment, before another knock on the door.

'Pip, Mr Sant doesn't want to come in, but he wants to talk to you, will you come out?'

Tom helped me back across to my bed and lifted my legs in for me, I was too drained to do it myself and I think he knew because I didn't have to ask.

'I can have a what?'

'It's a bagless catheter so you can open the valve yourself when you need to go...'

'It's a willy! I'm getting a penis?!' I couldn't stop laughing and my exclamation and excitement of a penis catheter set everyone else off, too. The catheter was half the size of the tube on the bagged one, it was yellow and had a little valve at the end that I could open and close whenever I needed, it also meant I could now wear trousers again! Look Geppetto, I'm a real live boy!

I was so happy I couldn't wait to try it out, so happy in fact, I had almost forgotten about not being able to wee on my own still, entirely. Whilst they put it in I made Tom wait outside, I wanted a willy reveal, but when they pulled the curtains back he was gone. I thought maybe he'd gone to the toilet or something so I took a quick picture on my phone of my new kit, another big sign post on the way to recovery.

'Right, put these on, we're going out!' Tom had waltzed back in to the room with a wheelchair, a pair of hospital trousers and a spring in his step. 'I've just spoken to Mr Sant and he says you deserve a trip out, so as long as you wrap up warm enough I'm allowed to take you out of this place for a couple of hours. I don't even have to bring you back in for tea because I've told him where we're going!'

My face was shell shocked in the best way. I couldn't feel my cheeks and I'm sure my eyes had reduced to slits, but I just couldn't believe the words coming out of his mouth. As long as I had my painkillers now and felt comfortable enough, I was allowed to leave this ward, leave this building and go outside. I don't even remember what fresh air feels like. Tom helped me dress and got me his spare coat from the car, I looked a right picture, I didn't take one though. A big man's coat, some mens hospital PJ bottoms and fluffy socks (I hadn't had shoes on when the ambulance had brought me through all those weeks ago and I still hadn't been brought any). I didn't want my slippers to get wet if it rained either so I just wore two pairs of slipper socks to make up for it. My hair was still unwashed and I had cried off all my make up, but Tom didn't seem to mind and it wasn't until we got in the lift I even realised how ridiculous I looked.

As the doors opened he kissed my head and pushed me out, down into the Brotherton wing.

'Where ARE we going?' I'd yelled back to him as he ran with me down the ramp into the other building.

'You'll see!' He pushed my chair and let me go speeding down the corridor on my own, chasing after me to stop me crashing in to walls, or people. We made noises like speeding cars around every corner and he pretended to struggle pushing up the slightest incline. Or at least I hope he was pretending, god knows how much weight I've put on in this place. For a few minutes we felt like a movie montage, I could even hear the background music as we laughed.

'Ta-da!' He pushed open the door and wheeled me out backwards on to the street. Across the road was the millennial square and I'd completely forgotten, being caged inside, it was the last day of November and the German Christmas Market was on.

'Madame, how do you take your sausage?' He was radiating happiness, as was I. It was dark and all the twinkly lights hanging over the huts were lit up in a yellow glow, there was a band playing and every now and then you'd hear someone shouting something in a terrible attempt at German then roars of laughter would follow. People were courteous, allowing the wheelchair through most of the time and giving Tom the eye. I bet everyone thought , "what a nice man bringing the ill person out". He was, is, a nice man. The best if you ask me.

He bought us currywurst and he had a small beer so he could still drive home. He parked me right in front of the band and they played some German songs mixed with a few English ones. The Pogues - Fairytale of New York came on, my favourite Christmas song, and mid-stuffing our faces Tom took the breaks off my wheelchair and started dancing with me, one hand on one handle so we kind of swayed together.

'This is my favourite Christmas song of all time, it would be rude not to dance!' He'd beamed.

'Mine too!' our eyes locked and for a moment it was just us.

After a minute a few others joined in with the dance, but we still had the best moves, the wheels helped my rhythm, of course. I didn't even feel the cold, everyone was wrapped in scarves and hats and gloves and shivering, but Tom and I were emitting a certain warmth that could've lasted all night. We finished our sausages and wheeled around the stalls, looking at the intricately designed toys and ornaments.

'Can I get you something? I want to get you something!'

'I don't need anything! You've already bought hot dogs, I'm happy just looking.'

'No, you've got to have something, what about this? You can't say no to Tortoise!'

In his hand a was a tiny handblown glass tortoise, it was beautiful and delicate and before I could protest he was in my hand. We didn't get a bag because we didn't want him to suffocate on the way back to my room. I didn't even want to go back. I was on such a high, too lost in this wonderful night to remember that's where I lived for now, staring up at the hospital again made me want to cry. Tom only had time for a quick crossword once we were back, he had to get the car and had work early in the morning. We'd been out for a couple of hours anyway and visiting hours would soon be over, I just didn't want him to leave. I clung on for dear life until he had to prise himself away from me, reluctantly, but still. I tried to indulge in the events of the evening instead of getting caught up in his looming absence.

'Let me know when you get home...'

'I won't.' He kissed my head and my lips and left. The sense of his mouth on mine lingered and feeling my lip fall back to me after his pulled away was enough to crack the lump in my throat.

I'd stopped no more than three tears streaming before a nurse appeared at my side.

'Pip, you're moving wards. Now.'

I didn't have a real answer as to why they'd made me move wards, yet here I am lying in an isolated bed on the stroke ward. And no, I haven't had a stroke. My new room consists of only my bed and one other, it looks like the storage room from ward twenty-four that's been turned into extra beds. There is a window, length and width of the wall to my left and a toilet directly to my right, I feel like I'm in a glorified box and I'm not even claustrophobic. Or I wasn't. On the move down they broke my tortoise from the Christmas market, they chopped off one of her little feet, supposedly a total accident, but I still cried. I'd not even had her more than two hours. Tom had assured me not to be upset and he'd replace her, but I didn't want to, broken or not she was mine. At least now we matched, I suppose, I only have half a leg too since the left side of me isn't getting much more sensation than before the op.

There's a woman in the other bed who seems friendly enough, but I didn't talk to her all day yesterday because I was too miserable to give a damn. I'm sure she thinks I'm a total bitch, but nobody is helping make matters any better. Every time another patient comes by to use the loo or pass through I get glared down and they have said multiple times, "Why is there a CHILD on our ward?" I'd tried to keep my curtain shut, I know it wasn't entirely their fault, but the stupid nurse insisted it stay open to "open up the room"... Not being funny bitch, but I've been here exactly three weeks today and it feels like a lifetime, the best thing I can get is personal space, especially down here, so leave it be... Grrr. It's not like I can get up and pull it around all the time either, but when nobody is around I use my Zimmer frame to yank it across as far as I can. Not only the privacy, but sleeping next to a bathroom on a ward full of old people doesn't smell the most pleasant.

Thankfully, it's still Alice and Rachel who have turned up for me for physio today so at least there's two friendly faces. Their little double act makes me smile and it's nice that they're not more than ten years older than me, still relatable and don't mind me bitching about being stuck here with nobody else my age. They are just about the only two people who seem to understand the frustration. Since there isn't much room in this ward for walking with a Zimmer frame, they wheel me down to their physio "headquarters" so we can use the space there. It's empty for us to use and full of gym equipment I don't think I'd know how to use if you paid me, if it's not a squat rack I'm not interested.

With my Zimmer frame as support they help me up, but once standing, they pull some crutches from behind them.

'How do you feel about taking these for a spin?' Alice ask as she practically threads my arms through them for me.

'Do you think I'm ready?'

'We won't know until we try. We'll support you all the way so don't worry, just tell us if you don't feel like you can do any more okay?'

I'd only had crutches once before in my life and I had preferred to crawl everywhere, finding it way easier than trying to understand them. Simpler times when you only sprain an ankle playing badminton in your schools sports hall, not exactly life changing for more than two weeks.

The first thing I did was use them to stand up straight, I

don't remember the last time I did that. Zimmer frames are too low to support you and keep you upright, you end up walking with a slight hunch that I'm sure is not good for anyone. Holding my shoulders straight and back, level with my hips, caused strain in my lower spine, but the kind that comes with a decent stretch first thing in a morning. It was a bitter-sweet relief and I had a sudden need for someone to pick me up and crack it back into place.

'One step closer to heaven, baby...' I'd started singing, in an awful tune, but the pair of them joined in and we laughed - the good old days when S Club 7 were the only important thing in life. Oh, how the times are a changing.

I really surprised myself on crutches, they were bloody hard work, but I did manage a couple steps away from my chair and back again, the primary goal was to learn how to use the sticks to stand up and sit down properly. I'd still only have access to the Zimmer frame for now outside of physio, but I was allowed to use it without supervision from today so I didn't have to have someone with me when I left my bed - not that I ever leave my bloody bed. Not only had I successfully used crutches today, Rachel had insisted she show me all the physio facilities, just to keep me out of confinement a little longer, I really appreciated that. It was a different kind of air out here than in my bed, not stuffy, a little bit more free - one step closer to home.

Once they had dropped me back at my ward, they'd made me walk through to my bed using my frame, just to prove I would really be okay without them. After using most of my energy on testing out the crutches it was knackering, but I powered through anyway because I had another request and wanted a greater chance of a 'yes'.

'Please could I have a shower? A wash my hair sort of shower?'

'What do you mean? Have you not been allowed to shower this whole time?!' In unison they recoiled in shock.

'Well no? They don't want to get my wound wet. One girl helped me have a body wash with the shower head on the shower chair last week, but I haven't been able to wash my hair or anything...' I trail off and they immediately ask me to get on the bed so they can have a look at the state of me.

'I don't see why you can't at least have a shower. I'm going to put a couple of the splash proof covers on and make sure it's covered really well, but it's been two weeks since the op now, I can't see why you're being made to sit like this!'

Not only was I allowed to shower, I was allowed to do it on my own, well, with my walking frame, but that's inanimate so it doesn't count. The only restriction was making sure I washed my hair over my face rather than down my back as much as possible, it didn't even sound too bad until I realised my blonde locks were thirty-two inches long and practically strangling me with every motion. Absolutely perfect otherwise, of course. I used my fancy Lush shower gel that Lily had bought me, it smelt like candy floss and bubble-gum and had glitter in the ingredients, I was sparkling like a bad vampire... Cough, Edward Cullen, cough.

Forgetting all these wonderful things, my absolute best part of this day was getting to shave my fluffy vagina! It wasn't easy, my Zimmer frame was soaked, but it didn't matter too much, it would dry. I even had to take a breather and sit in the shower chair when I got half way through, then three quarters of the way through, but it was so worth it. I still don't have great sensation in my saddle area, it's part of the Cauda Equina that may never recover so I could've easily cut something and not realised, it didn't seem like it though.

I let myself drip dry due to the aching and was in there for a good hour overall. It was one in the afternoon and mum and dad were due any minute so I thought I should make my way back to bed. My hair was so difficult to brush since it had been haphazardly washed the wrong way around to normal, so I opted to just plait it and hoped the knots would eventually fall out. If I didn't have two visitors coming I might have decided to sit in my chair for a while, but it was seemingly best not to try and do too much, I had already had quite a morning so far.

'What are you doing down here? It said stroke ward on the door?' Dad sounded genuinely upset by this and mum was staring at my view of the back of the hospital. They sat and as I explained that I had been told as little as they knew, dad handed me a card.

'This is your Christmas card, we were up all night writing them and thought you might like yours here to brighten up the place.' That was more thoughtful of them than normal and it made me smile, until I read the front. 'Pee Pee and Tom'.

'Why is it addressed to Tom and I?' I'd tried not to use my, "for god's sake I've told you this one hundred times" tone, but I'm not sure it came out as I'd hoped.

'Because you two are practically in a relationship Pip, don't start this now. You're together, you just need to get over yourselves!' Mum hated when I tried to tell her anything to the contrary. 'Your dad and I held hands once and we were official, so what's the problem? Have you ever even asked him?'

'It's not the same as it used to be when you met dad, mum!'

'No it isn't the same - women are supposedly bolder these days and I certainly thought you would be! Isn't he here all the time anyway? He wouldn't be here and doing things for you if he wasn't in love with you. People don't invest time like that for nothing, you know...' She kept on and dad and I exchanged a look, he felt like an ally for a change today. It was nice, as much as mums relentless ramblings were infuriating as we'd had this conversation on multiple occasions, I knew she just wanted me to be happy - and probably on the way to being married and out of her house. Mostly the latter, I imagine.

'Look, it's more complex than that, don't ask me how, it just is. We're not together and I really don't think we ever will be, if we've made it this far without it being anything I can't see it being anything else so what's the point in even asking?' I'd never actually said more than this about the topic before and I realised, for the first, I'd left a question out there for my parents to answer.

'Pip,' This time it was dad, he usually stayed pretty quiet on the matter. 'I know I don't ever usually chime in here, but do you not think your mum is maybe right? You've got balls, kid. And at the end of the day, if you are comfortable enough to sleep with someone and let them care for you like this, then do you not think you should be comfortable enough to ask them where you stand? You're worth more than the middle road and after all you've been through, that you're going through, you certainly have proved you don't need someone who doesn't need you. What's the worst that can happen?'

Even mum was quiet, he didn't speak loudly, but we both listened intently. I think that has to be the nicest, most caring, genuine thing my dad has ever said to me and I really believed every word.

'Look! I forgot to tell you...' I appreciated every word he'd just said and he knew it, we'd shared a look that had prompted his squeezing of my hand, but it seems I'd felt the pressure in my bladder, too.

'I have a willy!' Both my parents erupted into laughter when I pulled the catheter out from between my legs under my nighty.

'Well that's not something I ever thought I'd get to hear my daughter say!' chuckled mum, as she unzipped her coat and put it on the back of the chair. I was waving it around and I told them all about how I could now wear trousers and shower on my own and how I was so close to getting crutches and they really listened to me. They didn't look bored or like they wanted to leave and then finally mum said, 'Come on, let's take this willy for a spin!'

I hadn't actually used it yet, I hadn't really felt the need to go, but apparently my bladder had stretched to just over 1000ml so there was little chance I'd feel it until it was nearly full any way - because of the nerve damage. I didn't really feel able to go to the bathroom, my back had endured a lot already today so I was going to press my bell to ask the nurse for a bowl, before I could, dad hopped up and went to go and find one for me instead.

'Well she's a bitch, isn't she?' He was referring to the nurse and yes she was! In typical hospital Pip mode, I ask that one of them film it, they declined so instead I held my phone in one hand and my willy in the other, the only noise you could hear on the take was laughing and wee hitting the bottom of a cardboard tub. Success!

For the first time, once my parents had left, I was still feeling on top of the world. I'd had a productive day and although I was on a crappy ward with crappy, mean nurses and crappy, rude patients, I'd done well. Amongst all the good things, I couldn't help but think about what my dad had said about Tom and I and I opened our Christmas card. Inside was a voucher for the The Spa for the two of us, "For when you're out free! x" they'd written on the gift card and on the other side "Thanks for taking care of her!" Maybe they didn't hate me after all.

I texted them thanks for the visit and the voucher and sent a picture of it to Tom, the voucher that is, then checked my other messages. Just one from Lily. She'd asked me how my first outing had gone and I couldn't stop myself from gushing. I talked in great detail about how wonderful the night was and how I'd cried when he'd left, then I told her what my dad had said and how I think I'd decided he was right. I do deserve someone who wants all of me, all the time (or mostly!) I wanted a real relationship that was going somewhere and I think it's about time I did something about it.

Chapter Twenty-Eight

It's official, start with crutches today! Thank Christ. I'm getting so close to freedom I can practically smell it - so very close. I still need supervision, but it's actually easier than I thought as long as I go slowly. We went from one end of the ward to another and I felt like the queen of the corridor, if this is what it feels like being able to use crutches I can't begin to imagine how I'm going to feel standing on top of Mount Kilimanjaro looking out across Africa. THAT will be like being Queen of the World, not just a hospital ward.

Ollie had replied to my email and said as long as my specialist and other medical professionals could sign me off and my resting observations were fit to their standard, there was nothing stopping me from trekking. I cried tears of joy... and maybe fear. I had been given the all clear, as much as possible at this point, to follow my dreams and raise money for a worthy cause, I just felt like a bazillion dollars and I was too excited to let it go. All the way through physio Alice and Rachel and I talked about all the treks and hikes and climbs we'd like to do or had done, I was so inspired, if they'd have let me, I'd absolutely have attempted the trek to base camp that second.

My legs didn't agree with me though and I think I'd probably pushed it too far when I'd said I could easily turn back and do it all again. Thankfully there was a wheelchair for back up and after a good thirty minutes of strong effort I was sitting next to my bed having a rest. Well earned, though, and it meant I could get cracking on Tanzania research with my brain still in full swing. At least I'd still be using one muscle, not including the massive finger workout I was getting with my aggressive typing skills. That sounded way filthier than it should've.

The afternoon flew by so fast I'd hardly seen a thing other than a million different websites about Tanzania and Africa and some online shopping for good measure. I'd researched the best local places to buy hiking boots, one, right in the centre of Leeds, sounded perfect! I'd looked up boot styles I might like and what terrain I'd be on, the weather at the time of year I expected to go, the packing list and the best recommend products for each item on the list. There was a to-do page, a to-buy page and a questions I might have page in my notebook, all very neatly scrawled, tick boxed for when they'd been completed, bought, answered. I was more prepared than I needed to be considering I might not be going for another two years, but I was excited and on an absolute roll.

I suppose I'd better clear up all my mess, Annie and Alex are expected this afternoon and I'm surprised he's coming, too. She says he's bringing her across because he wanted to come in and say hello and it makes me wonder if maybe he's trying to make up for being quiet with her and working extra lately. She doesn't miss a trick that girl, but I think she forgets that I don't either. Something is off. She texts asking if I need anything bringing from home before she sets off and actually I do, I really would love a pair of leggings and a jumper. I miss being able to wear day time clothes and not bloody PJ's and hospital gowns all the time. Now I have a willy I can make half an effort and that's what I'd like to do.

They turn up with a Primark bag in one hand and a Marks and Spencer bag in the other.

'Surprise! We thought we should treat you to some bits, you deserve them after all!' Alex handed me the food carrier and hugged me before sitting on the chair with the bag of clothes. I'd got back on my bed before they'd arrived to make room. The bitch of a nurse wasn't happy when other people sat anywhere near it - GERMS! She'd insisted. Annie hugged me and pulled up the plastic chair next to my bed mates table.

'I'm sure she won't mind if I borrow this - sorry!' She spoke aloud to the sleeping woman, you could hardly see her under her pillow so she could've been awake for all we know. Annie was obviously covering her bases!"

'You know you didn't need to buy me things!' I protested as I opened the bag to find posh cheese, exotic juices and upmarket chocolates. A sneaky bag of Percy Pigs hiding at the bottom, too.

'Oooh, you know me too well, you spoil me, but thank you so much.' It all went in my cupboard apart from a circle of mature cheddar that I started unwrapping as they spoke.

'We have news, but first we bought you some bits, have a look in the bag!' Annie was practically squeezing with excitement and I felt like I was being left out of a joke that only they would find funny.

'Oh yay, you got me the cotton leggings, you're a saint, you know I hate the ones you wear, they're all stretchy and thin...'

'Yeah, yeah just get to the white t-shirt at the bottom' she grabbed the bag out of my hand, but quickly thrust it back and sat with her fingers between her thighs. Alex sat forward in his chair with his arm around her. The white top was folded rather neatly and I wondered what could be so bloody special about a plain white top... also it was very well folded for a retail cashier...

MAID OF HONOUR. It said right across the front in pink text and I just looked at her for a second, still not getting the punchline.

'We're engaged!' Alex took her hand to show me the ring and Annie immediately burst into tears - 'so will you?!'

'Will I what?'

'Be my maid of honour you absolute muppet?!'

'Of course, of course, ahh congratulations! Sorry I'm so slow! I'm so happy for you!' Annie had leant across for a big squeeze and then I hugged Alex, too.

'Eeeeeeek!'

'So how did it happen then?' I look at Annie as if to say "last time we spoke you thought he might cheating on you, woman?" She was still showing me the ring as she spoke and Alex would pipe in every now and then with details of why he'd been working overtime to pay for the diamond and how she wouldn't get off his back, they'd laugh and kiss and they were bubbling over with affection. It was the first time I'd ever really seen them naturally together without worrying about tea burning or what was happening next. They seemed to be smitten and it was so warming.

A corker of a ring, too. Just her type with the rose gold band and three stone marquise setting, not something I'd pick, but it fit her better than a glove and it seemed as though she'd never not worn it. They were the epitome of love birds. He'd been working extra and keeping his phone close so she wouldn't see the messages from her parents and his parents asking when he was doing it and had he bought the ring yet so on and so forth.

'It was SO romantic!' she'd told me. They'd gone out on a walk with the dog up Over Silton and clambered through the Christmas tree forest up to the top of the hill, she'd broken her shoe half way up, the entire sole had come off so he'd given a piggy back the rest of the way. By the time they'd reached the top there was nowhere to sit so he'd told her to wait there a minute whilst he fashioned a bench from rocks and branches for them to sit on. When she was seated he'd pulled her head on to his knee and they lay for a while watching the sun go down, slowly, when she looked up at him he'd kissed her and he says that's when he realised he had to do it. He was more excited to look at her face than watch the orange sun set behind the trees. Naturally she'd said yes and they descended down to go home and tell their parents.

'We wanted to tell you in person!' She said, as if I'd feel bad that she hadn't called me in that very instant.

'I'm just so happy for you, you deserve this. I can't wait to help plan the wedding. It's not like I've not got the time!'

I hadn't meant to make that last remark, I didn't really want to go back to how shit my reality was in comparison, but it felt like I couldn't think of anything else for a minute. My friends are engaged and I am overwhelmed by how happy I am for them, I really, truly am. I can't wait to help pick out a dress with her and spoil her and dance with her when they've finally sealed the deal, but when was I going to get to do it too? Would I ever get to ask her to reciprocate the honour? It just made me realise I had to do something about Tom. I want all of this and I deserve it, so it's time to find out where we're going once and for all. I AM happy single and I DO love myself, but I think I'm reaching a point where I want to be able to love someone else just as much. It's about time I let myself just be, and I want to be with Tom.

Chapter Twenty-Nine

If I have to suffer any more with this pissing catheter (pardon the pun) I may literally scream the place down. Five days I've had my willy in now and as much as it's super convenient and fun to play with - boys have it so lucky they don't even know - I am sick to death of it. I want MY OWN urethra to work, I don't need a crappy extension cable. Last night it didn't even do it's damn job. I am supposed to be the one who controls output, but somewhere between me falling asleep, finally, at 2am and waking up at 7.30am, my bed became saturated with my own concentrated urine and, yet again, BLOOD! It looked like I'd given birth and not even realised when I'd woken up and taken my top blanket off, I sobbed in utter dismay that something else could possibly have gone wrong.

'Oh it's just your catheter leaking,' the nurse had said... JUST?! JUST?!

Honestly, one of these days I'm going to be better and be able to laugh about how ridiculous my body has treated me (touch wood), but for now it's humiliating and frustrating as all kinds of shite. FUCK THIS! And not that I don't love being able to shower now, but the novelty wears off when you only seem to be showering to clean piss and blood from yourself at twenty-two years old, it's really not the same as showering for a hot date - not that I'd know I suppose.

Once again, Mr Sant is having to be consulted on where we go from here, supposedly they cannot remove it until he says so and that just makes me want to take it out even more. I drink copiously throughout the morning to fill my bladder to bursting point, just to make things messier and hoping that might push the proceedings along if I'm in a constant state of incontinence. At the very least I can prove when I go to the toilet that it's all coming out past the catheter and into the bowl rather than through the open valve, that's what I'll do next time. If I have to make someone watch me on the toilet I'll do it for the good of my sanity.

Thank the heavens for my physio.

'You are telling us that you woke up in your own wee and nobody gave half a damn?! Honestly, this ward isn't taking good care of you at all!'

'Do you know what makes it worse? That ginormous window that fills an entire wall might make the view pretty, but it leaves the room so cold that being sodden wet with wee didn't even keep me warm, it gave me chills more than anything!' It was true, too. The nights were so cold I needed extra blankets just to keep me at a normal temperature, and I'm usually the hot one (in a sweaty way, not in a sexy way-duh).

'Let's get you into warmer pastures, today we're thinking of taking you on a little walk with your crutches, we were going to take you up the ward corridor, but how about we go down the main hospital corridor to the lifts and back? Change of scenery?' Rachel sounded so hopeful I almost believed it would make me feel better just for not looking at this room any longer.

As they helped me stand, a rush of urine swept down my leg... ARGH! Poor Rachel and Alice didn't even bother calling for a nurse this time, they helped me change and found me some giant granny nappies to wear. Funny how I lose the Zimmer frame, but the old people lifestyle is still coming for me!

I won't lie, they're actually very comfortable and I asked them for another couple of pairs, just to be safe they wheeled me out of the ward and let me get out by the doors.

'Okay, so we're going to go from here, to the lifts and then back again okay? Alice will walk with the wheelchair behind in case you need to rest, got it? You must tell us because we don't want you collapsing!' I laughed and said I'd try my best and started with the crutches. Both arms in, using my good leg, my right one, to balance, I then moved the sticks a foot in front of me and brought my left leg through with them so i was standing in a triangle. Then repeat.

Crutches are more hard work than they look, kind of like pushing a pram, it seems easy because it has wheels and you can rest on it when you're tired, but actually it's extra weight and a nightmare to get going once you're stopped. Also, if you used too much weight on the crutches, the handles dig into your palms and cause blisters and sores and even just walking the 150 metres along the hallway to the lifts and back was causing redness and burning, I don't want to imagine what being on these full time at home would be like - or for the rest of my life potentially. I keep forgetting that's a real possibly that I may never be able to walk properly on my own again. A forgotten potential reality.

At the lifts it was funny to see visitors walking around, but I think they must've thought it more strange to see me because I felt like a lion in a zoo, all eyes at all times were directed at me. I almost think Annie and Rachel were encouraging me just to distract from the stares.

'You're doing so well, just a couple of steps more and you can sit down. Promise, you can have a rest!'

'No thank you.' I kept walking. I turned right around at the wall, trying hard not to noticeably lean on it for support and pushed back down the corridor until it was just us again and I slowed my pace. Apparently I wasn't feeling very people-y today and I think it had a lot to do with the fact I was sweating profusely from the exercise, what little it was, and wearing a nappy that I'm sure could be seen through the back of my gown they'd put on me. My other PJs' hadn't yet dried on the radiator from last night so it's all I was left with. My leggings were lost somewhere in my cupboard and I didn't fancy the girls going through all my stuff, as much as I like them, I still don't like the idea.

Finally back in my little shithole, there was still no news from Mr Sant about my catheter and it turns out he'd actually gone home for a family emergency - so I sort of had to let him off. I understand that he has a life and I absolutely hope that whatever is going wrong is okay very soon, but I also really wish there was someone else who could give me the okay to be comfortable right now. Instead of moping I decide it's probably a good enough time to clear out my cupboard, at least it passes the time and I will hopefully be able to find my leggings.

I can't just move like I used, sat cross legged on the floor was no longer an option, so I fashion a visitors chair in front of the doors and use my crutches to help me get across. That process alone takes five minutes, actually clearing all the crap took almost an hour, but I had time to kill and no visitors due. I put all my toiletries into a basket I'd found and all my pens and books and bits and bobs into the box Lily and Mick had brought. Clothes went into hospital carrier bags and everything else either went in the bin or got stacked neatly in the back. Food went in the top drawer and on my desk - I keep the most important stuff within grabbing distance of course.

Since it was all out, I decided I may as well make half an effort with my appearance and put some proper make up on. I'd only really been wearing the baseline stuff, foundation and some mascara and the odd hint of blusher depending on how dead I'd felt. The bronzer came out only a handful of times and I hadn't used my Naked palette more than once in this entire month. Disgraceful I know. I also decided to put my leggings on and the top I'd been wearing when I came in the ambulance, it was black like most of my wardrobe and written on the front it said "Girls do not dress for boys" - right now I wasn't dressing for anyone that wasn't me and I was just glad I looked half-human.

A nice smokey eye and some winged eye-liner to boot, I didn't feel remotely like myself in the best way. I didn't want to be myself today, that wasn't going to cut it, I wanted to be made of magic instead. They say positive thinking helps so surely positive practising does even more. I chose my favourite, all-rounder, red lipstick by Lime Crime that I completely adore, it fits all skin types and I should know because usually I'd be a total wash out, but now I'm a vixen... of sorts. I used both bronzer and blush to create a semi-contoured look and to hide my chubby little hospital cheeks that I'd grown since being here, my chins were only ever mode defined, too.

By the time I'd finished I took a good look at myself and thought "You scrub up good, Parker".

I'd done the entire face using the black screen of my phone as a mirror so I checked the damage on my phone camera once I was done just to be sure I hadn't been blinded by the light, I really looked a total dog.

Snapping a very quick selfie because I didn't want to be seen and judged for being a typical kid obsessed with her face, I sent it to Tom without a caption. He responded straight away:

'Beautiful as always, don't wash it off until bedtime.'

'You absolute numpty!! Why didn't you tell me you were coming?!' Tom arrived, flowers and an advent calendar in hand, just before tea-time.

'Well you just looked so good, how could I possibly let you sit here all alone like that? You deserve to be seen and I didn't want to miss out. These are for you.' He really is Superman I think to myself, although almost out loud, as he hands me the beautiful bouquet of red daisies. 'To match your red lips.' The advent calendar is my favourite kind too, milky stars. He knows me too well for either of our own goods.

'Now I'm glad you're dressed too, because I'm taking you out. Let me just grab a wheelchair.' I insist he doesn't have to take me anywhere, but he's adamant and says he has a plan up his sleeve that he won't let me ruin with my modesty. Cheeky git. For a second time, we tumble through the hospital wheeling at far too many miles an hour until we are again through the doors and at the Christmas market. We don't stop there though, not this time. We pass right through it, smelling all the same smells as before and hearing all the same sounds, if I didn't know better it could be the same night, I still didn't have shoes.

'It should be just up this hill...' His voice trails off as he searches the buildings beside us. 'A-ha, here we go!'

Pushing my chair into a door on our left, we enter a darkened foyer, lit up by red neons and I feel a bit like I'm in a strip club or something. They know who we are the second they see me in my chair and the hostess calls for a gentleman to take us through the back to what looks like a very secret lift. Apparently it's not usually accessible unless on booking request as they don't want people who don't need it to be using it. It's the first time that has ever really resonated with me, but how I appreciated it. I never used lifts because I don't like them, but know lots of people who do use them even when they don't need to. Funny how all sorts of things can change your perspective. Being in a wheelchair without choice is certainly one of them.

I chose to move from the wheelchair to my seat and let them keep it safe for me in the back, with my crutches down the side of the table for Tom to reach if I needed them. Thankfully it was relatively empty so I didn't feel like I was cramped and taking up space, I even got up with Tom to have a look at the food, obviously he carried my plate for me, I can only just stand up on the crutches let alone carry a full meal, too!

'So it's a 'Round the World' buffet, in case you'd not noticed. I thought that it's unfair the furthest you'll go is home, for a while, when you deserve more than the world, so the best I could get is a global buffet! I hope you like it.'

'Honestly it's perfect, thank you. They say the way to a man's heart is through his stomach and now I have a willy, you've got it just right!' We laughed and talked as we ate dinner, making jokes and I let him vent to me about work, it made me feel helpful somehow when I couldn't do much else.

It was still early when we left so we decided to take a stroll through the city whilst it was quiet. Living in such a small town you forget the shops in the city don't all close at five, on the dot, so we managed to get in to the shopping centres and do some window shopping. I'd brought my purse because I intended to buy him an advent calendar, I just didn't want him to know about it until we got back to my room.

The opportunity arose when we nipped into the shop I'd seen online that fitted hiking boots, I just wanted to have a look whilst I could, but ended up buying a pair. The shop assistant was maybe too friendly and cared far too much about my plans, it was easily a sympathy vote "aw the poor wheelchair kid thinks she's going to be able to climb a mountain". I didn't love it, but if it helped me bag some money off the final bill then I would let her try and make herself feel like a more decent person by patronising me. It didn't ruin my future plans, I was just ecstatic to be one step closer (literally!) to being able to do something worthwhile, I'd felt like a waste of space for too long now and this was just about the only thing keeping me going, and Tom if I'm completely honest.

I chose a Salomon pair in black and I couldn't wait to break them in, but I got them in their box and asked Tom to drop them off at my house instead. There's such little room at the hospital and with them breaking my glass tortoise I didn't want to risk anything else. I let him wheel me all the way back down to the entrance before I declared I'd "lost my purse". It was ten minutes before the place was due to close so I asked him to just park me by the Thorntons' window so

I could look at all the display whilst he ran back to see if I'd left it in the hiking boot shop. Of course this was a lie and I felt awful, but he'd parked me just close enough that I could shout the shop assistant.

'Excuse me? Hello? Sorry...'

'Are you okay?'

'Oh, yes, I'm fine! I'm just wondering if you would be able to make me an advent calendar with my friends name on in the five minutes it will take him to get back?'

'Of course. What name would you like? It goes on the big chocolate for Christmas day is that alright?' It was perfect and so I asked him to write "Tom" with a little heart, before bagging it up and hiding it under my boots, they were just large enough to cover it.

'When did you get this, little one?! Cheeky!' His face lit up when I handed him the chocolate before he left. Although I did have to make him promise not to eat it all at once. It was just past visiting hours when we made it back and I had to try so hard not to well up knowing he had to leave straight away. It had been such a wonderful night, yet again, and this time we couldn't climb into bed and have a cuddle or anything, he just had to drop me off and leave. It was always a proper British old movie farewell, the way we looked into each others eyes and lingered because neither wanted to leave. The "okay I REALLY have to go nows" and the "one extra hug, just one I promise. Please?"

I always made sure the last thing he saw was a smile on my face. Ever since I was a kid I've tried to always make sure when I say goodbye I am smiling, or I say I love you even if we've just been in a fight, regardless I need it to be okay because I'd seen this true crime drama thing when I was younger where someone had never made it home from work and the last thing his daughter remembers was him leaving the house that morning and saying that he loved her and she'd been in too much of a mood to say it back. I don't like to imagine that if something goes wrong the last thing I would've said to that person would've been horrible, or the last time they saw me I was angry or miserable. I know it sounds completely morbid, but we all have our own ways of sending our love.

He kissed my hair and left.

'Let me know when you get home, mister.' I smiled.

'I won't!'

Chapter Thirty

Aaaaand, it's out! It's finally been removed (hopefully permanently) from my body, and as much as I was semi-excited it went in, I couldn't be happier about anything else on the planet right now if I tried. Catheter free since two thousand and sixteen! Well, that's what I'd like to be able to say in ten years' time, it has a certain ring to it I think! Like Ted Mosby's "vomit free since ninety-three" thing in How I Met Your Mother, that I can't use because I wasn't even born then. Mine is more personal to me now any way, "Catheter free since two thousand sixteen". I like it so PLEASE body let's keep it that way, okay?

Mr Sant said that they'd have to monitor me and scan my bladder daily then measure the output etc, but once he had done it a few times and was happy he'd let me know, and that's good enough for me for now. I'll just make sure I'm drinking jugs full a few times a day and then I know I'll at least be able to go. It's just strange still because unless my bladder is full to bursting I don't have sensation so I need to regulate myself by going every three hours or so, to try and train it back to normal(ish). Whatever normal even is for a bladder. Eventually we're hoping I get full sensation back, and even though nobody can really say if that's possible, I'm still positive.

As a celebration of urinary continence, I was allowed to use my crutches down to Costa with Lily and Mick when they arrived. Today is a good day. I didn't really fancy anything by the time we'd made it down to the counter, but I was still glad to be out of the ward with my friends being semi-normal. Mick had an espresso and Lily had a fancy hot chocolate, just the smell made me feel queasy, let alone the mound of cream and marshmallows spilling from the cup. I put it down to motion sickness from being upright for so long from my bed to the lobby, when you've had spine surgery laying down becomes the only thing you really know, or most surgery I suppose.

The cafe was relatively quiet and we only stayed about half an hour, including standing outside the main doors for some fresh air for a few minutes. It took exactly 120 seconds before I'd realised how sheltered I had been in a heated hospital and how unprepared I was for the weather conditions of the looming winter. It certainly didn't stop me from taking deep breaths and enjoying watching the warm air leave my lungs, it was a nice change to see the last of the greenery and more colours than 'sterile white'.

Back at the camp, visiting hours were in full swing and my friends and I were being glared at like some kind of hooligans. Why is it that it's supposedly the younger generation with no respect for their elders, when we've done nothing but smile and be pleasant to all the people here without so much as a friendly turn of the eye? Drives me bonkers, but not for long because physio turn up within five minutes of us sitting down.

'And where do you think you've been you happy little wanderer?!' Rachel grinned and I could tell she was glad to see me not looking so glum.

'My friends and I just went down to Costa - we took the lift of course!' I continued to introduce them to Mick and Lily and everyone exchanged pleasantries.

'Well, if you'd like, you can come and watch as we try

and drag Pip up some steps, it's about time we gave them a go, if you're feeling up for it? And your friends can cheer you on with us, a whole cheer squad!'

I made sure Mick and Lily didn't want to leave instead, but they chose to watch the crutches novice attempt to climb some stairs, I thought it was for support, but obviously more for the laughs! There was so much cursing anyone would've thought I'd have joined a Captain's crew. Oh how un-lady-like of me. Rachel and Alice were great, they said if they were me they wouldn't even be bothered to apologise, it's tough stuff this learning to walk business and they're bloody right. First we had to discuss the types of stairs I had at home, I tried to play down the fact they're slightly spiralled, but Mick and Lily outed me and I was glad they did in the end. If these three steps up and down a physio staircase were hassle enough, then I had to be super prepared to take on my own.

I told them mum and dad weren't willing to give up the downstairs for me and had to narrowly avoid a conversation about how that attitude would remain the same whether or not I was seven or twenty-seven, they weren't nurturing people but I'm accustomed to it now. Following all the comments about how awfully sad that is, everybody else gushed about their relationships with their parents - the times they cared for them, funny anecdotes, how close they are and all their family traditions. It all sounded alien to me and so I promptly changed the subject to Kilimanjaro. I figured I was better off asking them what they thought before I disappeared and went home and then at least I had all the professionals concerns and opinions.

'That sounds like a really wonderful thing to be doing, it honestly does,' I sensed a "but".

'But... right now we just really need to get you home.'

'Once you're home,' Alice continued 'You'll be referred to your local physiotherapy team and they will work with you to come off the crutches completely - if that's something your body can manage. After that, it's all up to them on what you can and can't do.'

I looked to Mick and Lily and they immediately retorted, 'Don't worry we'll keep an eye on her. No running before you can walk, woman!'

God they know me so flipping well! The eye contact said more than I thought it had, it's like she could've seen the running track I was dreaming up before I'd finished building it.

The technique I had to practice to get up the stairs was entirely dependent on my crutches, since we have no banister at home, no hand rail or anything. If you'd never had to think about the way you walk, or the way you climb a staircase, your mind finds it particularly amusing to say the least. I feel like Ariel, trying to flip my fins, but not getting too far and my brain finding the entire concept of having feet at all, hilarious. The drug high doesn't help, when you're on morphine just about everything is hysterical, from food to farts and everything in between. Apparently I was laughing at how funny my own name sounded, but I don't even remember. Don't do drugs kids, mmmkay?

Using both crutches on the floor level with my feet, I had to step up onto the first step with my right leg (my good leg) and push my weight through my sticks to lift the left leg up to join it. Once both feet are on the step I have to balance on my right leg again and bring the crutches up to meet me, level on the same step. The best way not to forget this, they say, is to think "good up to heaven and bad down to hell", this means that on the way down the stairs you do the same thing only in reverse. Crutches down to the step below you, bad leg down to join them and then good leg to follow. It sounds easy enough, but I honestly nearly fainted by the time I'd made it up the three steps. I had to wait ten minutes at the top and sip some water Mick had run off to get for me before I could try and get down again.

Thankfully, by the time I did make it, a wheelchair was waiting for me. I'd noticed them bring it in since I was too busy concentrating on not falling to my death. I'd managed to crutch my way to the physio room to do the stairs in the first place, but there was no way I was getting back. Back to bed I think.

Mick and Lily didn't stay long once we'd made it back to my ward, and lucky for them they managed to miss my parents by all of ten minutes. Having visitors can actually be pretty exhausting sometimes, no matter how good it is to see the people you love, you can't help but feel the need to dress up, be chirpy and just generally more emotive. When you're dosed up to the heavens and constantly in pain, it can be hard to live up to the standards you set yourself for facing people and by the time it's the end of the day you feel shattered. It's only 4pm and I'm getting that way before I've even had tea, but I'm trying to give myself a break because physio worked me well and I had already done more than usual. Hopefully mum and dad don't take my lack of animation too personally.

Today the parents are relatively dressed-down, no suits or uniforms, just trousers and mum is even wearing tennis shoes. She doesn't even like wearing them to tennis!

'Have you spoken to Tom yet?'

'Nice to see you too, mum!' I say as I kiss dad on the cheek to greet him, apparently I still have my sass. 'And no, I haven't, but I'm too exhausted to talk about it today, I've just managed to walk up some stairs!'

'Oh really? How many?' Dad asks.

'Only three up and three down, but it's more than I could do yesterday.' They look at each other as if to silently discuss how big of a deal it is before dad replies. 'Not bad, not a staircase though is it?'

Sometimes I think they're just joking and have a terrible sense of humour and zero personality, but I always think about when I hear them together in the lounge and know none of that is true. They do know how to smile and how to make appropriate jokes using tone, they just don't bother with me.

'We actually came to see you before we go.' Mum stated, out of nowhere.

'And since you can't manage the stairs yet we know you won't be out before we leave.' Dad added.

'Oh right, so where are you going now then?' I tried not to sound too sarcastic and bitter, and I actually think I must've just about pulled it off because nobody batted an eyelid and mum proceeded to explain.

'We've booked a last minute holiday over Christmas to the States. We thought that you probably wouldn't be out by then anyway so we don't have anyone else to cook for at home or anything. Even if you do get out, we come home for the second of January so it's not like you'll be on your own for long. If you pulled your finger out with Tom you might not be on your own at all.'

'We go on the 19th and come back the 2nd in the evening. It's one of those tours you can book, they had a last minute opening so we booked it yesterday.' Dad sounded genuinely excited, but I was still hurt at the way mum had so casually brushed over the fact I was probably going to be spending Christmas in this bed, alone. Annie would be with Alex, Mick with Lily, Tom working like he does every year. Then there's my 'loving' parents swanning off to the bloody USA!

'It's a tour of Canada and New England and we spend New Year's eve in New York. You said how wonderful it was so now we're going too, but obviously everyone wants to go for New Year so I bet it will be even better than what you said!' Oh dad, when will you stop competing? They always have to do one better than me, always, and they're not even jealous siblings. I've seen my friends fight with their brothers and sisters like this, but never with their parents. I remember once, Annie's brother and her spent forty minutes arguing over who had the better experience in Cyprus based on all sorts of shit; where they'd stayed, activities they'd done, when Google said the weather was supposed to be better... honestly, madness! Always a pissing contest.

'That sounds great, I'm sure you'll have a really good time.'

'That's the plan!' They chimed in perfect unison.

Before I could give them time to go on about it anymore, I tried to talk about having my catheter removed and how I would like to think I'll be home before they leave. It is only the tenth now and if I can wee on my own and walk upstairs within a few more days, it shouldn't be long at all. Fingers, and everything else, crossed. Realising the date I also decided it was time to eat my advent calendar, too, I just didn't want to open it in front of the parents in case it lead to a "did Tom get you that?" conversation...

Once they'd reverted back to bragging and stopped for breath, once again, they jointly decided it was time for home. They promised to TRY and get to see me again before they went, but obviously there's just so much planning and packing to do in the meantime that they couldn't promise anything. If I didn't see them before, I wouldn't see them now for three weeks and I wasn't even that disappointed about it. I made dad shut my curtain when they left just to give me ten minutes of peace and quiet before someone inevitably grassed me up for hiding. According to the nurse it wasn't polite to shut myself away. Bitch, it's not polite to tell me I'm supposed to keep myself on display and be glared at, but that doesn't stop you.

Chapter Thirty-One

Jesus Christ this hospital is ginormous, it's a wonder more people don't get lost, I think I might be and I've lived here for over a month. Today marks the day of my first official "solo journey", as I'm talking my crutches on a walk to see Jill on Ward twenty-four (I hope she's still there, in the nicest possible way!) I'm only on ward twenty-one so you'd think it wouldn't be that far away, but actually, so far, I've managed to come up a floor in the lift and down two marathon length corridors and I'm still only at twenty-three... Exhausted doesn't cover it, but I'd say I'm doing quite well.

I'm wearing actual human clothes, not patient gowns and men's trousers. I've got my leggings on and my hand washed and dried t-shirt that's been hanging on my half-radiator for a couple of days. It feels a little crunchy, but that's the price you pay for hand washing with hospital soap and water. I feel clean, though. I even bothered to put on some make-up, too, just for Jill because I know she'll appreciate my smokey eye and bright pink lips if nobody else does. I've always said lipstick was made to be seen, I won't wear this nude, foundation lip look, I love brightening my smile with colour, especially when it doesn't feel all that bright these days. I still didn't have any shoes, I was almost wishing Tom hadn't taken my hiking boots home so I could wear them here, but I didn't really want them to get covered in hospital smells or stolen so instead I wore my slippers.

The closer to the ward I got the more I felt like I was in twenty-eight days later, it was eerily quiet and all I could hear was my own breath out of time with the clicking of my crutches on the cold, hard floor. I knew I was going too fast, but it wasn't causing me any more pain to start with so i carried on. Anyway, no pain, no gain, right? I'd already done the stairs with physio today and this time I managed without nearly passing out so that's good news. Lost in a world of being momentarily invincible, I didn't notice I'd reached the ward doors and a family were leaving, we practically bumped heads.

'I'm so sorry!' I boomed in their direction, they looked as startled as me, but the second they saw my crutches I was met with sympathy and an offer of an open door. I had wanted to try and open the door myself, seeing as I wasn't sure how it would work with my crutches, but now it was being held open for me I didn't have a choice. I politely thanked them and walked through toward the desk.

'You're walking?!' The nurse behind the desk announced when she saw me. 'Look, it's Pip and she's walking on her crutches all by herself!' She motioned to the others behind the desk to look in my direction and I smiled as I leaned onto the counter top.

'It's bloody hard work this walking business, but one step closer to home!' They laughed.

'You look fabulous too.' The care worker sitting behind the computer said, 'You must be getting better.'

'You do good! What brings you to this neck of the woods?' The nurse added, motioning for me to take a seat, but I shook my head despite my leg's will to accept.

Jill was still in the same bed I'd left her in, or she was supposed to be. All her things were still there, but she had gone out for lunch with Andrew - lucky bugger! There wasn't anybody occupying the bed where I had been moved from and I was miffed that I had been moved at all.

'Hi Jill, it's Pip. I just thought I'd come and show off my crutches and see how you're getting on, but I hear you're out for lunch! If I don't get to see you before either of us go home (which is soon I hope!) I have written my email on the other side of this napkin. Keep in touch and keep well!'

I drew a small mountain on the bottom with a stick figure, atop. Just in case she happened to know more than one Pip, she'd know it was me, the crazy 'can't walk, but I will climb' girl she had the displeasure of meeting in a hospital bed. We might be different ages in completely opposite stages of life, but we can at least find common ground in ill health. I left the note as a bookmark in the novel she was reading and gave myself a minute to enjoy being seated before the long walk back to my bed.

In my head I had a plan. I hoped that I would be out of here by Christmas, then back to work by January and be able to come off my crutches, start breaking in my hiking boots and form a training plan not long after. If I utilised the whole twelve months I had ahead of me, I should be fit as a fiddle for a New Year's climb. I should really look into one of those "GoFundMe" pages or something for the Charity, too, I've never been the most tech savvy so I think I'll enlist Annie's Alex to help with that. Or maybe dad if he's feeling generous, he is in the 'business' business after all.

Being entranced in the wonders of Tanzania and mountaineering for the afternoon had exhausted my mind along with my already exhausted body and I must've fallen asleep reading stories of adventures. When I woke, my laptop was gone, but I was being held by Tom instead. I said nothing, but instead pulled his arms around me tighter and breathed in the scent of his shirt, he'd been working, but, to me, he smelt just like home.

'Oh hello little one, you're awake.' I felt his lips press against the top of my head and I smiled lifting my face towards him. He kissed my nose and I nuzzled back into his chest.

'I hear you've been out adventuring today,' he whispered into my hair. 'The woman opposite said you'd been gone over half an hour after your physio had left, where have you been wandering to? You haven't done too much have you?'

I told him about going to see Jill and doing the stairs again, I loved hearing him tell me he was proud of me, and I equally loved hearing him scold me for doing too much, I think there was only one thing I didn't admit... That I loved him.

'I was going to take you out to eat today, but you're so sleepy and you've done a lot so how about we order some food and stay here and catch up on Mr Attenborough? How does that sound?'

'Sold!'

We ordered Pizza Hut, because it seems that's all I was really craving in the hospital. Dad seems to think it's because when mum was in labour with me she'd had him in a headlock screaming that that's all she wanted when she'd finished pushing, so the first words I must've heard leaving the womb were "Pizza Hut". Makes enough sense to me and so that's exactly what we had, although when it came I realised I wasn't as hungry as I thought and I only managed a slice. Such a disappointment on my end, because usually I can eat a large pizza to myself, but thankfully I had Tom here to finish the rest.

Even the smell was making me feel queasy tonight, so I had my face squished under a blanket against Tom's chest and wasn't even watching David, I was just listening to his familiar voice narrating the world's deserts. Everyone talks about Morgan Freeman having a great voice, but Sir David Attenborough does the job for me. Even with my eyes closed I can imagine his silver wisps of hair quivering in the wind as he watches the nature around him. That's a job I'd love.

Usually Tom would be prising my eyes open or pausing the programme if I was falling asleep, he didn't want me to miss the good camera shots or the animal chases, but tonight he let me rest and acted as my blind subtitles if there was something intense going on. I was cold and I had my entire face covered by blankets to keep in every ounce of heat I could, Tom was boiling and I had never been more grateful to have a personal radiator. Even though he said I didn't need one because I was too hot to touch.

I felt guilty that I hadn't really been conscious much of his visit, but it only cemented more of what I already knew about how I felt about him. I had wanted to talk to him, but I just couldn't bring myself to do it when I wasn't feeling myself entirely, I just needed him here and I didn't know how what I wanted to say would change that. I'm sure he feels the same, he must do. Everyone says so, no man would be this way if he didn't, I just wanted to be sure. And now, I think, I am. I was practically asleep when he had to leave and I still struggled to let him go. He turned off my laptop and closed my curtain and kissed my head, before promptly feeling it with the back of his hand and peeling one of my blankets half way down.

'You need to cool down,' he'd warned. 'I'll speak to a nurse on my way out and see if they'll check your temperature, get some rest and let me know how you feel tomorrow, okay?' My eyes still weren't open, but I reached out a hand to touch him.

'Let me know when you get home...'

'I won't', he chuckled, then kissed my extended hand and put it back under my blanket before leaving. The sound of his shoes getting further away made me sad enough I could cry, but I fell asleep instead.

Chapter Thirty-Two

Well. That was gross. Four days of passing out in the bathroom, throwing up and practically throwing my back out doing so. Not to forget the combination of diarrhoea one minute and constipation for the next sixty... Kids, don't do drugs, they fuck with your body in ways you never want to have to witness yourself, let alone have three nurses clean up after you. Bleurgh.

After Tom left the other day, I woke up before midnight, desperately needing a wee. I clambered out of bed and hobbled around to the toilet in the hallway, as someone was using the one in my room, and I locked the door behind me. I was only about twenty seconds into my wee when I suddenly felt dizzy, my head was spinning and my eyes felt like they had quadruple vision. I couldn't tell if I had two crutches or eight, so I kept feeling the air until I managed to grab the real ones and use them as an upper weight support, resting my arms on the handles in a bid not to keel over off the seat. Was I going to be sick? Did I need to get off the toilet and put my head in it instead? On a normal day that would be easily done, but now I could hardly stand or sit, I couldn't imagine how I'd get on the floor and up again so I just hoped I'd be able to projectile into the sink on my right. I couldn't.

My sticks clattered to the floor as I leaned as far forward as I could, I was sweating profusely and I slipped right off the seat, missed the sink, and proceeded to vomit all over the floor in front of me, the crutches flew so far they knocked the door and that alerted some of the staff on the other side.

I don't really remember much after that, but I could hear them saying how hot I was and I wasn't even in a funny enough mood to wish it had been a nice comment from an attractive surgeon. I felt like the Wicked Witch of the West, melting before everyone's eyes. I was certain I was going to be sick again for the next few hours. When I'd come to, I was writhing in pain and holding my head over the side of the bed so when I was sick it wouldn't mean a change of sheets.

Usually I'd feel sorry for all my bed neighbours, but not in that state, I didn't even feel sorry for my nurses, I could only think about how sorry I was for myself and how much I wish I could've just slept it all away. As expected, my temperature was through the roof and there was no doctor available to come and see me until the middle of the night, possibly the morning, so I was dosed up on painkillers and anti-sickness medication until I fell asleep again. It felt like years. Thankfully though, I wasn't sick again for at least eighteen hours so my throat had time to come round, I really hate throwing up and I hate it even more when it doesn't make me imminently skinny. I'm still a heff after day four of puking.

The doctors didn't visit until rounds, I had my bloods taken again and was given fluids and liquid drugs that just sent me into little sleep comas. I didn't even see a doctor on the third day and I expected somebody would've at the very least let Mr Sant know there was something clearly wrong. It was like I didn't really exist for a while. No doctors, limited nurses, only care support and two visits from physio who left when they saw the state of me - both times! I managed to text Tom, I wanted to know if he'd been feeling okay.

Maybe if he wasn't I could blame it on the pizza, but he was fine and he had eaten the whole thing, pretty much, so I had to accept, again, that my body was failing me.

What a drag this turning twenty-two business has been. Maybe twenty-three will be my year? Gives me time to recover from this awful illness and my operations and then I'll be turning twenty-three in the happiest place on earth to finish the next year climbing one of the prominent peaks in the world! It's definitely going to be better, I mean, it can't be worse can it?! Taking my life back by storm, I say! Or at least I will be when I'm physically allowed to.

If people know me for anything I'm fiercely independent and I can be sassy and stubborn when I need to be. Not as bad as Annie though, she might seem calm and collected, but Jesus of Nazareth, sometimes the woman won't budge! I do love her though, and I miss her. Being away from her, even though when I'm home we only see each other once every couple of weeks, I still know that she's just around the corner if I need her or vice versa. I feel like a useless friend being stuck in this place, in this tiny room. Especially now she's engaged, I should be spoiling her; taking her and Alex for drinks, buying champagne and planning a party, organising the world's best hen-do and booking bridal appointments after scouring magazines for the best boutiques. That's what best friends are for and now I can hardly afford to eat any more after buying everybody Christmas gifts and paying for a holiday. At least I should be back at work come January and then I can spoil her, and everyone else. Just got to make it last until then, let's hope the parents stock the fridge before they travel. I don't have the money to bet on it.

The thing is, it isn't just about money, not completely.

After all our years of friendship and talks about the future, we were supposed to do these things together. We were supposed to grow together, similarly, with engagements and have babies at the same time so they can be best mates. Our partners were going to learn to be buddies because we were going to double-date all the time. All my friends are in relationships and buying houses and thinking about those things and I'm leaving them behind and as much as I thought that would make me depressed about being on my own, it actually just makes me feel like I'm letting my friends down. We're old enough that these things are normal and I'm embarrassing them by not being anywhere close to what they need. How can they think I'll still be a good friend when I don't know what it's like to have a baby or get a mortgage, how can I be helpful and give them advice when I'm clueless? It scares the shit out of me and I resent it.

Not that being in a relationship should be the key to a good friendship, but when you're going steady with somebody, you're going to be less inclined to listen to my same old bullshit stories about the guy I'm seeing but not seeing... I really need to do something about that and not just for the sake of my friendships. I love Tom. I do. I love him enough that I want him to have everything he wants and I don't mean that I want to tie him down (maybe sexually, but that's all!) and marry him and have babies with him, Christ on a bike, with my spine can I even have babies? I just think I need him to know I love him, for my sake. I never liked the idea of changing somebody, or asking them to do something they didn't want to do, so I won't ask him. I'll tell him. I'll tell him that I love him and that I love us and that he makes me happy and he can make of that what he will, but whatever happens afterwards, nothing will change that. That's what I'm going to say.

'Thinking of you, I hope work is going well mister! X'

I press send and Alice and Rachel come through the door.

'You look better!'

'Look, there's even colour in her cheeks! And she's on her phone so the headache must be gone, I hope you're not still seeing double, or triple?!' These two really know how to make my day and just the look of their faces and cheerful tone made me want to hop out of bed.

'PLEASE tell me we can go for a walk today? I've been trapped in here for days and I swear I'm not going to pass out or throw up - pinky promise!'

'I'm glad someone else still uses the pinky as a valid contract these days - how do you fancy some stairs?' Rachel holds out her baby finger and we shake. Instead of wheeling me down to the physio department, they wheel me down past the lifts and through a door to the public staircase. That's a lot of bloody steps, I think to myself, but the look on my face obviously says a lot more than that.

'We don't have to do the whole lot today, we just thought it might be nice for you try and see how you manage more than three up and down...' Alice insists.

Fuck it. If I'm going to climb a mountain, I can't be scared of some stairs. I don't voice my assertiveness to the girls because if I then can't do it I'm going to feel a right blinking twat, but let's just hope I can do it. Cue a very dramatic rendition of Miley Cyrus 'The Climb' with two backup singers to help, we don't even stop when a doctor comes racing down the stairs and around me, we just laugh and continue.

'It's all about, it's all about the cliiiiiiiiiiimb!' If I wasn't using my hands to prop me up on my crutches, there would absolutely be some serious hand gestures and air microphones to play along with.

I honestly don't even remember which steps I took or what they looked like, but I do know that looking back down at my wheelchair and counting up to my feet perched on the edge of the first flight, those thirteen steps felt like nothing. It was almost so easy that I didn't even want to sit down or rest before trying the next thirteen. It was a Leo moment, stood on the Titanic. I'd never really thought about how incredible I could feel and how much progress I had made until I was 'The King of the World', looking down at the wheelchair I was, not too long ago, reliant on. Now I could use my legs to take me higher than anybody expected I would be able to go again and even though I thought I might, I didn't cry. Not even happy tears, I was in absolute awe. And it didn't feel selfish or big headed or embarrassing to be completely proud of myself for once. I had no belief I could do it and I still could, I proved myself wrong, now I just had to get back down!

I was rewarded with rest and a promise of my own bed when I made it back to my room. We were finally on the home stretch, if I could just make it a couple more days and manage the stairs a few more times then I was going to be out of there. Obviously, as Rachel had pointed out, they would have to discuss it with Mr Sant first, but I should absolutely be home for Christmas at this rate. I was immensely overwhelmed with what I had accomplished and to take it one step further, I opened up my goals diary and filled out the dates for not only the first time I completed tackling the stair case, but the first day in this entire six weeks that I had not cried. Now THAT was something to celebrate.

'What's the matter? What's going on? Pip you need to turn on your side for me now!' I must've dozed off having a flick through my goals diary after filling in the latest entries and I was rudely awoken by Mr Sant's voice barking orders to turn over so he could look at my scar. I obliged without question because I was still coming around, but the room was filled, him and two nurses and two care support and possibly a secretary of some kind. I didn't even bother to ask what he was doing when he started poking and prodding, I just winced and motioned to any sore points.

'Oh thank goodness!' He finally exclaimed, pulling my t-shirt back down and getting a nurse to help me turn back over for me to get comfortable.

'How are you doing? I was told there was something wrong with your wound and came the minute I heard.'

'Well I'm not dying as far as I know, it hurts as normal, but that's not new?' My eyebrows raised like the kids in that Dairy Milk advert a couple of years ago - I could feel them dancing around my face in comical confusion. At least I couldn't say he wasn't worried about me 'ey!

'I also have been with a fever and sickness the last few days, I don't feel 100%, but I did manage to climb the stairs today so that must mean I'm getting better, surely?'

'Oh my word, you climbed the stairs? And how do you feel? Super!' his little round face lit up and everything was calm again.

'So does that mean I can get out of here now?' I smirk, hopefully at him. He rolls his eyes all the way back into his head, practically, before informing me that as long as physio say I can go, he's happy with my progress and by all means I should get back to my own bed. Just hearing him say it makes me almost break my goal of 'no tears', and maybe if I hadn't written it so neatly in my diary I would've let the river run. He shakes my hand like the professional he is and says he'll let me know in the morning, but for now I should relax. So, that's exactly what I do. Feet up, Horrible Histories on, and a cup of jelly snagged from the care support staff to tide me over. This time tomorrow I should be going home and I've never felt better.

Chapter Thirty-Three

Waiting for the doctors to do their rounds this morning was like waiting for Christmas as a kid. I woke up far earlier than I normally would and I slept even less than the standard amount I get on a bad night. I was giddy as a kipper!

The night seemed to drag before it had even reached after nine so you can only imagine the pain of still seeing after one AM with no hope for heavy eyes.

I hadn't wanted to tell anybody I might be coming home today, just in case I didn't get to and then I would have to tell them I was wrong. Rather be a happy surprise than another disappointment. Mum and dad were leaving anyway, they should already be on the way to the airport so it's not like they could come and pick me up even if they knew. They probably would try and find a way out of it even if they were here and capable. I'm hoping that Tom will take me. I don't ordinarily like to assume (it makes an ass of you and me, you know) and I don't like to ask for favours, but he had said he was going to visit me today, so what would be the harm in seeing if maybe he would take me back with him when he goes. Annie would be calling me ridiculous right about now saying I shouldn't have to feel bad for asking for anything, especially in this situation and especially with Tom, he's made it clear enough it's not a problem and he wants to be here for me so I should let him. I'm trying! If I didn't have the balls to call him and ask, I'd call her instead, that's what friends are for.

Obviously, I wasn't trying to get my hopes up, I don't even imagine I'll be allowed to go home, the scare yesterday could've been more than that and he could've just realised. Maybe physio would like to do more than thirteen steps with me before they sign me off. So many things could've changed and if I get excited about going home before anybody confirms it I've only got myself to blame. Chill out, Pip, you've made it five weeks, what's a few more days?

'Good Morning, Pip. How are you feeling today?' Other than being completely anxious to get home, I had a feeling of intense nausea mixed with cold body sweats. That's what you get for being so overwhelmed with the idea of getting to leave the hospital you've been living in and also realising maybe you're not quite ready.

'I'm okay, I just want to get home!' I exclaimed, dropping my head backward on to my pillow and pulling the "urgh for god's sake" face; my eyes closed and mouth was in such a heavy frown it could've pulled my cheeks off. I didn't tell him I was feeling slightly skew-whiff just in case it compromised my escape. When I looked up from my pout, Mr Sant was smiling back at me.

'Well it's a good thing that physio have signed you off then isn't it. Is there somebody that can come and pick you up? You're a free woman!'

'Am I REALLY?!' the frown I'd been holding extended upwards to my premature crows feet and my face flushed. Was he having me on? I'm allowed to leave! My face felt hot and the minute he nodded I felt my eyes glaze with water. It's real.

'Sorry for crying, I'm such a baby. I just feel as though I've been here forever and like I might never leave. Are you sure I'm allowed to go?'

'Your wound looks good, like it's healing well as it can

be for now. It's still so fresh. Physio are happy with your progress and aren't worried about your technique or your strength, you've shown massive improvements and there's no point you staying here if you can be in your own bed. All your scans are coming back showing everything is where it should be and your infection has diminished so there's no reason for you to stay unless you feel like you can't go home?'

'...So what time should I get my lift to pick me up then?' I was dabbing my eyes with a tissue since I'd spent half the morning putting my face on to pass the time and I didn't want to ruin the eye-liner I had spent twenty minutes putting on. Especially now people in the outside world were going to have to look at me. Bad enough I'm smelly and in hospital clothes most of the time with ratty hair, the least I can do is spend time on my face.

'We'll get the pharmacy to get all your tablets together and then you should be free to go. Bear in mind it might take a couple of hours so it could still be tea time before you leave.'

I decided, still, not to tell anybody. I was going to wait for Tom to turn up and then surprise him when they tell me I can leave, even if he can't wait to take me home I can call someone else or a taxi I'm sure. I just wanted to see his face. Mr Sant explained to me about what to do if I notice any changes in my scar or any signs of infection. He was due to be away over Christmas too, he said he wasn't going to be back until the first week of January so in the mean-time I would have to contact the ward and they would let him know when he got back. He wasn't expecting anything would go wrong though, and neither was I. I think at this point we're all just waiting for the bone to fuse, as long as I rest, there shouldn't be any problems he said. If I know my friends well enough, I'm not going to have any chance to do anything other than rest. Mr Sant laughed when I said that.

'Just don't go running before you can walk, okay?'

'You know me so well by now.' He shook my hand and said he'd see me in the clinic when he was back from his travels. The second he turned his back I reached into my cupboards and started to pack my things.

All my clothes went in one bag, my books and paper and pens and bits and bobs went in my box from Lily and Mick and my toiletries went in a basket I'd acquired from Jill. Almost as if we were connected somehow, I heard my phone ping through with an email.

'Hi Pip,

Jill and Andrew here. Thank you for your note, so sorry we weren't there to see you. I got to go home yesterday and so I thought I'd email to say I'm so sorry we didn't get a chance to say goodbye. It would be lovely to meet up and catch up on each other's progress soon.

If you're still there next week I could come back in and visit you? How are you getting on?

Looking forward to speaking to you soon.

Love,

Jill and Andrew.'

What a gem. It made me happy to hear that she was finally home and to know that we would be able to keep in touch. I found such an unlikely friendship in Jill and Andrew that I felt this experience had bonded us more than I could've imagined. They were like funny little guardians.

My own Molly and Arthur Weasley, which I know makes me Harry Potter, but we do both have scars that define us. Mine was going to be a constant reminder of the last few months and I was going to have to get used to it. I only really had chicken pox scars before, but this one was much bigger and had a better story than just my mum enjoying picking my scabs when I was asleep. She would tell me off all day for scratching, but the minute I was in bed she'd sneak in and pick all my spots off! Gross or what! I made a mental note to reply to Jill when I'd got home, I was too excited to pack and be ready to go at the drop of a hat.

I heard Tom's footsteps coming down the corridor before I could see him and I just wanted to jump out of bed and run to him. I was bursting with excitement and so the second I saw his face emerge from behind my curtain I said, 'How do you feel about taking me home with you today?'

'I'm not sure they'd let me do that!' He replied, as he leant down to kiss my forehead, but his eyes scanned from me to the bags laid across the end of my bed and back to me again.

'Well if they'd rather you didn't take me home, they've got a funny way of saying it, because it sounded a lot like 'Get someone to pick you up, you're a free woman!' I quoted and mimicked Mr Sant making myself laugh.

'You're being serious?! You can go home? How? Are you well enough? Have you done enough work with physio and the stairs and your crutches?' His tone rapidly went from happy to worried and I pulled him close to me on the bed, nuzzling into his armpit.

'Don't worry. I'm fine. I promise. I can go.' He kissed me again on the head and squeezed me gently. Everything was packed and ready for us to leave. We just had to wait for my medication and I was good to go. In the meantime, we had crosswords to do.

Doing crosswords together makes us sound like an old married couple, but it's one of my favourite things to do in the world. On my own, I do love a good puzzle, but when Tom and I do them together, there's little else that matters. It's safe and it's fun and it just feels like home, I would spend another week in the hospital if that's how I could be guaranteed to spend every minute of it. I'm notorious for skipping ahead to clues I already know the answers to and he prefers to try and work them out in the right order, but he never gets cross with me for shouting out random words when he's been wrapping his brain around an anagram for five minutes. That's one of the many things I love about him, the fact he puts up with me when not even I would.

It's after four o'clock before we know it and the pharmacist has returned with a bag bigger than my fat head, full to the brim with drugs. An adult party bag, if you will. I didn't need an explanation of what to use and when because I'd had them all before so all I required was the list of numbers to call in case of the changes that Mr Sant had talked about. Once she was happy that I understand what to do in case of multiple emergencies, Tom went to fetch me a wheelchair to take me down to the car and I sat on my bed looking around the room taking it all in. Every inch of the place. With all my things bags it felt like the final episode of Friends, panning across the empty room and then fixating on the sign on the back of the door. I got my phone out to take a picture for my recovery album.

'Room thirteen. Pip Parker. Mr Sant. No allergies.' That

was me, that was my whole hospital identity and now I could go back to being just 'Pip', without a room number, and still without allergies. I'm an outpatient again.

Looking through the car window for most of the journey home I felt like a dog in awe of the world outside. I couldn't move my feet or stick my head through the open window or wag my tail (mostly because I don't have one), but I was ecstatic. I swear to the babe they called Brian that everything was green, even despite Tom's protest that everything was mostly brown because we are actually in Winter and that's how it should be. Of course, the fences were brown and the walls were mostly grey with stone, pebbledash or red with brick, but even so, all those colours were beyond brilliant. So very bright and vibrant, almost like they were talking to me, they were alive. The sun-set was so orange, I think until now I'd forgotten what orange was!

I glanced at the clock, it was 17:17, time to make a wish. Most people I know don't even know what wish time is, or they only do it at 11:11 because that's the 'real' wish time. I like to be more optimistic than that and use all the opportunities I can for a free wish, and right now was certainly one of them. I just wasn't sure what to wish for. I felt the last of the sun on the back of my neck as I turned to watch Tom as he drove us back into Harrogate, down the Harewood hill with views across the fields. There's something so wonderful about seeing the countryside again. And something even more wonderful about being here with Tom.

I looked back at the clock, still 17:17, closed my eyes and blew out my wish.

'So, what exactly are we?' It practically jumped from

my lips. My wish for courage had immediately followed through, but it didn't feel like it was going to stop for breath.

'I just... I feel like I need to know. I've had such a long time to myself and to my thoughts and they're constantly coming back to you.' I stare straight into the field before us, not wanting to lose track of where I might be heading with this conversation if I was to look at his face. 'We've been whatever we are now for two years and I love every second I get to see you. We go for dinner and have sleepovers and we talk every day. I always want to know how you are and what you've been up to, not in a mad stalker jealous way, but in a way that means I care about you and I want to make sure you're happy.' I briefly pause to inhale. 'I love spending time with your friends and I love knowing that we don't have to hound each other every second of the day. There is nothing I want you to change or alter, you're the most wonderful person I know.' I reach a hand to his knee. 'You make me laugh and smile even when I don't quite feel like it. You have been here for me every step of the way throughout all my shitty mess and I know it hasn't exactly been fun, but you've honestly surprised me. You didn't have to come and visit me, you didn't have to take me out or buy me things, or make me feel like I was the luckiest person on the planet, despite everything. You are wonderful and I am eternally grateful to you.'

I felt like I was rambling, but it just kept coming like verbal diarrhoea. My face was red, I could feel it and my hands were sweating, the nausea was excruciating and with every word I thought I might vomit, but I kept on going.

'I'm not asking for anything from you. I am so beyond happy, I don't want things to change. I'm not asking to live together or to get married or have babies or any of that stuff, you know how I feel about children...' I laughed and looked to him for a response. He cracked a faint smile, but didn't look at me. 'I just want to know where I stand, can we be exactly what we are, but with a clear understanding of the fact I do not want anybody else? I do not want to find anybody else or see anyone else or talk to anyone else. I want you and I want us and I want everything we already have. I just want to know that we are on the same page, you know? Does that make sense?'

We were on the straight road back to my house, in five minutes or so we'd be pulling up my drive. He was quiet and I worried I'd said the wrong thing, then I looked over again and there was a tear rolling down his cheek.

'I'm so sorry,' he whispered. 'I'm such a dickhead, I'm so sorry.'

I couldn't speak, but my stomach was churning. This isn't how this was supposed to go, why was he sorry? What had I done...

'I can't do this. We can't do that. I can't be in a relationship, you deserve better I'm so sorry.'

'I'm not asking for anything to change!' I protest, almost too eagerly. 'Just everything we have now, I just wanted to make sure that this wasn't going nowhere, that we had something I wasn't making up!'

I could feel my voice breaking watching him cry, but I refused to allow a single tear to fall.

'It's not you, I just can't promise that this is it. I can't give you everything you need. We can't be together.'

'But we basically are together, what's so different about saying so? What's so hard about holding my hand? Am I just an embarrassment, is that why? Is it just you don't want people to know you're with me?' I didn't know where this sudden insecurity was coming from, but that's what I felt he was saying, that I wasn't good enough to be with, just good enough to play around with behind closed doors or in places far enough away that nobody he knows would see.

'Don't say that! That's not what it is. I feel like such a dickhead!' He sighed heavily and for the first time, he looked me in the face. His eyes were red and his skin had reacted to his tears making his face appear blotchy and irritated. I tried to smile at him, but it fell flat.

'You're perfect. Honestly you are, you're far too good for me or anybody else...'

'Obviously not...' I scoffed and turned to look through the window before he could see me welling up. I was certainly not going to guilt him into thinking being with me would ever be a good idea.

'Don't say that!' He practically shouted at me and it shocked me, my heart was beating faster with every breath. 'It really isn't you. You're just too wonderful, I mean it, I can't tell you enough. You're my mighty one and you really do mean the world to me. Which is why I can't do this. I can't be with you. Or anybody. I'm not good enough, I'm not worth it. The world is full of shitty people and I'm just another one of them. You don't need me. Trust me.'

I couldn't understand where he was getting this from and I kept trying to protest. How could he possibly think he meant nothing? But he stood his ground fiercely. He kept saying I could never understand and that hurt me more, how could he say I wouldn't understand and yet not be willing to help me try. I know exactly what he meant, we'd talked about it before, about how being born had left us feeling guilty. We didn't ask to be here and the planet certainly didn't need us. It was over-crowded and full of morons, the world is dying and we can't do anything about it. We can't, individually, solve the crisis and so what was the point in us at all. It sounds so morbid I know, but he was the only person I'd ever met that understood things the way I did. I couldn't see why he would let that get in the way of us making the most of what we've got. Each other. I could see I wasn't going to win this and I felt my heart shatter into pieces.

So this was it then? We would have to stop seeing each other because I thought we could be in a relationship and yet he didn't want to live in a world without me in it. So what? We stay friends? It sounds like such a nice concept, but it doesn't work like that, how am I supposed to see him and not want to be with him. He wants to be Superman. He wants to feel like he's fixing me and helping me, but by doing that he makes me rely on him and I didn't want to have to rely on anyone. Would I have asked him if everybody else hadn't pushed me into believing this was more than it is? Or am I using them as an excuse to hide the fact what he's saying makes no sense at all. We WERE together, just without the label and I'm not crazy for thinking so. Even if I feel it.

How did this happen? The car was deathly quiet, other than the odd sniffle from either one of us. The more one cried, the more did the other and we were stuck in a soppy wet circle. I felt as though we hadn't reached a conclusion or even had a real understanding of each other by the time we pulled up in the driveway and yet here we were, at the end of the road. We got out in silence. I unlocked the door as he grabbed my things from the boot, I was grateful mum and dad were away to avoid it becoming any more awkward. The tears were still rolling silently down both our cheeks as he followed me step-by-step up my stairs, making sure I was steady and not rushing it. I'd forgotten how narrow they were and I was relieved he was behind me in case one of my crutches slipped.

Once in my room I didn't really know what to do, I just stood by my bed and he put my bags on the floor at the foot of it. Without saying a word, when his hands were empty, he pulled me in for a hug. We both lost it. I could feel his tears in my hair and I knew my makeup was washing off onto his jumper, seeping through the fabric to his chest.

He sniffled and I struggled to catch my breath, holding on to him for dear life, wishing I never had to let him go. But this time, I really would have to. We were probably stood for a couple of minutes, but I wish it could have been longer. He kissed my hair, where he'd saturated it, multiple times before whispering again how sorry he was. I looked up at him, knowing I looked a state and not even caring, what did it matter now?

'I should really go, I've got work in an hour.' He said as he wiped his eyes with his sleeve.

'I really don't want you to be sad.' He failed to smile as he said it, but I managed to smile back for him. 'There you go, just like that.' He pulled me in again, briefly, inhaling deeply and kissing me one last time before turning to descend the stairs. I perched on the end of my bed and watched.

'Let me know when you get home...' My face turned a half, toothless smile towards him.

'I will...'.

Chapter Thirty-Four

Tears were still falling as I heard the front door close. That was it. He was gone. I couldn't even dramatically fall onto my bed in distress like a Disney Princess, just in case I ended up stuck there with nobody to help me back up. Instead, I chose to sort out my bags, and by sort out, I meant shove them all in a cupboard until tomorrow so I could climb into bed and sleep the pain away. I used one crutch to balance on and the other to move the bags in to the base of my wardrobe, hooking the stick through the handles. Once all the carriers had been moved I was left with boxes that I'd considered just leaving as they are, until I noticed the one at the far side of my bed. My boots.

I'd forgotten all about my hiking boots and how Tom had brought them home for me and so I sat on the end of my bed and reached out to put the box on my knee. The sound of my tears, landing heavily on the cardboard, encouraged me to wipe my eyes and take a deep breath. I closed my eyes tightly to stop the flow and rubbed them hard with the palms of my hands. After four deep breaths, I opened the lid to find a note stuck to the inside.

'I am so proud of you, mighty one. I can't wait to see you wearing these on top of Kilimanjaro. You're the only person I know who could go through all of this and come out the other side 5,895 metres on top. You're perfect. Love Tom XXX'

I peeled the paper off the underside of the lid and held it to my chest for a brief moment before sliding it into my bedside drawer for safe keeping. Another deep breath to stop myself from tearing up. I picked up my boots, holding them out in front of me. I am home. I can breathe. I can stand and I can nearly walk. I can wee again, almost normally, and I am back in my own bed. I have been through what has felt like going to hell and back in such a short space of time and yet here I am, broken and alone, stronger than I ever thought I would be. I miss Tom already, I don't know what will happen... much like I don't know how well I'll heal or if I'll ever be able to come off my crutches. I do know this though, just one thing. Kilimanjaro I am coming for you by hook or by crook, I'm going to make my dreams come true because, well, cauda equi-not, right?

My name is Pip Parker, I have Cauda Equine Syndrome, I'm recovering from a lumbar fusion and I'm going to climb a mountain.

CPSIA information can be obtained
at www.ICGtesting.com
Printed in the USA
BVHW031722250619
551796BV00043B/1057/P

9 781910 406946